THE FINAL NOTE

**Center Point
Large Print**

**This Large Print Book carries the
Seal of Approval of N.A.V.H.**

THE FINAL NOTE

KEVIN ALAN MILNE

CENTER POINT PUBLISHING
THORNDIKE, MAINE

This Center Point Large Print edition
is published in the year 2011 by arrangement with
Center Street, a division of Hachette Book Group, Inc.

This book is a work of fiction.
Names, characters, places, and incidents are
the product of the author's imagination or are used
fictitiously. Any resemblance to actual events, locales,
or persons, living or dead, is coincidental.

The text of this Large Print edition is unabridged.
In other aspects, this book may vary
from the original edition.
Printed in the United States of America
on permanent paper.
Set in 16-point Times New Roman type.

ISBN: 978-1-61173-191-0

Library of Congress Cataloging-in-Publication Data

Milne, Kevin Alan.
The final note / Kevin Alan Milne.
p. cm.
ISBN 978-1-61173-191-0 (library binding : alk. paper)
1. Spouses—Fiction. 2. Marriage—Fiction. 3. Large type books. I. Title.
PS3613.I5919F56 2011b
813'.6—dc22

2011021246

ACKNOWLEDGMENTS

My best friend and wife, Rebecca, deserves more thanks than I could possibly express. She allows me to write, inspires me to write, encourages me to write, and once in a while even kicks me out of bed at night and *forces* me to write so I can meet deadlines! I am eternally grateful for her love and support.

My five kids deserve a round of applause too. Their laughter keeps me smiling.

Thanks also to my parents, grandparents, and siblings for their insights and words of encouragement.

The Center Street and Hachette folks know who they are, and I hope they know how much I appreciate all that they do. If not, let me spell it out: I appreciate you A LOT! That statement is doubly true for my editor, Christina Boys, whose patience and talents never cease to impress.

Much thanks to Joyce Hart—agent extraordinaire—for helping me find a niche.

And finally, thanks to the readers. Your comments, questions, and feedback make this all worthwhile.

PRELUDE

I am a sane person . . . I think. Which is why I feel terrible for going to her house and screaming at the top of my lungs like a raving lunatic. I wasn't even intoxicated, unless you count being drunk with rage, in which case my insobriety was well beyond legal limits.

"You ruined our family!" I yelled. "You and your stupid thumbs and your stupid phone!"

Okay, maybe that last part sounds a little crazy, but in context I swear it made perfect sense.

"Mr. Bright, I'll give you exactly two seconds to leave before I call the police! She's already apologized. There's nothing more to say!" That was the mother—the one with the shrill voice, like a feral cat protecting a wounded kitten.

But I wasn't there to talk to the mother. I was there for her daughter, the twenty-something college student. It galled me that she still lived with her parents, because it meant I couldn't castigate her without their getting in the way. She was standing between her mom and dad on the front porch, just a few steps up from where I stood. The way she was holding herself made it look like she was freezing to death, even though it was a warm summer evening—I'm sure she was just doing that to keep from falling apart.

I'd already berated her once, earlier in the day.

7

This was round two and, despite her mother's threats, I was just getting started.

"Really? Because I've got plenty to say! But first, I want to show you something." I was carrying a briefcase. In one swift move I swung it in front of me, rested it on my thigh, and flipped it open.

"Oh Lord, he brought a gun!" the mother screamed. She and her husband both jumped in front of their daughter instinctively, sheltering her from whatever evil deed my anger-induced psychosis was about to inflict upon them all.

"Oh, stop it," I barked, surprised that they'd actually think I was the kind of person who would do something like that. Of course, none of them knew me from Adam, so I guess I can't blame them. "I just want to show you what you took from me." I lifted one hand and waved a fistful of the briefcase's contents.

"Paper?" That was the dad—the one who sounded way too dumb to be making the kind of money he must've been making to live in that kind of house.

"Notes!" I shouted back. "The kind you can hold and touch. Some of them you can even smell, thanks to my wife's perfume. These notes are meant to be cherished and read over and over again, not like your stupid texting that you read one moment and delete the next."

"What?" That was Ashley—the perpetrator.

"This morning," I reminded her, "before you ran

off, you said your boyfriend sent you a *'note.'* What he really sent you was a two-bit text message, and like an idiot you answered it. So I wanted to show you what *real* notes look like. Deep, thoughtful, meaningful correspondence; the kind of communication that started—*and probably saved*—my marriage. *Love notes!* And I don't ever want you to forget what they look like, because *this* is what you took from me!"

The mom and dad were speechless. Ashley bowed her head and went back to holding herself, weeping audibly in the night.

What happened next is hard to explain, because it was mostly in my head. I took my eyes off the family for just a split second to glance at the wad of papers in my hand. In that brief instant memories came flooding back, from the very first note that Anna gave me, right down to the very last. The notes hadn't come as often in recent years, but that was mostly my own fault. And I was going to change, I swear—I *swore* to Anna that things would be different.

I broke a promise—she paid the price.

I looked back up at the family, and suddenly everything I'd wanted to scream at them—*at her*—just vanished. What was I doing here? Why had I let my hatred drag me away from Anna in the first place? I should have been back at her side, waiting for the beautiful artist to draw her last breath.

"I'm so sorry," breathed Ashley.

I didn't want to hear it. I wanted to be mad. I wanted her to live with the guilt of what she'd done. I wanted her to be as miserable as I was. But mostly, I just wanted to get away from there and go be with the dying body of my wife. "You should be." I turned abruptly and left.

Thirty minutes later I was sitting next to Anna's bed in the ICU. She didn't know I was there. I didn't know if she was there either. Physically, mind you, she was lying right there on the bed, breathing through a ventilator, living on borrowed time through the wonder of modern medical machinery. But the part of her that really mattered? For all I knew it was already gone.

"Anna." My voice cracked. "I'm back."

There was no reply. I didn't expect one, but I kept trying.

"Can you hear me? Honey, are you there? I ran home, but I'm back now. Hope is doing fine. Your brother is watching her. Grandpa Bright is there too. They're all praying for you."

Several IVs were dripping fluids into her heavily bruised arms. I watched them drip while I waited for a response—any response.

"I found something," I told her at length. "It's my briefcase. The one you got me when they moved me into management. The one I took to work exactly once. Did you know I found another use for it? I've been loading it up with your notes.

I brought them all with me. Isn't that great? I thought . . . maybe you'd like it if I read them to you . . ."

I wanted to cry.

No, that's being dishonest.

I *did* cry, especially when I stumbled upon her original note to me. It wasn't a love note then, but it certainly paved the way for love to grow. That was years ago. As I stared at her now, it felt like eons.

Reading the words she'd written took me back to another time and place. A different country, a foreign language. A hope, a prayer, and a guitar.

Back then we were young and naive. Everything seemed possible.

We fell in love.

We hardly knew what love was, but it didn't matter, because we had each other and we were happy.

We were dirt poor, but it didn't matter, because we had each other and we were happy.

In time we discovered that not everything in life goes as planned, but even then it didn't matter. We still had each other. And we were still happy.

All of which is a very long, redundant way of saying *I screwed up.*

Eventually, I let the most important things in life take a backseat to more trivial pursuits. I somehow lost sight of—maybe even forgot altogether—just how good things had been in the

11

beginning, back when life was simple. Simple . . . and perfect.

Anna's notes reminded me of everything we'd had and everything I was about to lose. I wished I could tell her how sorry I was. Actually, I did tell her, over and over, as she was lying there, but she didn't hear. She just lay motionless, breathing artificially.

"Remember how it used to be?" I asked her as I wiped a fresh batch of tears on the cuff of my sleeve. "I thought ours was a fairy-tale, once-upon-a-time story. How did we get from there to here, Anna? *How?* Where is our happily ever after? How did I let this happen? I wish we could back up and do it all over again. Maybe then I'd get it right . . ."

Long before our lives fell apart, my wife dreamt of writing and illustrating books. It didn't exactly pan out. My dream was writing music, which was also a bust. But in the end, none of those things mattered. The only things of any consequence were the moments we had together and the memories we shared. Maybe that's why it's so important for me to tell our story, no matter how much it hurts to dig up past mistakes. We once had something great, and I don't want to ever forget it. Nor would I want to lose sight of where I went wrong, lest I make the same mistake again and lose the precious few things I have left.

Not long ago, my grandfather—who owns all the blame for getting me hooked on music as a kid—encouraged me to not just tell my story, but to write it down, so the memories remain fresh. "Writing your story is just like writing a song," he explained. "Start with the first verse and take it one note at a time."

If Grandpa's counsel is right, then I've already messed up. Rather than starting with the first verse of my song, I have taken a giant leap to the bitter end. But I suppose even a dismal tune like mine can easily be rewound . . .

FIRST VERSE:

SOLO, *ALLEGRETTO SCHERZANDO*

Chapter 1

"Let's start at the very beginning; a very good place to start." Julie Andrews sang those words while methodically strumming her guitar in *The Sound of Music*, just before she and the kids broke into their famous do-re-mi's. Then together they danced, climbed, sang, spun, and pedaled their way up and down through the rolling hills of the Austrian countryside. When concerned friends (and a few nosey acquaintances) have asked how my life got to the point it's at now, I've been reluctant to share the excruciating details. Instead, I tell them simply that, like Captain von Trapp and his musical wife, it all began quite wonderfully in Austria with a song and a guitar, but somehow it ended up in San Francisco . . . with nothing.

Okay, *nothing* is a bit of a stretch, but that's how it feels sometimes when your entire world is crumbling before your eyes.

A lot has transpired since Austria—most of my life's biggest disappointments, for instance. But if we're to follow my grandfather's (and Fräulein Maria's) admonition, then the snowcapped Alps of Europe's cultural heart is a very good place to start, because that's where everything fell into place. That was *the beginning,* the place where I received my very first note.

I'd just graduated from the University of

Rochester's Eastman School of Music and was on my way overseas for graduate studies at the University of Music and Performing Arts in Vienna, Austria, when Grandpa Bright announced he was loaning me Karl.

As odd as that may sound, it really wasn't. Karl was the name of Grandpa's guitar, though why he'd given it a name was anyone's guess. More importantly, Karl was the instrument I'd been openly coveting since I first heard Grandpa play it when I was a kid. Not only did Karl sound great, but it carried a certain reverence and mystique among the Bright family, mostly because Grandpa was so tight-lipped about how he'd acquired it and why he'd named it Karl. All he would say was that he owed his very life to that old guitar, and that he'd cherish it "until the great conductor of the universe calls me home to play in his symphonies on high."

Taking all that into account, I was more than a little surprised when he lent it to me. I was also deeply honored. But it was nonetheless fitting that Grandpa's beloved six-string should accompany me on my journey to Austria, if only for nostalgic reasons. We all knew he'd gotten it there while serving in the war. We just didn't know *how*.

I'd chosen Vienna over other possible graduate programs for the express reason that I wanted to see and experience all of the places Grandpa must have traveled with that guitar, as a soldier.

Nobody had a greater impact on my life than Grandpa, and Karl was part of that legacy, so going back to Austria, where Herbert Bright and Karl the guitar first met, was like a dream come true.

After arriving on European soil and settling into my two-year music program in Austria's capital city, I began soaking up as much as I could of the sights, sounds, and culture of my new surroundings. During my first semester abroad, nearly all of my spare time was spent playing tourist. If there was something to see in or around Vienna, I saw it. There were frequent visits to the opera houses, countless hours staring at the intricate details of St. Stephen's Cathedral and Karlskirche, and more than a few excursions to the Imperial Palace—the monstrous home of the Habsburgs, rulers of the Austrian Empire for more than six hundred years. I saw the Lipizzaner horses, the Vienna Boy's Choir, the Sigmund Freud Museum, and enough first-century castle ruins to last a lifetime. Before the weather turned cold, I took a paddleboat ride along the Danube River and during a long holiday weekend, I hopped on a southbound train through the Alps to the city of Graz, just so I could see the home where Arnold Schwarzenegger grew up.

Like I said, if it could be seen, I saw it.

Unfortunately, all such tourist activities cost money, which was something I didn't have a lot of. And so, on the day before Christmas, after paying an exorbitant price to see Diana Ross perform live with the Vienna Symphony Orchestra and two of the Three Tenors, I realized that I was flat broke. I'd secured loans to cover the big-ticket items, such as tuition and housing, so that wasn't a worry. But money to get around town? Cash to buy groceries? Funds to simply exist? Those coffers were empty.

Other students might have called their parents for financial assistance, but that wasn't an option for me. My mom couldn't help because she was "gone." That's how Dad explained it to me when I was five and she didn't come home from the hospital. Not passed away. Not dead. Just *gone* . . . and not coming back. And my dad? Well, after Mom left, he just sort of died too. Not physically, but in every other way—stopped going to work, lost his job, slept most of the time, started drinking heavily. After three months of depression he decided that raising a child by himself was more than he could handle, so he handed me over to my grandparents.

Dad pulled out of his tailspin a few years later. He never asked to take me back, though. In fact I rarely saw him. He became the Bright family ghost, appearing unexpectedly to say "hi" and then disappearing again for a couple of years at a time.

Following where my mother had gone,

Grandma Bright "left" just before I turned seven, so Grandpa and I had to learn to look out for each other. Grandpa was a psychologist by trade, but his passion in life was music, and he shared everything he knew about it with me as often as he could. When he wasn't seeing patients and I wasn't busy with schoolwork, we'd immerse ourselves in all kinds of music. Sometimes we'd listen to the radio and he'd have me write down the lyrics that spoke to me the loudest. Other times we'd learn about the classical masters and their contributions to musical history. But more often than not, we'd sit and play the guitar.

Grandpa began teaching me how to play as soon as I moved in with him and Grandma. By the time I was ten I was pretty good, and by the time I was thirteen, the student had become the teacher. Eventually I got my own guitar, though not as nice as Karl, and together we would write songs and play music until the wee hours of the night. Those were the experiences that helped mold and shape my dreams. It wasn't until college that I set my sights on a particular career goal, but it was those late nights playing music with Grandpa that convinced me my future was tied to the musical arts.

Although my childhood wasn't perfect, it could have been worse. I survived, which is the important thing, but only thanks to Grandpa. So naturally, Grandpa is the one who got the call when I spent myself into the poorhouse in Austria.

"You spent *how much?*" he asked after I explained my predicament.

I was on a pay phone, spending my last pocket change at a rate of two dollars per minute, so I had to speak quickly. "All of it," I repeated. "I'm really sorry. Can you just wire enough money to tide me over so I don't starve? By then maybe I can figure something out."

I knew I was in trouble when Grandpa suddenly switched to his thoughtful psychologist voice. "I would, but I think this will be a good growing opportunity for you. Here's my advice. *Use Karl. It won't let you down.*"

The automated female voice of the pay phone chimed in. "*Noch eine Minute.*" One minute left.

"What is that supposed to mean?"

"Why don't you play the guitar for money? I'm sure tourists will appreciate music from a skilled street musician. At least they did last time your grandmother and I visited."

I'd seen grungy-looking musicians playing at various tourist locations all the time, sometimes to good-sized crowds, but I'd always assumed those were just deadbeats trying to siphon liquor change from other people's pockets. And the thought of doing that myself? Well, it hadn't yet occurred to me that I was a deadbeat. "Really?"

"Ethan, why do people visit Austria? Why did *you* go there? For music! It's the heart of classical music in all the world. They want to hear music everywhere. I'm willing to wager if they hear you play, they'll pay. I would."

"*Dreissig Sekunden.*" Thirty seconds.

"Seriously? Even in this cold weather, you think people will stop and throw money in the hat?"

"Isn't it worth trying?"

"Yeah, but . . . what if you're wrong?"

"What if I'm right?"

"This doesn't sound like a very good plan. Wouldn't it be easier if you just sent me a little cash to get me through New Year's?"

"That *would* be easier. But the easy way isn't always the best way. You got yourself into this mess, and I think it'll do you some good to get yourself out. If you want to stay in Austria badly enough, you'll find a way to make it happen. If you don't, call me back and I'll arrange a flight back to the States—which you can pay me back for."

The phone beeped three times in my ear. I had just enough time to say, "Goodbye, Grandpa," and then it clicked off.

The next day, following an afternoon practicum with a small ensemble at the university, I hauled Karl down to Stephansplatz, an upscale pedestrian area surrounding St. Stephen's Cathedral in the center of the city. I'd seen musicians there before when it was warm outside, and I figured it was as good a place as any for a solo performance.

I laid a small piece of cardboard on the ground at the base of a building to protect my backside from the elements, then sat down. Ignoring the butterflies in my stomach, I checked to make sure Karl was still properly tuned, then I propped the hard-shell case open in front of me. It wasn't a hat, but there was ample room in there for donations. Finally, with a few curious onlookers already gathering, I closed my eyes and started to play.

I loved playing that guitar. I always had. Given its age, Karl wasn't the most stunning instrument to look at. Its wood was heavily worn, with nicks here and there from decades of use. But what really mattered was the sound, and in that it was a masterpiece.

Whenever I held a guitar—plucking strings, pressing frets, making music—I entered my own little world, like a private sanctuary in my head. There, in the middle of Vienna, with strangers gawking and making breath-clouds in the chill December air, it was no different.

Grandpa's old guitar sounded as good as it ever had. Its nylon strings were perfectly suited to the classical selections I'd chosen to play. I began with "Clair de Lune," a piece by Claude Debussy that I'd learned when I was sixteen. I knew it backwards and forwards. When I was done, I lifted my eyes to see the crowd's reaction. Only . . . there wasn't a crowd.

No money in the guitar case either.

The only person remaining was a man in his early twenties. His hands were shoved as deep as they would go in his pockets, and he wore a thick, handwoven scarf around his neck. "Dat was wery *güt*," he said with a heavy Austrian accent. "You are *Amerikaner, ya?*"

"How could you tell?"

He shrugged. "You look it. May I offer adwice?"

"Okay."

"Do you know songs dat are more . . . eh . . . *femiliare?*"

"Familiar?"

"*Ja.* Und faster. Wit more *zing.*"

"Zing?"

"Zing."

"Um . . . sure." Mentally, I raced through the list of songs I'd prepared, but they were all as lethargic as the one I'd already played. They were plenty difficult, but they lacked speed and intrigue, which probably meant *no zing*. Then my mind landed on one of the earliest neo-classical pieces I'd ever learned. "I got it," I said. " 'Bohemian Rhapsody,' by Queen."

He smiled with a nod. "Dat should do it."

I blew into my hands to warm them up, and then started into the song. It was slow at first, but clean and crisp, with enough notes to make it interesting. I kept my eyes up this time to better assess the response from pedestrians. Sure enough, when they heard the familiar tune, people stopped to listen. And as the melody kicked in and the tempo flared, with notes flying off my fingers like fiery darts, the crowd of onlookers grew.

And grew.

Some of them closed their eyes to focus on the sound. Others keyed in on my hands, obviously impressed with the speed of my fingers along the neck of the guitar. A few mouthed the words. The man who'd offered his "adwice" was bobbing his head in time with the music; he took several steps back to make sure he wasn't distracting from the show. Before the song ended at least five people stepped forward and dropped money in the case. When the last note sounded, another three lined up to reward my efforts. I thanked them all with a courteous nod or smile.

"Vell," said the man as the happy crowd moved on, "I tink you found your moneymaker."

"*I tink* you may be right," I replied. "Thank you."

I didn't count it right then, but I could see at a quick glance that there was at least two hundred fifty schillings in the case, a mixture of coin and cash. *Twenty-five dollars! From one song!*

From that moment on, finances were no longer a problem. I certainly wasn't swimming in dough, but neither was I destitute. At least I had enough to buy food on a regular basis, pay for transportation around town, and I even had a little extra for an occasional show.

Several days a week, I would lug Karl onto the subway and ride around to various tourist sites in the city, mostly the same places I'd frequented before going broke. I didn't always have as much success as my first time on Stephansplatz. Sometimes the crowds were thin and the cash even thinner. But then there were days that money flowed from pockets like air from a flute, which more than compensated for the down times.

I soon discovered that three or four compelling songs were plenty for one "show." Most people wouldn't stay and listen for more than ten or fifteen minutes anyway, so periodically I would just start my set all over again. To make sure I maintained sufficient zing, I always ended with "Bohemian Rhapsody." Even if the other songs produced nothing more than a few interested onlookers, that one always seemed to draw out loose change.

Thank heavens for Freddie Mercury.

I continued playing and studying throughout the remainder of that semester and right on into spring. During the summer session, my class load was light, allowing me more time to make money as a street musician. As expected, the warm months brought a marked increase in foreign tourists, and it showed in the amount of cash I was taking in. By the start of my second, and final, school year in September, I had enough saved in my bank account that I could cut back to playing once per week without any fear of straining my budget.

By my second Christmas in Austria, I was in the thick of my master's project, which kept me busy all the way through the end of the semester in April. That left me with just one capstone course and a summer practicum before graduation ceremonies were to be held in August. I'd been in college for six straight years—four in Rochester and two in Vienna—so it was hard to believe the end was so near. Time had flown by, and I wondered if it would ever slow down.

Then, in the middle of June, as my schooling was winding down, the passage of time suddenly shifted. In fact, for a couple weeks it seemed to stop altogether, as though God's metronome was somehow broken. But what I perceived as a slowing of time was actually just a side-effect of a strange illness I'd contracted. This particular infirmity hit me like a drummer on steroids. Physical symptoms included high blood pressure, shortness of breath, fever, and occasional chills. Heart palpitations came and went too.

I knew what I had was rare—lovesickness of such severity only comes around once in a lifetime.

I also knew that the *cause* and the *cure* were one and the same: *Annaliese Burke*.

Chapter 2

I guessed as soon as they got on the tramcar and sat down behind me that one of them—the one whose hair wasn't in braids—was an American tourist. It was her faded USC T-shirt and Bermuda shorts that gave her away. Well, that and the friendly way she said "hey there" or "hi" to every stranger who happened to look at her, including me. Her friend was harder to place, but her demeanor made me think she was either German or Austrian. Both women were in their early twenties, and neither unattractive.

I didn't mean to listen to what they were saying, but they sat right behind me, so it was hard not to. American tourists are always the loudest people in a crowd anyway, so I'd have been lucky to hear anything else.

"Where to next?" the American asked, but didn't give her friend a chance to answer. "Oh my gosh! Look at that building! It's got to be, like, three hundred years old!"

"Probably older," the other woman responded flatly. Her English was impeccable, showing just the slightest hint of an accent. "Most of them are. Remember, we're not still in California. But don't get too excited about that one; it's just an apartment building."

For the next several stops I listened as the tourist

29

asked questions about every little thing she saw, while her friend tried hard to be enthusiastic with her answers. Every once in a while I changed positions in my seat so I could sneak a glimpse of the USC-clad woman without being too obvious.

At least twice she caught me looking. I pretended not to notice when she smiled.

Three stops away from my apartment, the American let out an excited squeal that startled me. "Ooooh! There it is! We have to stop and see it!"

"We're not getting off the Strassenbahn for *that*. It's just a garbage incinerator. And it stinks."

"It's not *just* a garbage incinerator. It was designed by Friedensreich Hundertwasser. It's legendary! A perfect complement of art and industry, beauty, and function. I don't care what it smells like, we have to stop."

I knew without looking what building she was referring to. I rode past it every day, and every day I marveled that someone had spent the time and money to make something as ordinary as a garbage-burning factory look so inspiring. Its tall, mosaic-tiled smokestack was encompassed by several large protrusions along its length, including one bulbous shape that resembled a four-story golden egg. The roofline of the plant sported an odd arrangement of peaks and angles, each topped with spheres the size of small cars that glistened in the sun. All of the exterior walls were painted with random shapes and colors—black and white checkers, red squares, and yellow amoebas, just to name a few—while the top of the structure donned what can only be described as an enormous, red-and-blue striped newsboy cap that would have fit over at least fifty heads.

"*Ich bin aber müde*," whined the friend under her breath.

"What did you say?"

"*Nichts*. Forget it. If you really want to stop, fine. We'll stop."

A moment of silence passed, and then I felt a hand tapping my shoulder. "Excuse me," said the American. "Sir, do you speak English?"

I turned and looked at her, this time without needing to hide it. She had beautiful light brown hair, penetrating eyes, and an inviting smile. I nodded.

"Good. Did you hear what my friend said a second ago in German?"

I nodded again.

"Care to translate?"

I smiled awkwardly, then cleared my throat. "My German's not the best, but I'm pretty sure she said she's tired." I glanced briefly at the woman sitting next to the American, who looked like she'd just been betrayed.

The American's eyes lit up. "You're from the U.S.! Imagine that." She turned to her friend, raising her eyebrows questioningly. "Tired?

Really? Our trip is exactly one day old, and you're already pooped?"

The woman smiled weakly. "Jet lag?"

"I know this stuff is boring to you, because you grew up here. But I don't want to miss a single thing."

"But I know you. You'll want to stay there forever, until it's imprinted on your brain. By then our clothes will smell. Why don't you just take a picture from here?"

The American looked at her watch. "I've already seen pictures. As long as I'm in Vienna, I want to see the real thing. So why don't you run off and take a nap. I'll just go see it by myself, and then catch up with you in time to change my clothes before dinner."

The one with braids gave the other a pensive look. "Can you find your way back?"

"Probably not, but I'll figure something out."

That's when my first heart palpitations began. They came on very suddenly and didn't subside until I cleared my throat again and spoke. "Um . . . I could get you wherever you need to go. I mean, if you'd like. I know my way around. I'm a student here." I forced a smile before adding, "I'm Ethan, by the way."

A slow smile spread across the woman's face. She turned once more to her friend. "Magda, this is my *new* best friend, Ethan, who will be escorting me to view an iconic Hundertwasser."

She stuck out her hand as she turned back to me. "Pleased to meet you, Ethan. I'm Annaliese Burke. I go by Anna."

"You're not going over there alone with this . . . *stranger,*" Magda glowered. "You don't even know what he's like. He could be a crazy person. *A psycho.* Just because he's American doesn't mean he's a *good* American."

"So you'll come then?"

Magda cursed softly in German, then mumbled, "Yes, I'll come."

Anna turned to me again with a grin. "You're still invited too, if you're interested. I'm willing to bet I can tell you at least twenty things about that building that you never knew."

"Which would be twenty more than I know right now. How could I pass up an offer like that?"

In the years since that fateful summer day in Austria, more people than I can count have asked me how my wife and I met. I quickly discovered that "eavesdropping on a tram car near an artistic waste incinerator," only spawned more questions. Instead, I learned to say simply, "In Europe," which usually sufficed. If not, I would add that I helped show her around Vienna while I was a student there, and that the rest, as they say, is history.

Incidentally, history had a lot to do with Anna and me. Specifically, art history. She was a recently graduated art history major whose purpose in traveling abroad was to experience Europe's rich artistic past firsthand. When we got off the Strassenbahn that afternoon, she admitted to having done a lengthy report on Friedensreich Hundertwasser during her junior year. As we walked, with Magda trailing sluggishly behind, Anna rattled off a litany of things I "absolutely needed to know" about the man in order to fully appreciate the smoke-spewing factory before us. For example, the fact that he was the son of a Jew who posed as a Catholic during the Second World War. Or that he joined the Hitler Youth to avoid being sent to a concentration camp. Little things like that apparently influenced his architectural achievements.

Anna spent two hours studying the strange factory, frequently pointing out intricate nuances in its unique design and artistic form.

I spent two hours studying Anna's form and the intricacies of her physical graces.

She was a beauty from head to toe. Flowing hair. Brilliant eyes. Soft neck. Gentle hands. Perfect legs. When she walked, she glided. When she smiled, it was sincere. When she spoke, she did so with passion and conviction. And when she occasionally caught me staring at her rather than Hundertwasser's creation? She acted humble and flattered, rather than having the egotistical haughtiness one might expect from a woman of her allure. Music aside, I didn't know a lot about art, but I dare say that she was a Da Vinci compared to the rest of the Etch-a-sketch women I'd ever known.

Once Anna decided she'd seen enough of the garbage dump, the three of us made our way back to the tram stop, waited for the next tram to arrive, and then transferred a few stops later to a subway line that went right to the heart of the city. We found a quaint café with umbrella tables along Mariahilfer Street, not too far from the Leopold Museum of Modern Art, where we could sip drinks and chat in the warm summer air.

Anna was stirring the ice cubes in her *Limonade* with a straw. "So let me get this straight," she said, piecing together a few things I'd mentioned earlier. "You've got a degree in music theory, but you don't want to teach music. You earned a minor in guitar performance, but you don't want to play professionally. And now you're finishing a master's in music, and you don't plan on doing anything with that either?"

The last time I'd spoken with my dad—more than two years earlier, in the months leading up to Austria—he had made similar comments, but they sounded much less judgmental coming from Anna's lips. "It's not that I won't benefit from what I've learned along the way," I told her. "There's just not a direct correlation between my education and my career aspirations. What I want to do can't be taught in the classroom."

"Ooh, sounds exciting. Care to share?"

I took a long sip of my Almdudler soda. My family—aunts, cousins, and the like—had been trying for years to figure out what I wanted to do with my life. I'd been reluctant to tell them because I figured they'd say I had no chance. Even Grandpa Bright didn't know for sure what my plans were, though I think he could have guessed. "You promise not to laugh?"

"Cross my heart," she said, making an imaginary X with her finger atop the C on her T-shirt.

"I'll probably laugh," remarked Magda, who was still brooding about having to chaperone our trip to the dump.

We both ignored her.

I don't know why I felt comfortable telling Anna about my future plans. I'd never told *anyone,* and here I was discussing my dreams with a woman I'd known all of three hours. Perhaps it was my surety that I'd never see her again that made it easier to share. I took a deep breath. "I want to write songs."

Contrary to her promise, she let out a little snicker. "And what's wrong with that? Sounds like a perfect career for a well-educated musician like yourself. What type of songs? Classical music? Like symphony type stuff? Or were you thinking something more contemporary?"

"Uhh . . . contemporary, I guess you could say."

"How contemporary?"

"As contemporary as possible. I'm sort of partial to rock ballads, but I'll probably dabble in country songs too."

"Ahhh," she said, as if by instinct. She stared at me again for several seconds, focusing her big blue eyes on my slightly smaller brown ones, and then she said, "Good for you, Ethan. If that's your dream, then go for it." She paused and tilted her head questioningly. "But if that's what you've always wanted to do, and it doesn't require an advanced degree, then why go to school for so long?"

"To fine-tune my music skills? To expand my horizons? To get out of Podunk? Take your pick."

She chuckled. "That sounds eerily familiar."

It turned out that Anna's educational background wasn't so different from my own. She'd always been passionate about art, particularly painting, so it wasn't a surprise to anyone when she graduated from USC with a degree in art history. Yet she had no intention whatsoever of pursuing a career in art history. Instead, what she really wanted to do was write and illustrate children's books.

"But who'll tell future generations about Frieden-something Hundertwasser, if not you?" I teased.

"I'm quite confident that Herr *Frieden-something's* work will speak for itself," she shot back. "Just like Beethoven's ninth will do perfectly fine without you theorizing about it for the next thirty years."

"Touché."

We talked and laughed for another thirty minutes before Magda finally called it quits. "My parents are taking us out to eat in half an hour. If we don't go now, we'll be late."

Not wanting our time together to end, I rode with the women for several stops on the U6 train to Magda's apartment building. Before they went in, Anna pulled Magda aside to speak to her in private. When she turned back to me she was beaming. "We're both in agreement: you're *not* a crazy psycho. And you may have noticed that Madga's heart just isn't into playing tour guide in her home city. We're leaving Vienna in a couple weeks to see some other cities, but until then she wouldn't mind at all if I had someone else to show me the sights. How about it?"

My heart palpitations returned instantly. And chills. And shortness of breath.

Anna wanted to see Vienna . . . *with me.*

"Consider me yours," I said, not realizing how that might sound.

She didn't skip a beat. "Thanks . . . I think I will." She paused just long enough to make me wonder what she meant by that. "Can you be here at nine? I want to get an early start."

"The sooner the better." I didn't care if I

sounded a little too eager. I *was* eager. I was thrilled. My heart was pounding. I could hardly believe it.

Anna was going to see Vienna. With *me!*

The next morning I arrived at Magda's apartment building promptly at 8:59.

Anna was already waiting for me near the front door. "You sure you've got time for me today?" she asked. "I hope you're not skipping something important, like school."

I tried not to grin too sheepishly. "I called in sick; told my professor I had a fever." *And trouble breathing, and chills* . . . "Besides, it's just one class today. It's no biggie. Really."

"Good," she responded emphatically; then she asked where we were going first.

"Don't you have some specific places in mind?"

"You're the tour guide. Surprise me."

The first half of the day was spent looking at a church—*a single church*—from every different angle possible. It was called Karlskirche, and she seemed to know everything about it—who had commissioned it to be built and when, who designed it, which of its characteristics most exemplified the Baroque movement—everything. I found it astonishing how she could look at one gilded pillar for fifteen minutes straight without blinking an eye. When I asked her what she saw in it, she sweetly replied with a question of her own.

"What do you see—or hear—when you play Mozart's *Requiem* or *The Magic Flute*?"

"Easy. Pure genius."

She winked. "Exactly."

Over lunch we shared an Italian gelato from a street vendor, then hopped a subway out to Schönbrunn Palace, the 1,441 room summer home of the former Imperial family. Miracle of miracles, we were in and out of there in just under two hours, but only because self-guided tours were not permitted, and our paid tour guide would not allow us to fall behind the group.

At dusk, Anna inquired again about my availability for the following day. My practicum—which I couldn't miss—was over by ten thirty, so we agreed to meet at eleven o'clock for lunch, followed by more sightseeing.

We followed that same basic pattern every day thereafter. We would meet as soon as my classes were through, explore the city together until it got late, say goodnight, then start all over again the next day. After calling in sick on our first excursion, I never missed another class at the university, but even while I was studying, my mind was daydreaming about what awaited me after class.

By our fourth day together, Anna consented to spend less time at each new location, just to insure she had enough time to see all that there was to see at least once. So we systematically made our way from one location to the next, day in and day out. I didn't care that I'd already seen all of the places a hundred times; they were infinitely more interesting with Anna.

By the end of day nine we'd covered all of the must-sees, so I began taking her to places that many tourists either don't have time for or don't know about. Like Zentralfriedhof, the massive cemetery where Austria's musical luminaries such as Mozart, Beethoven, Schubert, Brahms, Strauss, and Schönberg are memorialized. Or Schatzkammer, the Imperial treasury that houses the Holy Lance, believed by some to be the lance that pierced Jesus's side. And Eroica Haus, where Beethoven lived while composing *Symphony No. 3*.

The only times we saw Magda were when she occasionally joined us for dinner; otherwise she was content to let us pal around by ourselves while she spent time with her family, whom she'd been away from for nearly eighteen months. But on day thirteen—the final day before Anna and Magda were skipping town to explore other European destinations such as Paris, Berlin, Budapest, and Venice—Magda suddenly decided that it was unfair that she'd "neglected" her best friend, so she didn't leave our side the entire day.

The entire day!

Her timing couldn't have been worse. I had been carefully strategizing for a full week about how, on our last night together, while we strolled along the far shore of the Danube River arm in arm, with lights from the Reichsbrücke Bridge glistening on the water, I was going to finally man up and steal a kiss from the most amazing woman on planet Earth. Instead, what I ended up with was an annoyingly long shopping trip with our Austrian third wheel so she could pick up supplies for the train ride to Berlin. And when the sun started to set, Magda was adamant that they turn in early, so as to rest up for their long journey.

Really? You need to be rested to sit on a train all day?

When we parted ways outside Magda's apartment building shortly after a sit-down dinner at Schnitzelwirt 52 on Neubaugasse, famous for its absurd portions of schnitzel, Magda gave me a sturdy handshake. "*Auf Wiedersehen*, Ethan. Good luck to you."

I sensed that Anna wasn't quite ready to say goodbye, but at Magda's prodding she gave me a quick hug. "Thanks for everything."

In the rush of the moment I couldn't formulate a decent response, so I just nodded. Anna even hesitated, like she was expecting me to say something, but all I did was tip my head and smile politely. Soon the moment passed, and they were gone.

That's it, I thought as the door closed behind them. *I'll never see her again.*

Two weeks trying to charm Annaliese Burke, and what did I have to show for it?

Nothing. Nada. *Gar nichts.*

No "Call-me!" or "I'll write!" or "Gee, it was fun spending so much time with you and I sure hope to see you again." No indication whatsoever that she expected our paths to cross in the future, let alone an address to look her up at when I got back to the States. Heck, I didn't even know which town she was from, only that it was somewhere in rural Idaho.

My heart slowed to a crawl as a fresh wave of chills rolled across my skin. All of a sudden I really did feel sick.

Anna was gone—or at least going away, and not coming back—and there was nothing I could do but kick myself for having believed I had even the slightest chance with a girl like that.

I stood for a moment by the curb, hovering over a storm drain just in case my nausea ripened into vomit. When the feeling passed, I took another long look at the apartment building, hoping beyond hope that . . . oh, I don't know . . . maybe that she'd run out at the last second and jump into my outstretched arms.

Your life is not a chick flick, I reminded myself.

The door remained closed.

Annaliese Burke was officially a memory.

Chapter 3

*B*roke. That's what I was again after playing tour guide for two weeks. With the cupboards getting bare and plenty of time on my hands, the only sensible thing to do was tune Karl and head back out on the street.

July is the peak month for tourism in Vienna, which meant there was money to be made no matter where I chose to play. However, competition from a whole host of street performers—solo musicians, jugglers, magicians, clowns, trashcan drummers, Peruvian flute bands—was greatest at the big cathedrals and civic buildings downtown, so I tended to stake out locations where I could have an audience all to myself, even if the size of the crowd was a little smaller. Outside the opera house before the evening show proved to be quite good. The train station wasn't too bad either. But my favorite place to play was called the Basilisk House, which happened to be the oldest building in town. I didn't make quite as much money there—three or four hundred schillings a night—but the acoustics were excellent, and the history of the place made it ideal for dreaming about Anna and wallowing in self-pity.

The Basilisk House earned its name from the sandstone basilisk figure protruding from the second story façade. Medieval legend has it that a horrible monster, hatched from the rotten egg of a chicken-toad, lived in the nearby well and made people sick with poison or killed them by looking at them. Pretty typical basilisk stuff. One day an apprentice baker, who was smitten with the baker's beautiful daughter, elected to prove his love through an act of bravery. Taking heart in the affections of the young maiden, he confronted *der Basilisk* in the well. When the monster attacked, he averted his eyes and cleverly held up a mirror. Repelled by its own appearance, the creature instantly turned to stone.

Each time I sat in front of the historic old building, playing my guitar, I thought about the legend. In my mind's eye, Anna was the baker's daughter. But what was I? The brave young apprentice? I wish. More likely, I was the geeky minstrel across the street, who was never mentioned in the tale because all he ever did was admire the fair maiden from afar, never once mustering the nerve to tell her how he felt.

On a clear July evening, exactly two weeks after Anna's departure, business in the shadow of the stone basilisk was unusually good. A large group from Ireland had come to visit the old house, but their tour bus was having mechanical problems. While they waited for it to be fixed, many of them gathered around to listen to my one-man acoustical show. Their bad luck became my good fortune, as they doled out the equivalent of more than a hundred dollars in my guitar case, made up of a mixture of Austrian schillings and Irish pounds. It was already getting late when the Irish blokes' bus was fixed and they left. There were hardly enough tourists remaining to make it worth my while, so I called it a night.

As I was bending over to put Karl away, I heard footsteps approaching quickly.

"Ethan?" It was a woman, her local accent slight, but detectable.

My head jerked up in surprise. "Magda? What are you doing here?" As nice as it was to see her, I was disappointed that she was alone.

She rolled her eyes. "Believe me, I didn't want to come."

"Then why . . . ?"

"Because *I* wanted to hear you play."

My heart froze. Magda's mouth hadn't moved. The words came from someone standing right behind me whose voice was even more familiar.

No accent. Pure Amerikanish.

I turned slowly, disbelieving what was happening. When my neck finally made it all the way around, there was Anna—*the baker's daughter*—smiling nervously back at me as she stepped out from behind a car.

"Hi," she said softly.

In my state of delighted shock, it was all I could do to form an intelligent response. Out of the corner of my eye I spotted the basilisk looming overhead. It reminded me that *this* was my chance. I could still be the apprentice, if only I was willing to be brave. Drawing a deep breath, I blurted out the first fearless thought that came to mind, "You are so incredibly beautiful."

The comment caught her off guard, I think, and for a moment I worried that I'd completely blown it. Her cheeks turned crimson. "I missed you too."

For several seconds we just stood there staring at each other, neither of us moving a muscle. We didn't even blink.

I finally asked her the same question I'd already posed to Magda. "What are you doing here? I didn't think you were coming back."

"We weren't planning on it. But there were two trains to choose from to get to Hungary, and one of them came through Vienna."

"So how long is your layover?"

She checked her watch. "About thirty minutes left," she said, frowning.

My heart sank. "The train station is like twenty minutes from here."

"I know. I'm sorry. I tried calling your apartment as soon as we got in. Your roommate said you were probably out playing the guitar somewhere. He gave us a list of the places you've been playing at the most, so we've been making the rounds. This was our last stop."

"Great," I mumbled. "You found me just in time to . . . what? Say goodbye again?"

Anna walked around me to join Magda on the other side of the guitar case. "No, just in time to say *hello* again. And just in time to hear you play the guitar. All those days we spent together wandering around town, and I never even got a chance to hear you play."

I nodded with a shrug, then picked up Karl and sat down on the stool. "Anything special you'd like to hear?"

"You choose. But make it something memorable. I want a song that I'll recognize, so I can listen to it in the future and think of you."

At first I thought maybe I should favor her with one of my staples, but neither Queen nor Beethoven felt suitable for Anna. Staring at her beautiful face, a melody came to mind, and I instantly knew that was the one for her. Closing my eyes, I began gently plucking the notes to perhaps the most romantic of classical tunes, Pachelbel's "Canon in D." I let my fingers feel their way from string to string, not bothering to look up until I was halfway through the melody. Anna was still there watching me, smiling, apparently pleased with what she heard. Magda was smiling too. A small group of five or six others gathered around to listen to the familiar tune.

When the notes reached their maximum velocity, several people clapped quietly, and a couple stepped forward to drop bills into the guitar case. As the melody wound down, an old woman dropped in some loose change from her purse, then the crowd dispersed once more. Only Anna and Magda remained.

"You're *amazing*," Anna said.

"So are you." My voice cracked just a little.

Magda rolled her eyes. "We have to get going."

Anna shot her a warning look. "*I know.* But first I have to give this fine musician a tip." From the front pocket of her jeans she pulled out a small slip of paper and took several steps forward. Standing over the guitar case, she was about to drop the paper in with the money, but stopped short. Instead, she took another step closer to me and slid the note beneath the strings of my guitar, near where my hand was still gripping the neck. Her fingers brushed mine for just a moment, sending a welcome shiver up my arm. "There," she told Magda. "Now we can go catch our train."

I watched them start to walk away. "Uhh . . . wait!" I shouted when my brain registered that they were really leaving. "Will I see you again?"

Beaming, Anna motioned to the "tip" she'd left in the strings of my guitar.

"I hope so." She waved once more, then turned past the corner of an adjacent building and was gone.

I carefully unfolded the paper. It was a napkin, folded in fourths. When I reached the center there was a brief, handwritten message.

It was a note that would change everything.

Ethan,

I can't tell you how much I enjoyed spending time with you in Vienna. To me, you've been the best part of Europe! On July 23rd I will have one final stop in Austria. I know it's out of the way, but if you'd like to see me as much as I'd like to see you, meet me at 10:00 a.m. at the birthplace of Austria's most famous musical prodigy.

Hope to see you there!
Anna

P.S.—If you're unsure which musical prodigy I'm referring to, just hum a few bars of Falco's greatest hit, and it will come to you!

I knew all four words of Falco's song by heart, and I sang them happily as I folded up the note and tucked it in my wallet for safekeeping. "Ooh, rock me Amadeus!"

Chapter 4

I was up bright and early on July 23rd and at Vienna's Südbahnhof by 5 a.m. There was a westbound train leaving at 5:30, but it was traveling on a circuitous route that had lots of stops in little towns and villages along the way. It wouldn't have gotten me to Salzburg until 9:45, which I thought would be cutting it too close. But an express train was departing at six o'clock, which would put me in Salzburg by 9:00. The choice was a no-brainer—wait a little longer in Vienna for the express train, but arrive at my destination earlier, and with plenty of time to meet Anna at ten.

I'd brought Karl along for the ride, thinking that Anna might want to hear another song, so with a little extra time on my hands I found an empty bench near the base of the escalators inside Südbahnhof and started to play my regular set. It was too early for many tourists to be passing through, but a few people dropped in coins as they walked by. By the time I put the guitar away to board the train, I'd earned enough money to buy a fresh baguette for breakfast and a couple of Almdudlers for the ride.

There were plenty of empty seats on the train. I chose to sit in a small booth that had two cushiony bench seats facing each other. A young couple and their curly-blonde daughter occupied one bench, but the other one was unoccupied. After stowing Karl on the luggage rack overhead, I sat down and anxiously checked my watch.

"Five fifty-five," I whispered to myself, feeling anxious to get rolling.

A minute later, as I was checking my watch again, a loud commotion erupted on the platform outside the train. Near my window stood a stout train conductor in his blue jacket and black-brimmed hat, waving and shouting to another conductor a few cars up. His Vienerish dialect was too thick for me to translate everything, but I did manage to pick out a few key phrases. "I'll stay here . . . ! You call for help . . . ! Hold the train . . . !"

Hold the train?

"*Wun-der-bar*," I moaned aloud. "*Das klingt nicht gut.*" That doesn't sound good.

The little girl across the aisle giggled at me.

Seven minutes later—a full three minutes (and counting) past our scheduled departure time—an ambulance rolled onto the platform with sirens screaming. A man and woman with emergency gear jumped out and were led by a conductor to the rear car of the train, three back from where I sat.

Twenty minutes later, the ambulance was still there.

It wasn't warm out yet, but I was sweating profusely.

The little girl kept herself busy by trying to mimic my terrible accent.

Another half hour and our train was still motionless at the station. I wanted to scream. Now I was officially late. Even if we'd left right then, the best I could hope for was to get to the Salzburg station by ten o'clock, and from there it was still another fifteen minutes to get to where I was meeting Anna.

After five more minutes, the woman sitting across from me asked her husband to go find out what was taking so long. He soon returned to inform us that an elderly woman from Switzerland had passed out in her cabin and cut her head on the metal-rimmed windowsill. When she came to, she also had pain in her neck. But instead of going for a quick trip to the hospital to get checked out, the woman was adamant that she was staying on the train and returning home to Switzerland to be with her grandchildren. That left the transit authorities with two equally bad choices: forcibly sedate a feisty, eighty-year-old foreigner and take her away against her wishes or let her stay on the train and risk having another injury along the way.

I never did find out what their decision was. All I know is that fifteen minutes later the "express" train finally started to roll. By then I knew my date with Anna was sunk. The soonest I could get to Mozart's house was 10:45, nearly an hour after our scheduled rendezvous, and by then she would be gone.

I silently prayed that they'd be able to make up lost time along the way, but it didn't happen.

When I arrived in Salzburg I hailed the first cab I could find and told the cabbie I had an extra fifty schillings for him if he could drive fast.

"Dat's vat . . . five dollars American?" he asked in broken English. "Not vorth fees from *Polizei* for too fast driving."

"*Wun-der-bar,*" I mumbled.

I think he went extra slow just to spite me.

It was a few minutes after eleven o'clock when I finally arrived at Getreidegasse no. 9, the birthplace of Wolfgang Amadeus Mozart. Aside from the large golden letters across the front of the building that read *Mozarts Geburtshaus*, it looked like every other building along the narrow street. I quickly scanned the crowd of people who were admiring the historic site from ground level, but none of them were Anna. I continued looking outside for several minutes, double-checking every face, but she wasn't there. Then I went inside and checked every room of the third-floor museum, but she wasn't there either. After redoing the entire search once more from the start, I finally concluded that she was, in fact, gone.

Can't blame her, I thought, then silently cursed the old Swiss woman for delaying my train.

On the off chance that Anna might come back

later to check for me, I took up a post a little ways off and stayed on constant lookout. After an hour of waiting, I gave up.

She'd given me a chance, and I blew it.

I picked up my guitar case and walked slowly toward the center of town, kicking myself the entire way for being such an idiot. Why didn't I just get on the slower train that left at 5:30? Or, for that matter, why did I even wait until this morning, when I could just as easily have taken a train last night? I wondered how Anna reacted when she realized that I hadn't come. Did she spend time looking for me, hoping that the next brown-haired guy was me? Was she upset? Was she indifferent? Was she at least mildly disappointed? Or was she like me, heartbroken and sick over what might have been?

Whatever she was thinking or feeling, it seemed unlikely that I would ever know.

Chapter 5

I'd already seen Salzburg on a previous visit, and I wasn't in the mood to stick around and see it again. Not without Anna.

After getting a quick bite to eat at a deli, I decided to kill time waiting for the next train back to Vienna by trying to make a few bucks. Karl was still in tune when I opened up the guitar case. I found a good spot at the base of Horse Fountain, a famous statue in the middle of Residenzplatz, and began playing. At first the Salzburg pockets seemed a little tighter than those in Vienna, but it wasn't long before a decent-sized group had gathered around to watch and listen.

By my second song I'd already earned enough to cover my long eastbound ride back to Vienna. I tried not to think about how lonely that ride would be.

During the third song I heard a well-to-do American say to his wife, "Dang if that Austrian can't pick a lick better'n anyone I've ever heard." Based on the size and shape of his belt buckle, I guessed he was from the Lone Star State. He dropped a crisp U.S. fifty-dollar bill in Karl's case and gave me a Texas-sized wink and nod.

That was the biggest single tip I would ever receive during all my days as a part-time guitarist on the streets of Austria.

I acknowledged the tip with an equally generous smile and said, "*Danke schön!*"

The fourth and final song of my set was the ever-popular "Bohemian Rhapsody." It didn't disappoint, either in terms of its appeal or in the number of wallets it cracked. By the midway point, five or six people had already dropped coins or cash into the hopper. Soon thereafter, a French-looking couple nudged their son and daughter forward, each with money in hand, to add to the haul. By then the song was really flying. All of my fingers on both hands were moving as quickly as they could, pounding frets and plucking strings.

I closed my eyes and thought of Anna and how affectionately she'd smiled when she heard me play in front of the Basilisk House. I tried to remember every detail about her as I lost myself in the song. There were a million things about her that I would miss. Her gentle voice. Her even gentler eyes. Her easy laugh. Her honest heart.

My eyes were still closed as the song was winding down. The last note had not yet sounded, but the crowd could tell it was almost over. Small flurries of clapping erupted from all around. While the clapping continued, a voice called out above the dying din. "I'm not sure you deserve a tip for that, Sir. Since when does Queen qualify as classical music?"

The comment pulled my eyelids apart and yanked me immediately to my feet. "Anna!" I shouted, completely ignoring the onlookers. "You're here!"

"You're late."

I put down Karl without taking my eyes off of her. "Too late?"

She tried to cover up a grin. "That depends on how good your excuse is . . . and whether or not you'll join me on the *Sound of Music* self-guided tour."

I tried to match her mock-seriousness. "Okay, then first let me assure you that I had every intention of being on time, but was waylaid by a very old woman who desperately needed medical assistance."

"You stopped to help her? Even when you knew you'd be late getting here? How noble."

"Well no . . . actually I was praying that she'd get off the train as quickly as possible so we could get moving. But, if absolutely necessary, I would have helped her too . . . probably."

Anna laughed. "At least you're honest. That makes your excuse almost believable."

"Thanks—I think. Now, about *The Sound of Music*. Is there really a self-guided tour? I thought I'd already done everything there was to do here."

She unrolled a small paper pamphlet with a picture of Julie Andrews dressed as a nun. "Sure is. Are you game?"

"With you? I wouldn't miss it for the world." I paused and looked around in every direction. "What about Magda? Is she coming too?"

"Aww, you miss her. How sweet. I'll let her know the next time I see her."

"When will that be?"

"Tomorrow, in Venice. She's on her way there now, along with most of my luggage. Our train came through Salzburg just before ten this morning. I got off, she stayed on."

"I didn't think Salzburg was on your itinerary."

The way she was smiling lit up my heart. "It wasn't. I gave up a day in Venice so I could spend one here."

"Excellent choice. I can totally see how walking around here in the stifling heat, hunting for decades-old scene locations from a Rodgers and Hammerstein musical would be *so* much more interesting than, say, a private gondola ride to St. Mark's Square to see the Basilica or Doge's Palace."

At that, Anna slugged me in the arm. Playfully, I think. "I had no interest whatsoever in *The Sound of Music*, or anything else in Salzburg." She inched closer. "I came to meet someone. *A guy,* if you must know. A guy who I couldn't stop thinking about."

I moved closer too. "A super nice, really handsome guy?"

"As a matter of fact, he is. And he's someone who I was sure would want to see me again, even if it was only for a few hours."

"Did he show up?"

Reaching out, Anna placed her hand on my arm and leaned in. For a moment I thought perhaps she intended to kiss me. *I hoped she would.* But when she was close enough that I could feel her breath, she let out a mischievous little whimper, and said, "Sadly, no. He stood me up. Too bad for me; he was really something special." She threw up her hands. "Oh well, at least you're here. Right?"

What a tease.

"Yeah, lucky me. I can be your shoulder to cry on."

"Exactly!" She patted me on the chest and then stepped back.

We spent the next couple of hours walking from site to site around town, trying to imagine which scene from *The Sound of Music* was filmed at which spot. My favorite was the Abbey, where we sang a rousing rendition of "How Do You Solve a Problem Like Maria." But mostly we just talked. And laughed. And teased. And talked some more.

Along the way we stopped by the train station and paid a few schillings to have them hold Karl until I could pick it up later. That not only made it easier to get around, but it also freed up my hand for when Anna decided to hold it.

In the afternoon we found a cabdriver who was willing to drive us the thirty or so miles to Bertchtesgaden, a small town just across the border in Germany. From there we took a tour bus up to the top of the Alps to tour the Eagle's Nest, Hitler's Bavarian hideout. It was a sobering experience to walk the same halls as one of history's greatest fiends. The view from up there was as majestic as any in the world, but the place still gave me the creeps.

To lighten the mood, we scoured the compound's many restrooms, looking for one that might be missing a door handle. As strange as that may sound, it wasn't. My grandpa didn't talk a lot about World War II, but he did claim to have been part of the brigade that took over the Eagle's Nest in 1945. He also insisted that while he was there he'd helped himself to one of Hitler's bathroom door handles as a souvenir.

Much to our disappointment, the restrooms that were open to the public had all of their handles accounted for.

Late in the evening, Anna and I returned to Salzburg, where we enjoyed a candlelit dinner at a Tirolean restaurant near the Salzach River. By the time our stomachs were full it was time to make our way back to the train station to catch Anna's southbound line.

While waiting for her train to board, I fetched my guitar from the luggage hold. Anna wanted to hear "her song," the "Canon in D," once more before she left.

Before I played, she scooted closer on the bench we were sharing. "Ethan, how far would you go to see me again?"

"When?" I asked excitedly.

"No, I mean just hypothetically. How far would you travel to see me?"

"Well, that depends."

She slapped my knee. "*Excuse me?* Depends on what?"

"On how far away you are."

Her smile said my answer was the right one.

Anna's train was already boarding, but there was still enough time to play the canon one time through. While my fingers were working the guitar, Anna's fingers took a moment to scribble something on a piece of paper. When the song finished, she stood up in front of me and slid the paper through the guitar strings, the same as she'd done in front of the Basilisk House in Vienna. Only this time she leaned over the body of the guitar, which was resting on my knee, and added something more—a soft peck on each of my cheeks, followed by a perfect, pensive kiss on the lips. Standing up, she adjusted her backpack on her shoulders and began walking slowly toward Platform Number 6.

I quickly grabbed the note from the strings. It took me all of two seconds to read.

Octavius Burke—Moscow

I recognized the name as that of her father. But . . . ? "Moscow?" I called. "You want me to find you in Russia?"

Anna turned and crossed her arms. "Is that too far for you, Mr. Bright?"

"No, but . . . why *Moscow?*"

"It's a little place I like to call home. Good ol' Moscow, Idaho."

The light bulb in my head finally clicked on. "And you're sure it won't be hard to find Octavius?"

"It shouldn't be hard at all. He's the only one in the entire state, the last time we checked. Find him, and you'll find me." She waved once more and was gone.

"You can count on it," I whispered.

Chapter 6

T he rest of the summer passed much slower than I would have liked. Not that I wanted my time in Austria to be over, but I could hardly wait to embark on the important business of locating Anna Burke. Eventually my classes concluded, graduation ceremonies were conducted, and I was officially declared a Master of Music. While my peers were interviewing for respectable jobs—teaching positions at universities, conducting musical theater in Paris or New York, or playing in renowned orchestras around the globe—I was packing up Karl and flying back to my grandfather's home in the quiet coastal town of Garibaldi, Oregon—population 881, give or take a score of seasonal crabbers who would only be counted as residents if the census were conducted late at night at the local pub.

I stayed there exactly one week, which was the amount of time it took to persuade Grandpa to loan me his beat-up truck for a trip to Idaho.

"You just got here and now you want to run off again?" he asked when I raised the question over dinner on my first night home. "What's Idaho got that Oregon doesn't?"

"Would you believe it if I said there's a shortage of professionally trained guitarists there?"

"*Pfft*. I'm neither young nor naive, Ethan."

"What if I said I'm interested in growing potatoes?"

Now he laughed out loud. "Ethan Bright, the spud farmer. That'll be the day."

And so I admitted to having met an exceptional woman from the Potato State and that I wanted to go see her.

"How long you do plan on being there?"

I swallowed an undercooked baby carrot. "Depends on how it goes. Maybe a week or two."

"I'll think about it."

I knew he'd end up letting me go . . . eventually. He didn't admit it, but I think he really missed having me around. He was only stalling as a means to keep my company for a little while longer.

On the evening of my sixth day there, he finally gave in.

The next morning, I was gone.

By six o'clock that night I rolled into Moscow, just across the border from Pullman, Washington, along the eastern edge of the Columbia Plateau. The welcome sign coming into town said there were just over twenty thousand residents, which, compared to Garibaldi, was quite a lot. Based solely on what Anna had described, I'd expected to see nothing but farmland. What I found was a vibrant town, bustling with cars, and with a charming university at its core.

It only took me five minutes to find a 7-Eleven with a public phone book. The cashier was more than happy to offer basic directions to the address of Octavius Burke, one of seven Burkes listed in the white pages. Ten minutes later I parked the rusted-out F-150 in front of a two-level home on Ponderosa Drive.

My stomach did somersaults as I waited for the door to open. When it finally did, I was greeted by a tall man with wire-rimmed glasses that rested squarely on a narrow nose. His mop of graying hair curled slightly just above the shoulder. He squinted at me like his glasses were out of focus, then he examined me from head to toe. "Can I help you?"

I felt strangely like a teenager arriving for junior prom. "Er . . . Hello. Is Anna home?"

He shifted uncomfortably. "Perhaps. Is she expecting you?"

"Probably not."

"Then may I ask what your business is?"

I wanted to say, "This isn't business . . . it's pleasure," but I doubted that would get me in the door. "I guess you could say I'm just following up on some unfinished business from Austria."

The man nodded slowly, and as he did so, his demeanor softened considerably. "So you're Ethan?"

"I am. You must be Mr. Burke?"

He nodded again. "Octavius."

"Anna told me a lot about you," I lied. "All good, I might add."

That put a smile on his face. He motioned for me to come inside, then closed the door and asked me to wait there. After climbing most of the way up the staircase that rose up from the edge of the entryway, he called out, "Annaliese! There's someone here to see you."

"Who is it?"

A chill coursed through my veins at the sound of Anna's muffled voice.

Octavius turned his head and looked at me, flashing a mischievous smile that reminded me of his daughter; then he called back over his shoulder, "Oh, nobody important." Focusing once more on me, he whispered, "Just between us guys, if I mentioned your name I bet it would take twenty minutes of hair-doing and makeup before she'd be ready to be seen. Better off just surprising her."

I suddenly liked Octavius Burke very much.

A moment later a door opened on the second floor and out came Anna, looking as gorgeous as ever in a maroon sweatshirt, gray pajama pants, and a pair of fluffy pink slippers. When she saw me she stopped mid-stride and did a double-take. She also glanced down at her slippers and pajamas and, by the look on her face, she regretted her choice of evening attire. But rather than act embarrassed or awkward, she just lifted her head and walked confidently down the stairs, as though she knew I wouldn't care what she was wearing.

Anna didn't say a word until she reached the bottommost step, making her the same height as me. With a familiar smile she reached out, wrapped her arms around my shoulders, and gave me a friendly hug. "You came," she said, with a mixture of excitement and contentment.

I chuckled. "Did you think I wouldn't?"

"I hoped, but it's been almost a month and a half, so who's to say you didn't forget about me? Or find some other unsuspecting tourist to charm? Wasn't your graduation two weeks ago? After a week passed I started to worry."

"Well, I am quite charming."

She nudged me in the ribs. "Yes, but suddenly less so than I remember."

"Actually, graduation was only eight days ago. And once I was back in Oregon it took me a little longer than expected to scrounge up wheels to drive out here. Before I went to Europe, I sold everything I had, including my car, so my options were somewhat limited. Convincing my grandfather to lend me his truck was like getting Magda to visit the Hundertwasser garbage dump. He caved in last night, and I hit the road this morning."

She tilted her head at an angle. "So it wasn't two weeks ago?"

"Maybe you have me confused with that other guy who stood you up in Salzburg."

"That's probably it. Oh well, at least one of you made it here."

Octavius and Anna lived alone in the home. Julia, Anna's mother, had succumbed to cervical cancer when Anna was a freshman in high school. The fact that we'd both lost our moms earlier than anyone should was one of the things that had helped us really connect back in Austria. Her older brothers were already out of the house. Lance, the oldest, was living in Pocatello, on the opposite end of the state, where he taught junior high shop class, solely as a means to fund his exotic summer adventures around the globe. The middle sibling, Stuart, was some sort of techno-geek running his own start-up company in Silicon Valley.

Rather than sending me to a motel, Octavius surprised me by offering up Stuart's old bedroom, directly across the hall from Anna's. "As long as you're in there," he told me, pointing to my designated sleeping quarters, "and Anna's in her room, then everything is copasetic. Call me old-fashioned, but this is my house, and even though you're both adults, in my house we play by my rules." He pushed his glasses up on his nose to emphasize the seriousness of the matter.

I made up my mind immediately to follow the house rules. If anything serious were ever to come of my relationship with Anna, I wouldn't want to be on anything but good terms with her father. "Understood," I said. "And, thank you."

I only intended to stay with the Burkes for a few

days (not that I had anything else on my life's agenda than to spend time with Anna, but I didn't want to become a bother). However, when a few days were up, Anna convinced me to stay for a few more. And then a few more. And a few more after that. Moscow, Idaho, was certainly not Vienna, but on her home turf it was Anna's turn to play tour guide, and she filled the role perfectly. Each day she took me to see something new—the university, a meticulously groomed apple orchard, whitewater rafting, a farmer's market, and an alpaca ranch, just to name a few. We even spent time poring through the Idaho Forest Fire Museum, giving special attention to what must be one of the largest collections of Smokey the Bear memorabilia in the world. Much like our time together in Europe, if there was anything worth seeing or doing, we saw or did it. And if there was ever a moment where we didn't have something on the schedule, Anna took me to meet the countless friends and family she had in the area. In the evenings we would try new places to eat, walk along the river, or simply sit in the park and talk.

No, it definitely wasn't Vienna, but with Annaliese Burke at my side, the experiences in Idaho were every bit as memorable.

At the two-week mark, Octavius shocked me over dinner by offering Stuart's room on a longer-term basis. "You've earned my trust," he said, "and should be commended for that. I don't know what your immediate plans are, but if you need a place to stay while you're figuring things out, you're welcome here."

"Thank you," I said coolly. "I'll think about it." *Yeah, right,* I thought, my mind already made up. *As if there's anything to think about.*

The next day Anna and I caravanned back to Oregon to return my grandfather's truck. We stayed nearly a week, allowing Anna time to get to know Grandpa Bright and a couple of my aunts, and allowing me time to pack up my few personal belongings. On the morning of our sixth day there we said goodbye, loaded the boxes into Anna's Jetta, and returned to Moscow.

I had no car and very little money, but at least I had a place to stay.

And I had Anna.

Knowing that I had to do something— *anything*—to start earning money like a respectable adult, I registered the following morning as a substitute music teacher with the local school districts, both in Idaho as well as across the border in eastern Washington. It wasn't what I considered ideal use of my master's degree, but at least it provided a paycheck. Between that and private guitar lessons, I was able to afford my own transportation very quickly, which was a huge relief. Soon thereafter I was making enough to afford rent payments for a single-room apartment on the other side of town. Octavius

71

assured me I was welcome to stay under his roof rent-free so I could save more money, but I knew I needed to be on my own, if only for the self-respect.

While I was busy teaching, Anna spent her days taking a few courses in writing, publishing, and children's literature at the university. She was still very determined that she was going to write and illustrate children's books as a career, and she hoped the coursework would give her an edge. In the evenings we often got together to nudge one another along in the pursuit of our artistic dreams—she would sit on one end of the sofa, thinking up catchy story lines or sketching characters, while I sat on the other end with Karl, trying to write pop hits. Periodically we'd stop to share notes and a quick kiss, and then it was back to work.

With each passing day, Anna and I grew steadily closer. Being around her was easy. She described our comfort level with one another as "uncommonly natural." It required no pretense whatsoever. We just seemed to *fit,* kind of like a two-part harmony. On account of how well things were going, it wasn't very long—a few months, tops—before we began openly discussing the possibility that our relationship might have the makings of something special—maybe even something that could stand the test of time.

Octavius was a philosophy instructor at the

university, so most of his days were consumed teaching undergraduates how to reason like the great thinkers of the ancient Greco-Roman world. But occasionally, when I was visiting, he also waxed philosophical at home. "Let me just remind you," he told us one evening over dinner, "that should you eventually decide that love exists in the natural world—and then, should you further conclude that you are, in fact, experiencing love firsthand, and not some delusion of the mind— that you are both sufficiently old to get married and start a life of your own." He paused to grin. "No rush, of course. Just laying out a few tangential things for you to consider."

By my fifth month in Moscow, a short seven months after meeting Anna on a tram car in Austria, I decided that the time for speculation and conjecture about what our future might hold was over. One night at Anna's house, after Octavius had gone to bed, I grabbed the globe that he kept on his desk in the study and brought it to Anna on the living room floor.

"Do you remember what you asked me before you got on the train for Venice?"

She dipped her head and smiled. "Of course. I asked how far you'd travel to see me again."

"And my answer?"

"Depends on where I am."

"Exactly. And I still feel that way. More so, actually."

Anna wrinkled her nose. "So what's with the globe?"

"That, Ms. Burke, is just to help you keep in mind how big the world is. Because I want you to know that wherever you are, that's where I want to be."

Her eyes smiled at the comment. "I'm here now." She leaned forward, expecting me to kiss her. When I didn't, she rolled her eyes and pretended to pout.

"The thing is," I continued, straight faced, "I'm more than a little interested in how far *you'd* go."

She chuckled dryly. "Why? You going somewhere?"

I raised my eyebrows but didn't say anything.

Anna sat straight up. "Oh my gosh. Are you?"

"Maybe."

"Where?"

"Well, that depends."

She chuckled again. "Everything depends with you, doesn't it?"

"Hey, I'm trying to be serious here."

After taking a moment to read my face, she politely played along. "Okay. Depends on what?"

"On how far you'd go to be with me. Would you search the world to find me? To find true love?"

"Is that what we have?"

"I think so."

"You *think?*"

"Okay, I *know*." I paused to let that sink in. "Do you?"

With her eyes locked on mine, she tipped her head almost imperceptibly, then calmly stated, "Yes."

"Then how far would you go?" I repeated.

"As far as I have to."

I smiled, and she reciprocated. "Okay, then since we've got the globe here, let me give you a few examples of different locations around the world, just to make sure you understand what you're saying. Because some of these places are pretty far."

She shot me a quizzical look. "Okay . . ."

I spun the globe and stopped my finger on the panhandle of the US. "Would you go all the way to Miami?"

"Absolutely."

I spun it again, this time to Europe. "How about Rome?"

"Definitely, I'd love to go back there."

"Berlin?"

"Sure."

"Greece?"

"Uh huh."

"Edinburgh?"

"You do realize that most of those places in Europe are about the same distance away from here, right? At least in terms of traveling time. So I wouldn't be going any farther to prove my love."

"Just answer the question, smart aleck."

"Fine. Yes, I'd go to Edinburgh."

"What about Lisbon?"

"Portugal? Sure."

"What if I said I was going to Australia?"

"Ooh, are you?"

"Would you go?"

"Without question."

I paused and spun the globe one more time, watching until it came to a stop, then looked at her until I had her full attention. "Anna, I *am* going to one of those places that I just mentioned. But it wouldn't be the same without you there."

Her face tensed instantly. "You're serious?"

I nodded.

"Which one?" she asked, then quickly added, "And don't say 'it depends.' "

"But it actually does."

"On what?"

"On two very important things. First, it depends on which of the cities that I mentioned sounds the most interesting to you."

She pulled her knees to her chest and wrapped her arms around her legs as she considered the matter. "I've been to Europe already, so . . . I think Miami would top the list. I've never been to Florida, and I love the beach."

"Okay. Then secondly it depends on . . ." I let the words trail off as I forced a giant yawn.

"Depends on?" she pressed, obviously concerned about why in the world we were going to Miami.

As the yawn tapered off, I deftly scooted closer, positioning myself on a single knee on the carpet right beside her. "On whether," I continued slowly, "you agree to marry me."

For a minute I feared her bulging eyes were going to pop right out of her head. And though I wouldn't have thought it possible, her eyes got even bigger when I produced a small engagement ring from my jeans pocket. Then she began to tear up, whether out of happiness or eyestrain, I wasn't sure.

Anna was trembling. She took a moment to compose herself while wiping the moisture from her eyes. "Yes, but . . . why are we going to Florida?"

Now I grinned as big as I could. "We have to go somewhere on our honeymoon, right?"

Wrapping her arms around me, she whispered, "Florida is perfect."

"Not to sound cheap or anything," I added, "but Florida was my first choice too, because I think I can afford to take us there without major debt. So thanks for that."

Without letting go of me she said, "We can go to Boise for all I care. It doesn't matter, as long as we're together."

SECOND VERSE:

DUET, *ADAGIO DOLCISSIMO*

Chapter 7

T he wedding happened six months later at an old church near the university campus in Moscow. Only a handful of my family could make it to Idaho for the occasion, but the ones that mattered most were there—Grandpa Bright, aunts Jo and Beth, and my cousin Seth, who was also my best man. To everyone's astonishment, my dad made an appearance too. He only talked to me briefly, offering whatever fatherly wisdom he could; I didn't put much stock in it, but it was a kind gesture on his part. It would be the last time I saw him for many years.

In contrast to my limited family support, the church was packed to overflowing with Anna's friends and family, who'd come to celebrate the occasion. Her mother's side of the family was thrilled that she chose to wear her mom's elegant white wedding dress.

One grandmotherly type, upon seeing Anna before the ceremony, proudly exclaimed that Anna was, "a spittin' image of Julia . . . God rest her soul." She also added, "No doubt about it, this is little Annie's finest moment."

The old woman couldn't have been more right. Anna was *fine*. She was a rare sight, with her long satin train and flowing hair. Though the church decorations were amazing in their own right, with beautiful white lilies and burgundy roses dotting the chapel from floor to ceiling, they paled in comparison to the living gem at center stage. Once she started walking down the aisle with Octavius, to the sound of a violin quartet playing the "Canon in D," I couldn't take my eyes off of her.

The minister gave a brief sermon on the sanctity of marriage, but I was too wrapped up in admiring the woman who was about to be my wife to catch many of the details. I do, however, remember vowing before God and the congregation that I would love, comfort, and honor Anna always, no matter what.

That evening, after the reception, we caught a late commuter to Boise, and from there boarded a red-eye to Florida. At thirty thousand feet, I added an extra vow or two to the ones I'd made earlier at the church. "There's only one way I could ever really express how much I love you," I told her. "I'm going to write a song, just for you. You deserve a ballad that's uniquely yours."

"That's sweet. But what happens if you write a song and then the way you feel about me changes? You'd have to rewrite it."

"*Huh?* Didn't we just tie the knot? How could you possibly think I could ever love you less?"

"I was hoping," she snickered, "that five, ten, fifty years from now, you'll love me *more*."

I kissed her gently on the cheek, then again on her forehead. "I will."

"I'm counting on it. I'm also counting on you serenading me at least once a week on the guitar. And if you happen to write a song just for me along the way, all the better."

"Only once a week? Easy."

"For the rest of our lives?"

I smiled and kissed her. *"Forever."*

She kissed me back. "So when will this song of yours be done?" Before I could answer, her gaze narrowed on me suspiciously. "Are you going to try to sell it to some music producer, so a big-time singer can turn it into a huge hit?"

"Do you want me to?"

"No."

"Not even if you can star in the music video?"

"Ugghh, double no."

"Good. Because I want it to be yours, and yours alone. It'll be like a gift that only you can open."

"A gift, huh?" She laughed softly. "After today's reception, I think I'm all gifted out." Anna sat quietly for a moment, and then her eyes lit up. "It can be an anniversary present! You can work on my song for the next year, then sing it to me one year from today, on our first anniversary. That's all I want, and it won't cost you a dime."

"It won't cost *us* a dime," I corrected, "and good thing, because after this honeymoon an extra dime might break our budget."

"Hey, for richer or poorer, right?"

I took a long sip of my ginger ale. "So it's

settled then—I owe you a song one year from today. But since you know what you're getting next year, I want to request an anniversary present too—assuming you were planning on getting me something."

"Okay."

"I'd like a painting. An original Annaliese Bright. On canvas. Something we can frame and put up in our home."

She tapped the tip of my nose with her index finger. "Consider it done."

"Excellent. Then when you're a world-renowned author-slash-illustrator, and people are clamoring for your work, I can put it up for auction and make a killing. I think that'll be my retirement plan."

"Oh really, Mr. Bright? You're going to sell your anniversary present? Fine, then when you're a famous songwriter, I'll sneak into the bathroom and record you singing one of your hits in the shower, then send it in to all the radio stations so everyone can hear the true voice behind the music. I bet someone would pay me for that, right?"

Anna had overheard me singing in the shower exactly one time, back before I found my own apartment, and had teased me mercilessly about it ever since. Although I loved music and lyrics, my own voice was not an adequate tool to put the two together, which was the very reason I'd aspired to be a songwriter rather than a singer. "You wouldn't."

She patted my leg. "Just keep my painting on the wall. Or else lock the door when you're in the shower."

It was already late at night and the flight to Miami was long. Anna eventually fell asleep. I stayed awake long enough to write down a few of my thoughts from the most important day of my life, but the only thing I could find to write on was the white throw-up bag in the seat pocket in front of me. I took it out and jotted down whatever came to mind: impressions from the wedding, how I felt about Anna, things my family had said to me, and the promises I'd made to Octavius before the ceremony. When I got to that last one, it occurred to me that I'd made many promises in the last twenty-four hours, and not just to Anna's father. I flipped the bag over and itemized each of them.

Promised Octavius:

- that I will always put Anna's happiness ahead of my own.
- that I will take care of her.
- that I will never break his little girl's heart.

Promised Grandpa Bright:

- that I will always treat Anna as a treasure. "For where your treasure is, there will your heart be also."

Promised my Dad:

- that I will learn to be forgiving, even when it's hard. (Note to self: why would I promise that man anything? Oh well, forgiveness in a marriage still sounds smart.)

Promised Aunt Jo:

- that I will remember to put the toilet seat down (note to self: a 2-bath apartment might be worth the expense).

Promised God, "in witness thereof by those in attendance" that I will love, comfort, and honor my wife:

- in sickness and in health
- for richer or for poorer
- for better or for worse
- in sadness and in joy
- to cherish and continually bestow my heart's deepest devotion upon her
- to love her, and none other, as long as we both shall live.

Promised Anna:

- that I will serenade her on the guitar at least once a week.

- to write a song just for her and sing it to her on our first anniversary.
- that my love for her will be greater with each new tomorrow.

Satisfied that the list was complete, I tucked the vomit bag in my carry-on, leaned back, and closed my eyes. Sitting there in the airplane's narrow seat, a strange sense of contentment washed over me, like everything was right in the universe. At least in my universe, it was. I'd found *her*—the only woman I would ever want or need; the woman who'd stumbled into my life on the streets of Vienna, and who agreed to become my wife at a church in Moscow.

I opened my eyes once more to look at Anna. She was leaning against the window, oblivious to the world around her. Yet even as she slept I could see the makings of a beautiful smile on her lips.

After my mom died when I was a kid, I often wondered where heaven was located, assuming that's where my mother had "gone." I never really came to a solid conclusion on the matter. But my final thought that night on the airplane, before succumbing to the lull of jet engines and dim cabin lights, was that I'd finally found heaven. It was hiding right beside me in Anna's perfect smile.

Though our flight ended in Miami, our resort was further north, in West Palm Beach. When we arrived late in the morning, exhausted from a long night of travel, the beach at our back door seemed the perfect place to sit and relax. We lounged on the white sand for almost an hour, jointly planning out the rest of our week. Hanging out at the beach, doing next to nothing was our top priority, but we also wanted to have some fun and see the sights. When our planning session was through, our short list included parasailing, deep-sea fishing, driving south to explore the Keys, an airboat tour in the Everglades, and a trip to a gator farm.

With our plans sketched out, we grabbed a late lunch at a beachside cabana, then went back to our room and finally unpacked our luggage. The bulkiest of our belongings was Grandpa's guitar. Although I'd wanted to leave it back home in Idaho, Anna insisted that I bring it along so I could play for her late at night on the beach. After hanging a few outfits in the closet, I took Karl from its case and casually plucked out a medley of classical pieces, followed by a country song I'd recently written; then I laid down for a much-needed nap.

When I awoke just before three o'clock, Anna was curled up beside me, sleeping like a baby. Next to my side of the bed, propped up against the nightstand, was Karl, even though I distinctly remembered having put the old guitar back in its case on the floor before falling asleep.

Tucked beneath the strings of the guitar was a small pink envelope. On the front, written in Anna's distinctive hand, were the words *True Love Note*. On either side of the inscription she'd drawn a pair of musical notes.

Hey Hubby! Do you like the sound of that? I can hardly believe we're actually married! What a trip, huh? I can also hardly believe that you're taking a nap on the first full day of our honeymoon!

Just kidding . . . I'm worn out too, and will be joining you soon. But oh, what I wouldn't give right now to be that pillow that you're cuddling so tight!

As the envelope states, I've named this a "True Love Note." I know how much you love playing musical notes, and I've always had an affinity for writing love notes (hee, hee), so this is my attempt at bringing those two things together. Hopefully it will bring us closer together too! Okay, in case you're worried, I haven't written all that many love notes . . . but I did write a few over the years, to guys whose names I no longer remember. Which is why I'm calling this a True Love Note, the difference being that you're the first person where I know the love is true!

So here's the deal: every time you play the guitar for me, I promise to leave you a True

Love Note in your guitar. Yes, I know, that means at least once a week (you promised!). They won't always be long, but they will always be true. And hopefully they will always be a reminder to you that you are truly loved.

You've made me so happy, and I can't wait for that happiness to expand as we grow old together.

In every way possible, I am yours.
Anna

Chapter 8

Octavius was kind enough to move all of Anna's belongings from his place to ours while we were in Florida. All we had to do to settle in when we returned was find room for the pile of wedding presents. He also surprised us with a brand new queen-sized sleigh bed, which was waiting for us in the bedroom, complete with warm flannel sheets and a thick feather duvet.

Once September rolled around, substitute teaching and a part-time job at a music store kept me busy about four days a week. The other three days were spent writing lyrics and melodies from the comfort of our tiny living room. It was working out so well that in the first few months of marriage I'd already composed eight songs that I was sure would catch the interest of producers in either Nashville or L.A.

Anna worked evenings at a department store. Not her dream job, by any stretch of the imagination, but it was enough to help cover the bills, and it left her mornings free to focus on writing and illustrating children's books. All of her stories were terrific, but the best was a heartwarming series about a scrawny little boy named Luke Warm and his heroic quests to find friendship. Anna used the kitchen table as her art studio, but she kept all of the completed artwork on the top shelf of her closet in special binders. The books were progressing so well that she expected to have them polished enough to send out to publishers by the end of the year.

For the first few months after our wedding, the daily grind of life was overshadowed by the naive bliss of matrimony. The newness of marriage made it seem as though nothing would ever go wrong. It was as perfect a beginning to our new life together as I could have imagined.

I faithfully played the guitar for Anna at least once a week, as I'd promised, and in return I received a *True Love Note* woven into the strings of my guitar, to be found the next time I played. Sometimes the notes were several pages long, and other times they were only a sentence or two. But even if all she wrote was, *I love you more today than yesterday,* that was enough.

In addition to honoring my vow to play the guitar for her, I'd diligently lived up to all of my other marriage-day promises too. Well, maybe I left the toilet seat up a few times, but in the Garden of Eden we'd created for ourselves, such trivial things were easily overlooked and instantly forgiven, so it was as though it never happened.

Wouldn't it be great if the honeymoon period never ended? If everything stayed perfectly divine and unbelievably dreamy forever? After Adam and Eve got the Supreme boot from their little garden paradise, I bet they thought that exact same thing. But eventually, every marriage succumbs to the realities of life.

Our formal honeymoon in Florida ended on a Sunday. The honeymoon period, however, ended almost four months later . . . on a Friday.

An all-call page was made over the intercom at the middle school where I was substituting. "Mr. Bright, please come to the office immediately. Mr. Bright, to the office please."

When I got there, the school secretary was waiting anxiously with a phone outstretched in her hand. She mouthed, *It's your wife.*

Even before I said anything I could hear Anna crying.

"It's me. What's going on?"

"It's my fault," she whimpered. "I thought I turned the oven off."

"What happened?"

She was quiet for a second, and then the whimpers turned to sobs. "The chicken *burned,* Ethan . . . I was trying to c-cook you a nice dinner."

"Sweetie, it's okay. Take a deep breath. I don't care that you burned the chicken. We can spare a few bucks tonight to go out for dinner. How does that sound?"

The wailing on the other end of the phone intensified. "It's not the *ch-chicken!* It's everything else! I th-thought I'd t-turned it off when I ran to the store. And when I c-came back . . ."

The muscles in my throat tightened around a new knot. "Anna, what happened?"

I could hear her sniffling. She took a big, calming breath, and while slowly exhaling she said, "It's gone, Ethan."

"What is?"

"*Everything*. Our furniture, our clothes, the apartment—it's all gone. The fire spread so fast. Too fast . . ."

My mind was reeling. I'd been living in a postnuptial dream world for so long that I found it hard to process what she was saying. I tried focusing on the key words.

Chicken.

Fire.

Apartment.

Burned.

Everything.

"Everything?" I asked.

"Yes!" she howled.

"The bed from your dad?"

"Gone."

"Your stories and artwork?"

She cried loudly, then mustered another sorrowful, *"Gone."*

I tried to swallow but my mouth was too dry, and the lump in my throat just wouldn't budge. "What about Grandpa's guitar? And all of my songs?"

"The guitar was near the f-front door. I was

able to grab it. But your sheet music was on the n-nightstand." Anna broke into another fresh round of sobbing. "I'm . . . *so* . . . sorry," she managed to get out between tearful breaths.

"But you're safe, right? You're not hurt?"

"I smell like smoke, but I'm fine. Can you come home?"

The vice principal filled in for me in the classroom so I could go be with Anna and survey the damage. The fire trucks were still there when I arrived, but the work of putting out the blaze was all but done.

The property manager was on the scene talking to Anna when I approached. "The building is covered with its own fire policy," he told me. "But do you have any sort of renter's insurance to cover your things? Your wife wasn't sure."

I focused on Anna and tears filled my eyes. "No," I whispered, as I wrapped my arms around her. I held her as tight as I could. "I meant to . . . but it slipped my mind."

Anna sobbed some more. Not only was everything we owned gone, but without insurance we had no way to replace it.

Later, when it was safe enough to enter, the fire chief gave us a quick tour of the apartment. What had been my home when I left earlier that morning was now just a smoldering shell of ashes and charcoal. The refrigerator was melted. The walls and ceilings were scarred with soot. The bed was a heap of rubble. Our dressers were cinders. Anna's illustrations—the product of untold hours of work—were now piles of silt on the scorched floor. And there wasn't a single shred of evidence left that I'd ever written any music.

We were both shaking when we left the apartment. The sense of loss was demoralizing. All of our hard work—*our dreams*—had literally gone up in smoke. I didn't blame Anna for "burning the chicken" any more than she blamed me for not getting insurance, but the fact remained that we suddenly had nothing, and the thought of it shook us to the very core.

But the trauma of the day was not over. Once we were alone in my car, Anna had more details to share.

She fumbled around in her purse. "This isn't how it was supposed to turn out."

"You mean extra crispy? No kidding."

"No, I mean *today*. It's all wrong."

I exhaled slowly, staring up at the car's sagging ceiling liner. "What could possibly be wrong with losing everything you own?"

She ignored me. "When it didn't come this week, I feared the worst. That's why I was so anxious to make a quick run to the store. I didn't think it would take so long."

"Huh?"

She'd found whatever it was she was looking for, but her hand remained in her purse, trembling. "I don't know quite how to say this, Ethan. This clearly isn't the best time for mistakes of this sort . . ."

"Would you just spit it out already? For crying out loud, our house just burned down. What could be worse than that?" It was the first time in our marriage that I'd spoken to Anna in a way that was anything less than adoring.

I regretted it instantly.

Her free hand shot up to her face, covering her eyes as a new wave of tears began.

Realizing my mistake, I gently apologized and she seemed to settle back down. "Please," I said, "just tell me what's wrong so I can help."

She brushed at the fluid on her cheeks with her sleeve, then steadied herself and looked me straight in the eyes. "The thing . . . Ethan . . . is that . . . there is more in the oven than just some lousy chicken."

"What, like a side dish?"

"You could say that," she deadpanned as she withdrew her hand from the purse and dropped an odd-looking stick on my lap. It was shaped like a tongue depressor, only made of plastic and with a small picture window at one end.

I just stared at it, too nervous to pick it up. "What didn't come this week?"

"Do I really need to say? I think the plus sign there pretty much explains everything."

"So . . . rather than keeping an eye on the chicken you were . . ."

"Taking a pregnancy test. I couldn't wait to find out, so I found an empty stall in the grocery-store bathroom and sat there waiting for the results. That test there is actually number three. The first time I didn't believe the results, so I went and purchased a large water and another test, but it said the same thing. I'm sure the cashier thought I was nuts when I came through a third time for another Dasani and my third pregnancy test. Anyway, after I saw the plus sign on that last test, everything is sort of a blur. Somehow I ended up back at the apartment and there was smoke coming out of the windows and people in the complex were starting to run around. I quickly grabbed your guitar, but that was all I could get to. The neighbors wouldn't let me go back in to try to save anything else."

"It's going to be fine," I assured her.

But in the back of my mind, all I could think was, *the honeymoon is definitely over.*

Octavius was more than happy to let us move back into his house, this time without any rules about not being in the same room at night. He didn't even charge us rent, so we could save our money for all the things we didn't have—clothes, bed, furniture, art supplies, bedding, dishes, towels, just to rattle off a few.

It took several weeks for it to happen, but the shock over the fire eventually faded enough that we were able to focus our attention on Anna's pregnancy. Thankfully, she wasn't sick at all, so her spirits remained high. At night we would lie awake in bed, trying to sort through the details of our sudden state of pre-parenthood. I tended to focus on what I viewed as the more pressing, tactical concerns: *How soon can we move back into a place of our own? How much does a baby cost? Can we adjust our budget to make ends meet? And how in the world can we earn enough money to pay the doctor bills?*

Though she didn't dismiss the practical realities of our situation, Anna stewed more heavily on things like who the baby would look like, would it be a boy or a girl, and would it prefer Dad's music or Mom's art?

"He, *or she,* might not be artistic at all," I pointed out late one night. "He could end up like your brother, a brainiac techno-gadget whose only creative outlet is programming video games."

She gasped. "Can you imagine us raising a little Stuart? No way. I'll just have to immerse him in the arts from day one to make sure nurture has more sway than nature." Though it was already well past midnight, she threw off the covers and climbed out of bed.

"Where are you going?"

"I have some fun ideas for paintings of animals to hang in the nursery—assuming our baby has a nursery. They'll be bright and bold and daring, just like our child. I want to start working on them while the images are fresh in my mind. You just go to sleep."

"Anna," I called before she slipped out through the bedroom door. "You're really liking the idea of being a mom, aren't you?"

She glided back to the bed and gave me a final kiss goodnight. "I'm scared," she admitted, "but I couldn't be happier."

Out of practical necessity, our individual dreams of the future had to take a backseat to the immediate, collective needs of the present. Both of us were determined to pitch in to make things work. I accepted every substitute teaching job that came up, whether for a music class or not. I also took on more hours at the music store and added three additional students to my regimen of private lessons on the weekend.

Anna bumped up to almost thirty hours a week at the department store. She asked for even more, but they didn't want to be on the hook for benefits, so they kept her just beneath the threshold. Twice a week she also taught an evening watercolor class at a local craft store. Anna considered the craft-store money as her own little slush fund, to be spent however she liked. Usually it went to something for "the baby"—booties, sleepers, shoes, and even an occasional matched-set outfit.

"I don't get how you can already buy newborn clothes," I told her once while she was hand-modeling the latest deal she'd found at Gymboree. "We don't even know what we're having yet."

"It's very simple, dear. Mint green and yellow are neutral colors. Just like rabbits, puppies, and teddy bears are neutral animals. As long as I stick to a combination of those things, it doesn't matter if we have a boy or a girl."

"You've really given this some thought, haven't you?"

She looked down and touched her belly, which was just starting to show, and smiled peacefully. "I think about it all the time."

During the first trimester I noticed a steady decline in the number of True Love Notes I was receiving from Anna, but only because the frequency of my guitar serenades had dropped. Whereas during the early months of our marriage I would play for her almost daily, by the twelfth week of her pregnancy I felt good if I pulled out Karl twice in a seven-day stretch. But every time I did, she left me a note, without fail, even if it was just to remind me that she wished I would play for her more often.

Although we still felt as poor as dirt, early in the second trimester we found a suitable two-bedroom apartment across town and moved back out on our own. In order to tuck away a little money for after the baby arrived, I added four more hours of private guitar lessons to my weekend schedule. It wasn't a lot, but it helped.

With the amount of hours we were working, it felt like Anna and I hardly saw each other. Sometimes, late at night, she would say that I needed to slow down, that I'd taken on too much.

"It's only temporary, until the baby comes," I would tell her. "Just to make sure we've got enough money to get by. Then who knows, maybe after the baby arrives I can finally sell a couple good songs and get us out of this financial mess."

"Just until the baby comes?"

"I promise."

Honestly, I intended to keep that promise. And I really think I would have. Unfortunately, I didn't get the chance. Before the end of the fifth month of the pregnancy, Anna miscarried.

The baby never came.

Chapter 9

*F*or me, the miscarriage was an unfortunate event. For Anna, it was an emotional avalanche. Sure, the pregnancy was a bit of an "oops," but that didn't prevent her from becoming very attached to the infant that was growing and kicking inside her. As the pregnancy progressed, she'd started to view and define herself as a mother, and the idea of adding a new member to our family thrilled her to no end. She'd narrowed down a long list of baby names to a handful of her favorites; she'd pinched pennies to begin stocking up on diapers; and she'd painted enough watercolor animals to fill Noah's Ark, let alone the walls of a single nursery. But now that was all just wasted effort. One day everything was perfect, and the next day all of her fantasies of motherhood were yanked away without cause or warning.

The obstetrician's explanation, which he offered along with a twenty-five hundred dollar fee for his services, was, "Sometimes these things just happen."

Really? Thanks for clearing that up, Doc.

Without health coverage to defray the costs, the unsuccessful pregnancy sucked up every last cent in our savings account. And what did we have to show for it? A few fuzzy sonograms of a child we would never meet, baby outfits that would never be worn, and heartache that felt like it would never go away. To deal with the loss, we settled back into a routine that included heavy doses of concentrated "me time," during which both of us refocused our efforts on our as yet elusive dreams of writing songs and children's books.

I was genuinely happy to see Anna spending more time on her artwork. I didn't say anything when she'd sequester herself in our apartment's second bedroom—the one we'd planned for a nursery, but which now served as her art studio—until all hours of the night. I just figured she was trying to paint and write herself out of the doldrums she'd been in over miscarrying.

When I came home from work on the day of our first anniversary, I was surprised to find the lights turned down, with candles lit throughout the apartment. Anna was waiting for me at the kitchen table, wearing a beautiful red dress and, more importantly, a smile that spanned her entire face. It was the same smile I'd fallen in love with back in Austria; the same one that reminded me of heaven. Ever since the fire, and even more so after the miscarriage, that particular smile had been noticeably absent from her repertoire of expressions; not that she hadn't smiled since then, only that I hadn't seen *that* smile.

I bent down to give her a kiss. "Look at you . . . I think you look more beautiful tonight than ever before. No joke. But I guess I didn't get the memo that we were having a fancy dinner. Should I change into something nicer?"

"Nope. You look perfect to me just the way you are. Have a seat."

"Something smells terrific. What's on the menu?"

She let out a muffled laugh. "It's called Chicken Fuego."

"*Fuego*? Doesn't that mean fire?"

"Uh huh. *Fire chicken,* to commemorate our sizzling first year together. But don't be fooled by the name. Unlike the last time I attempted to cook chicken, this recipe is heavy on the fire sauce, but light on the actual fire. In fact, I haven't seen a single flame."

"We could always go to the store for a while and see if anything ignites while we're gone."

"Hmm. Do we have renter's insurance yet?"

I let out a little laugh myself as I stared in awe at the woman sitting across from me. "You're incredible, Anna. Do you know that? I love you so much."

"I know you do. And for some crazy reason, I feel the same way about you. Which is why I have something to show you. I was going to save it for later, but now I can't wait." She stood up and grabbed my hand, then pulled me into our bedroom. On the wall above our bed was a large, framed oil painting. "So? What do you think? It's your very own, original, Annaliese Bright. On canvas."

I was speechless. The painting was an absolutely stunning portrayal of her and me on the night I proposed. It showed the two of us sitting on the floor holding hands, curled in perfect symmetry around a globe. The way we sat, with our bodies and legs curving in opposing directions around each other, it gave the appearance of a human yin and yang. Where one ended, the other began, each giving rise to and completing the other.

"It's the most amazing thing I've ever seen," I said at length. "Is this what you've been working on late at night?"

She nodded excitedly. "It's been so hard keeping it a secret from you. And I wasn't sure I would actually get it done in time. But . . . well, I wanted to keep my promise."

As the last words hit my ears, my heart sank. I'd been so preoccupied with everything else that I'd failed to keep my end of the bargain. Though I'd written plenty of good songs, she'd already heard all of them, and none of them were written especially for her.

I think she could see the anguish in my eyes. "It's okay," she said gently, squaring up to me and touching me softly on the arm. "It's been a rough year, and you've been beyond busy. Please don't feel bad that you didn't write me a song."

"But I promised," I said lamely.

A serious look crossed her face. "I know. And there are other things you promised as well. If it's okay, I'd like to talk with you about them while we eat."

I nodded, and we returned to the kitchen.

While we were eating Chicken Fuego, Anna surprised me again by sliding a white airplane vomit-bag across the table for me to examine. I recognized it instantly.

"Where did you find this? I thought it burned up with everything else."

"You must be getting old; you're already forgetting things. I was taking Karl out of its case about a month ago to leave you a note, but the button for the shoulder strap caught on a piece of the felt padding. It pulled it right out. This was tucked in there behind it."

"That's right! I completely forgot. I put it there, thinking it would be safe."

"You were right. It was safe from you ever finding it again."

"Maybe I am getting old. But I'm glad at least one of us found it."

She smiled affectionately. "Me too. But why didn't you share this with me before? I love what you wrote about our wedding day. And about me. It's very sweet."

I scanned the words I'd written three hundred sixty-five days earlier. "Yeah, well. That's how I felt. Still do, as a matter of fact."

"And how do you feel about what's on the other side of the bag?"

I flipped it over to find the list of wedding day promises I'd made. I took the time to read each one before responding. "Well . . . some of these I think I've done okay on. Not perfect, but pretty good. For the things I vowed during the ceremony, I believe I've kept each of them. Same goes for what I promised your dad."

"What about the things you promised *me?*" she asked softly.

I read those ones silently again. *Promised that I will serenade her on the guitar at least once a week. Promised to write a song just for her and sing it to her on our first anniversary. Promised that my love for her will be greater with each new tomorrow.*

I met her gaze and tried to force a smile. "Well . . . one out of three's not bad, right?"

"Nice try."

"I can do better."

"I know."

"Now that things are a little less stressful, I should be able to start playing for you again. At night, before we go to sleep."

She raised her eyebrows. "Ooh, sounds romantic."

"And as for your special song, I won't work on anything else until it's done. Okay?"

She crossed her arms and rested them on the

table. "I've been thinking about that, actually. And I've decided that I want you to hold off. I don't want you to rush it. I don't want it forced. I know you love me, and I know eventually those feelings will spill over into a song that's just for me. But until then, I'd rather you focus your attention on . . . *something else.*"

I sat up. It wasn't only the way she said those last two words that caught my attention, but also her sudden nervous demeanor. "Something else?"

"Uh huh."

"Do you have something specific in mind? Or just something other than writing you a song?"

Clearing her throat, Anna reached across the table for my hands. Once she had them, she squeezed gently. "I want us *both* to focus on having a baby."

I resisted the urge to pull my hands back. "Wow . . . I mean, so soon after . . . Are you sure?"

She nodded resolutely. "I know it's crazy, given where we're at financially. But I want to find a way to make it work. If that means I work full-time for a while and spend less time on my books, I'm okay with that. And if I have to wait a little longer to get my song, that's okay too. It's just . . . after being so close once already, I know I want to be a mom. And I don't want to put it off."

I rubbed my thumb softly on the back of her hand, buying some time to evaluate my own feelings on the matter. It was obvious that she'd given this a great deal of thought, and I seriously doubted I could get her to change her mind, even if I had good reasons to object. But *did I* have good reasons to object, if this was what she really wanted? Wasn't I upset too when we found out we'd lost the baby? Didn't I wish things had turned out differently? Before saying anything, I made double-sure that my reasoning was sound, that I wasn't leaping into something of such significance without fully weighing the ramifications.

Was I was really ready to commit, wholeheartedly, to whatever came out of my mouth? Was I prepared to make the necessary changes in my life to adequately support a family? *Was I . . . ?*

With a deep breath and another squeeze of the hand, I stared into the face of my best friend, and said, as sincerely as I could, "I'm with you one hundred percent."

Anna had no idea that I was even looking. Rather than get her hopes up prematurely, I decided to wait until there was something positive to report. That moment came about six weeks after our one-year anniversary.

"I have an interview," I announced one evening.

"For a new job?" She tried to curb her enthusiasm, but her eyes betrayed her excitement. We hadn't specifically talked about it, but we both knew that the best way to embark on starting a family would be with steady employment, complete with an insurance plan and maternity coverage. Having already experienced the alternative, we knew our budget couldn't take another hit like that.

"Yep. It's time to put my education to work; join the big boys in corporate America."

"Corporate America has openings for classical guitarists. I had no idea."

"Cute. Actually, I expanded my search a bit for things that loosely fit my skill set, and I stumbled across a marketing firm that's looking to hire what they're calling a 'creative marketing specialist.' The posting says the candidate needs some musical training."

She snickered. "And what exactly is a creative marketing specialist?"

"Basically, entry-level jingle writing. It's helping the marketing team come up with slogans for customers, and then putting them to a catchy tune."

"Sounds right up your alley."

"I know. It's like writing really short songs. How hard can it be? I spoke with the hiring manager and he's willing to give me an interview. He actually sounded reasonably impressed with my musical experience. But . . ."

Anna tilted her head. "What's the catch?"

"He's got lots of applicants already, and he wants to make a final decision by the end of the week, which means I have to be ready for the interview in three days."

"Aren't you ready now?"

"Yes, but . . . it's in California. San Francisco, to be exact. And they won't pay to fly me in. If I want the interview, I have to start driving early tomorrow morning."

If she was moderately enthused at the prospect of my getting a new job, now she was on cloud nine. "Oh, we *have* to make this happen!"

"So you wouldn't mind moving if I got the job?"

"Mind? What self-respecting USC grad would say no to going back to Cali? Plus, we'd be closer to L.A., so maybe that would help you get the right contacts to finally sell your music. I couldn't be happier."

The next morning, at 4 a.m., Anna and I both piled into her Jetta and started driving south. Two days and nearly a thousand miles later, we pulled into San Francisco.

My interview was scheduled for the following day at 10 a.m. When I entered the firm's lobby, I was met by a dozen other men and women, all dressed in suits, who were applying for the same position. The hiring manager, Mark Lloyd, swept into the room at precisely ten o'clock, wearing khakis and a polo. He was in his mid thirties, with thick hair and a confident demeanor. He seemed sharp, immediately commanding the attention of everyone in the room.

"Hello, and thank you all for coming," Mark said loudly. "You are the third and final group to be interviewed. If you're here, it's because I liked what was on your resumé, and you didn't embarrass yourself when we spoke on the phone. But please understand that there is only one opening, and roughly forty interviewees, so keep your expectations in check."

Given the odds, I couldn't help thinking I'd wasted a lot of money driving all the way from Idaho.

"Here's what's going to happen." He glanced at his notepad. "You'll each get a twenty-minute interview, with either me or my boss. At the conclusion of your interview, we'll tell you if we'd like you to move on to the next round or not. Any questions?" When there were none, he checked his notes once more. "All right, then we'll go alphabetically. Ethan Bright, you'll be with me, and Brittany Davis, follow us and I'll escort you to Mr. Schleger's office."

My twenty-minute interview went as well as I could have expected. Mark was easy to talk to, and I didn't say anything that I thought was detrimental. At the end of it, he stood and shook my hand, thanked me for coming, and then told me he'd like me to proceed to the next step of the hiring process.

It took them a little more than two hours to get through the first round of interviews. By then there were only four people left—two other men whose names I didn't catch, and a chatty blonde from Santa Cruz who was "totally, like, going to freak out," if she got the job. Mark treated us to lunch at a nearby restaurant, and then we started round two.

"This will be very simple," Mark explained. "We're going to go back to a conference room where we have a piano set up for you. You don't have to use it, but it's there if you want. Our creative team, which includes basically everyone who reports up through my boss, will be in the room observing. When it's your turn, come in and find a seat. I'll introduce you to everyone. Then I'll give you the name of one of our customers and tell you a little bit about them. You'll have five minutes from that point to come up with a jingle to be used for that customer's radio advertising. Make sense?"

We all nodded.

This time he took us in reverse order, which meant I was last. Every seven or eight minutes one of the other candidates would return from their "jingle-view" (Mark's term, not mine). Both guys looked a little green when they came through the door, but the blonde was sure she "totally nailed it. *Totally*."

When it was my turn to go, I felt oddly at ease as I took a seat at the long rectangular conference table. I attributed my comfort level to the countless hours I'd spent in Austria performing for strangers. After brief introductions, Mark reiterated that I would have precisely five minutes to come up with a jingle, and then he asked once more if I had any questions.

"Yes, two," I responded. "First, do you have a guitar? I can work with the piano, but my mind thinks best with a guitar in hand."

He shot a questioning glance at a female employee near the door. She nodded back, then stood up and left the room. "Susan prefers to work with guitar too. She'll lend you hers."

"Great. My other question is about singing. I can hit most notes—in my range at least—but I'm not what anyone would describe as a singer. What's more important to you, that I come up with a good jingle, or that I sing it well?"

A few people in the room chuckled. "You won't find many good singers here," Mark said. "Susan's probably the best, but the talent drops off quickly after her. We're definitely more interested in your *jingleability*. We have professional singers we contract with for the actual recordings, so you just have to be able to create something catchy that they can work with."

Susan returned a minute later and handed me a twelve-string Martin electric–acoustic.

"All right," continued Mark. "The company we'd like you to *jingle* in the next few minutes is the same one we've given to every other candidate. It's called Nick Jensen Auto Body. They specialize in repairing cars that have been damaged in accidents. They're not a huge national outfit, but they do have a growing number of shops in California, and they're trying to create a brand name for themselves as they prepare to expand. So your job right now is to come up with something catchy to help them accomplish that." He looked down at his watch, clicked a button, and said, "You may begin."

Up until that point, I'd been fine—no worries, no stress, just sort of letting things happen. But with the clock ticking, my mind went as blank as the faces staring at me around the table. For the first thirty seconds I just sat there, cradling the guitar, quietly looking back at them. Soon, my armpits began sweating. That's when I knew I was in trouble. As my temperature rose, my fingers began plucking nervously at the strings of the guitar, without any conscious direction from my brain. It wasn't until they'd been moving for almost half a minute that I realized I was playing Queen's "Bohemian Rhapsody," my old staple from Vienna.

Rather than let them think the song was a mistake, I decided just to let my fingers keep playing. At least it seemed to have everyone's attention. A few heads were bobbing, and previously blank faces were now smiling.

At four minutes, Mark quietly announced that I

had one minute left to share my jingle. I wracked my brain, trying to think of something . . . *anything,* but nothing came to mind. Time pressed quickly onward. With thirty seconds remaining, and with my fingers plugging through the guitar solo as fast as they could, I remembered the advice Anna had given me earlier that morning: *If it comes up in your interview, just remember that the best jingles are the simple ones—simple words, that are sung in a memorable way. Even a company's name can be interesting if it's got the right music.*

Mark was looking disappointed. He mouthed the words, *Fifteen seconds!*

The company's name, I repeated in my head. Just then my fingers reached the end of a key stanza in the song. With no other options, I strummed the last chord as loud as I could, and then implemented Anna's advice to the best of my ability. "Nick . . . Jensen . . . Auto . . . Body . . . ," I sang, plucking one string of the chord for each syllable. I held out the last note as long as I could, and as it started to fade I added quickly, "Collision repair . . . in the *nick* of time!" The words bounced from high to low through a warm major key.

All around the table, men and women exchanged excited glances, speaking to each other with their eyes. Mark finally stood up to translate the nonverbal conversation.

"Mr. Bright, if you don't mind, we'd like you to move to California to join our team."

"You mean I got the job? Just like that?"

"Just like that." As he explained later, even though they thought the phrase "nick of time" worked well, it wasn't the words I'd chosen for the jingle that impressed them so much as how the words *felt* with the music. "The whole package just worked. And the killer guitar performance didn't hurt either," he added with a slap on the back.

Immediately following my interview, the marketing team began working on radio and TV spots built around my eleven-word jingle. It would end up being my first recorded "song."

Two weeks later we waved goodbye to Octavius as we drove out of Moscow, Idaho, for a brand new life in sunny California—a life that included a full-time, salaried job.

Which meant benefits.

Which included health care.

Which meant . . .

Pregnancy.

Chapter 10

When I was in fifth grade, my dad showed up at Grandpa's house one day, completely out of the blue, insisting that I join youth basketball. I'd hardly seen him at all in the past year, and he was concerned about basketball? It eventually became clear that this was his attempt to steer me away from "artsy" pursuits like playing the guitar and writing music. I didn't have much interest in basketball, but I signed up anyway, just to appease him. Not surprisingly, he was gone two days after I joined a team and he never saw a single game.

Frankly, I was glad he never watched me play, because I was terrible at it. But I did learn a thing or two from the experience. Notably, early in the season I remember struggling to make a simple layup. Everyone else on the team seemed to be able to do it, but my arms and legs couldn't get the motion right. Every ball I tossed up was a catastrophe, going anywhere imaginable, except through the hoop.

The coach pulled me aside one day during practice and gave me some excellent advice. "You're thinking too hard. Stop thinking and just have fun. It's not as complicated as you're making it."

I made the very next layup, to thunderous applause from Grandpa, who was watching from the stands.

Six months after moving to California, I gave the same basic advice to Anna. "Sweetie, we must be thinking too hard. Let's stop *thinking,* and just have fun. Billions of people have done this, so it can't be as complicated as we're making it."

She growled softly while fiddling with the pregnancy test in her hand. It was the sixth such test in as many months. "Maybe I just *can't* get pregnant. What if the miscarriage permanently messed me up?"

"Oh, c'mon. You don't believe that."

"Well then maybe it's *you.*"

"Or *maybe,* our heads are getting in the way. Maybe we're thinking too much. How many books have we read on this subject? I honestly think we just need to relax a bit. Slow down and have fun." I poked her in the ribs. "Let's not force it and see what happens."

Apparently, that was the trick. Five weeks later I was in my office at work when the call came.

"Guess who's finally expecting!" she practically screamed into the receiver.

I played dumb. Anna would say I wasn't playing. "Expecting what, hon?"

"What else? A baby!"

"Ooh! Could it be . . . Heather and Stuart?"

"Not even close."

"Lance's new girlfriend? What did your dad say her name was?"

"You're not very good at this, are you?"

"Fine, one more guess. Could it be . . . you?"

"Yes, genius. It's me!"

"That's awesome! Honestly, I'm so happy for you—for *us*. And you successfully took the pregnancy test without burning down the condo?"

"Amazing, huh? I guess I'm getting good at this pregnancy thing."

She should have knocked on wood.

At sixteen weeks, Anna had another miscarriage.

Emotionally, going through this for a second time was a major blow to both of us, though our individual coping mechanisms were quite dissimilar. Whereas Anna refused to do much of anything but cry and mope for the better part of two weeks, I dealt with it by drowning myself in long hours at work. Ironically, my perceived dedication to the company's success turned out to be a huge boon for my career. When management saw how hard I was working, they rewarded me with a promotion, backfilling as a first-line manager for Mark, who had accepted a new position. Unfortunately, that meant that the long hours were no longer just a Band-Aid to cover the pain of another forfeited pregnancy, but rather an expectation of my new responsibilities.

Once Anna got all of her tears out, she gradually returned once more to her happy self. Not wanting to sit around the house alone all day, she busied herself with a part-time job at a craft store. In her free time she rekindled her dream of getting published by sending her books out for evaluation. Sadly, the kindling never ignited a fire. Three months after shipping mock-ups and manuscripts to nearly one hundred publishers of children's literature, she'd received nearly one hundred rejection letters. It wasn't too much longer before her paintbrush and pen were even less active than my fingers and guitar.

One night over dinner she announced that she was throwing in the towel for good. "I guess I just don't have what it takes to make it as an author–illustrator."

I could tell by the look on her face that she was really just vocalizing her frustrations, and maybe looking for a little support from the one person in the world who she should be able to lean on. And I knew, deep down, that I should have encouraged her to keep trying, and to never give up. But then I considered my own lifelong dream, a dream that seemed to be fading just as fast. Was that ever going to become a reality? Would anyone ever want to buy one of my songs?

Probably not.

So instead of telling her the truth, that she was a rare talent and that if she just kept at it somebody would eventually publish her books, I simply nodded.

I nodded!

Of all the things I regret as a husband, that was

one of the worst. A stupid, heartless nod that said, "You're right, honey, you don't have what it takes," even though I fully believed she *did*. I was simply too tired of dealing with disappointment to make the effort.

Her eyes filled immediately with water, a sure sign that I'd just broken her heart.

She tried to remain stoic, willing the tears to keep from falling. "And since I won't be painting or writing anymore, I want to try to get pregnant again," she said calmly.

Again? Aren't two failures enough? But I'd just told her she should give up her dream, and I couldn't bear to break her heart twice in the same minute. So I shrugged and said, "Okay . . . maybe third time's the charm."

We'd only ever been to see an obstetrician during or after the pregnancies, never before. But this time around, Anna was bound and determined to do everything in her power to go full term, which included an obstetric consultation before we even started trying to conceive.

It took several tests, both internal as well as ultrasonic, but eventually the lady doctor had a prognosis. "Your cervix is incompetent." She stated it as a matter of fact, as though that explained everything.

"So are some doctors," I muttered under my breath.

Anna scowled. "Don't mind my husband. He can be incompetent too."

The doctor waved it off. "Oh I don't mind. Mr. Bright, cervical incompetence means the cervix has difficulty holding the weight of a fetus on its own. Nearly a third of all miscarriages in the second or third trimester are a result of an incompetent cervix."

"What's the cause?" asked Anna.

"Usually it's tough to assign a definite root cause. But in your case, it looks like there has always been some malformation of the cervix, probably since birth. I saw in your medical history that your mother died of cervical cancer."

"That's right."

"Well, that may be linked somehow. It's potentially a defect that you inherited, and this is how it's presenting. But we'll certainly want to keep a close eye on it as you get older."

The room went momentarily quiet. Anna stared at me, letting the weight of the bad news pass between us. Finally she asked the question I knew she was thinking, "So there's no way for me to have a baby?"

"Well," the doctor said, "it certainly presents some complications. *And* greater risk. But with some assistance, I think you stand a reasonable chance to reach full term. No guarantees, of course, but we do have a decent rate of success. The plan will be to perform what's called a *cerclage* in week fourteen; basically, sewing the cervix shut. Then we'd remove the sutures once the fetus is fully developed. This should give your body the extra support it needs to carry into week thirty-six or thirty-seven, which should be plenty."

The smile on Anna's face was one of hopeful optimism. "That's the best news I've heard in a long time."

With newfound vigor, Anna laid out an optimized plan for getting pregnant, using special charts and graphs, brochures, and a stack of books recommended by the OB.

Six weeks later she was taking a pregnancy test. The results were positive.

Fourteen weeks later the doctor performed the cerclage, which caused an alarming amount of spotting.

Two weeks later the spotting stopped.

One week later the spotting resumed.

Three days after that, Anna miscarried for the third time.

Three weeks after that, Anna stopped crying.

Our next two years in California were frightfully similar to the first two. I worked hard establishing a name for myself at the marketing firm, while Anna worked hard getting pregnant. *Twice.*

Both pregnancies ended prematurely.

Eventually, I think we both became numb to it all.

In the middle of our sixth year there, Anna woke me up late one night. She'd obviously been crying. "One more time," she said.

I rolled over and rubbed my eyes. "One more time for what?"

"I want to get pregnant one more time."

"What's the use? We already know what the outcome will be."

"Sixth time's the charm?"

"Not likely."

Anna flicked on a light, I think so I could see how serious she was. Then she pointed up at the painting above our bed; the one of us encircled around a globe. "You said you'd search the world to find me. Where I want to be in the world is a place that includes children. It's the one dream I'm not ready to give up on."

Fully awake now, I sat up on my elbow so I could see her better. She was as beautiful as ever, but there were pieces of her—her heart, mostly —that seemed more frail than in years past. A lot of that was a result of the immense loss she'd endured through five miscarriages. *Who wouldn't be a little scarred after that?* But part of her hurt, I knew, was caused by me, through many little acts of thoughtlessness. Things like leaving the house without kissing her goodbye because I was in a rush, or staying late at work when I knew she needed me at home, or choosing to watch a show to wind down after a long day when she wanted me to play her a song on the guitar. Little things that I took for granted, ignored, or simply forgot.

Sometimes little things, when added together, aren't so little.

"You're not kidding, are you?"

She shook her head once, then asked a question she should have never had to ask. "Do you blame me, Ethan?"

"For what?"

"For losing so many babies. Do you resent it?"

"Heavens, no!"

"You don't ever consider the possibility that if you'd married someone else, you could already be a father by now?"

"Of course not. I wouldn't want to be married to anyone else."

She locked eyes with me, as though trying to catch me in a lie. "Okay . . ." she said slowly, "but even if you don't want to be married to someone else, are you still sure you want to be married to *me?*"

"Where is this coming from, Anna? I love *you,* pure and simple. I've always loved you, and I always will."

She didn't blink, but finally her face relaxed and I thought I caught a trace of my favorite smile. "You promised me you'd serenade me on the guitar. That was all you needed to do to say you love me. But since you hardly play anymore, I guess I need to hear the actual words now and again."

"Anna, I'm sorry. I love you like crazy, even if I don't show it or say it like I should. I'll do better. But as I've said before, I'm in this with you one hundred percent. And if you're still willing to keep trying for a baby, then I'm all for it too."

She pulled me close and hugged me tight. "I was hoping you'd say that."

One month later, Anna left a note in my guitar informing me that she was pregnant for the sixth time.

We were careful not to get too excited about it, having learned through experience that the more you hope, the worse it hurts when it ends. Anna waited until she was two months along before going to see a doctor. That's when we learned this pregnancy was going to be a little different than the previous five—if not qualitatively, at least quantitatively.

"Twins!" Anna shouted when I walked in the door after work on the day of her ultrasound. "You should have canceled your meetings and come with me, Ethan! Two little hearts beating side by side right there on the screen."

"You're kidding."

She wasn't. She handed me a black-and-white image showing the telltale signs of two lives growing inside her.

Given her history of miscarriages, combined

with the added risk of carrying twins, the doctor took extra measures to ensure a viable pregnancy, including bed-rest starting with month three. Lying in bed all day got old very quickly, but throughout it all Anna remained upbeat, telling herself it would all be worth it in the end.

When we moved into the seventh month, her modest optimism changed to hopeful enthusiasm. "We're gonna make it this time, aren't we?" she asked one morning as I was getting dressed for work. "We're really going to be parents."

"With two babies, we're going to be the busiest parents on the block."

"I don't care if we're the busiest parents in the world, I can't wait," she said dreamily. "And not just because I'm tired of sitting around in bed like a bump on a log. I just want to see them and hold them and hear them cry."

"Me too . . . minus the crying."

"Oh c'mon. After all we've been through, what could be more wonderful than the sound of two little babies screaming at the top of their lungs?"

She had a point. After years of hearing tearful cries from my wife over babies that never came to be, the sound of little ones crying for a little attention would be welcome indeed.

The excitement of parenthood was growing each day. Grandpa Bright called frequently to see how things were going. Knowing that Anna was feeling like a cooped chicken, he also poked around now and again about her mental well-being, but all indications were that she was getting through it like a true champ. Octavius called often too, checking to make sure his little girl was weathering the ordeal all right.

In the middle of the seventh month, Anna's brother Stuart and his wife Heather came by for an unexpected visit.

"Did Dad send you to check on me?" Anna asked as they filed into our smallish master bedroom.

"Nope. I just wanted to share my good news in person," Stuart replied.

Anna's face dropped. "So you *didn't* come to check on me?"

"Well . . . sure . . . I mean, of course we want to know how things are going. Er, how are things going, Sis?"

Heather swatted him on the back and rolled her eyes. "*You* were our primary purpose for coming, Anna. But we do have some really good news, so we thought as long as we're here that you'd like to hear it in person."

"I'm just teasing," replied Anna. "What's up? I want to hear all about it."

"Why don't we wait," Heather offered, "until you've had a chance to bring us up to speed on the pregnancy."

"What's to tell? I just lay here all day in bed, waiting to pop these kids out. Now c'mon, what's your big news?"

"At least show us the nursery first," said Stuart. "Dad says you've had Ethan working late at night getting it ready."

"Sorry, doctor's orders are that I not get out of this miserable bed to show anyone the absolutely *adorable* matching cribs, or the collection of priceless paintings by yours truly. So out with the big news. Don't keep a pregnant lady waiting."

Stuart and Heather smiled eagerly at each other, then Stuart's smile widened into an unstoppable grin that looked like it might keep expanding until it breached his earlobes. "Okay, here it is . . . I'm retiring!" He threw his arms in the air like he'd scored a touchdown. (If that's what he meant to do, I'm impressed that he knew the football signal at all. Just saying.)

"Can you believe it?" Heather asked.

I shot a quick glance at Anna, whose jaw had dropped just as far as mine. "What do you mean?" I asked. "You're like, thirty-five years old. You can't just retire."

"Thirty-four actually. And I just did. Yesterday."

"Isn't it terrific?" said an ecstatic Heather. "We feel so lucky. Almost like we won the lottery!"

"*Did* you win the lottery?" I pressed. "How else could you just up and quit your job?"

"Didn't quit, exactly," Stuart replied. "We sold our start-up to a big technology firm, and I didn't see the need to stick around after the merger.

Figured I'd enjoy raising my kids while they're still young. So I'm going to be a full-time dad for a while."

"Wow," I said, genuinely stunned by the news. "Mind if I ask . . . How much did it go for?"

"Three hundred."

"Thousand? That doesn't sound like it will last you long. You sure this is wise?"

"*Million,* Ethan. This is big-time."

My jaw dropped the rest of the way to the floor. "But you . . . I mean . . . Don't you have like a twenty percent stake in the company?"

The peaceful satisfaction that settled into his face made me want to gag. *Nobody should look that happy.* "Twenty-five percent, making my take an even seventy-five million. Of course, they're going to tax the heck out it, but I don't care. We'll still have plenty."

I don't think I said another word during the rest of their visit. I vaguely recall hearing Anna say how excited she was for them, and I thought I heard Heather mention something about making a cash offer on a new home, but the rest was a blur. I was reeling. Sure, I was happy for their success, but at the same time I suddenly felt woefully inadequate. My own dreams had always included fame and fortune, and yet here was Stuart Burke, a socially backward über-geek who devoted multiple hours each week to chat room discussions about the '80s movie *Tron,* suddenly swimming in money and without a care in the world.

Was I jealous? Absolutely.

I silently vowed right then that, one way or another, I was going to be a success too. It's not that I felt I was a failure. I didn't feel I'd have to retire early and never have to work again, like Stuart. But I was going to make sure that Anna and our two little babies had everything they wanted.

A little more than two weeks after finding out my in-laws were now multimillionaires, we received some very good news of our own: we'd hit the eight-month mark, and the doctor was ready to remove the sutures that were holding Anna's cervix together. To everyone's amazement, the cervix held strong even after the procedure. Before we knew it, we were at eight months one week. Then in a few more blinks of the eye we reached eight and a half months, and the doctor decided the safest thing for Anna and the babies was to deliver.

On a drizzly Wednesday morning we held our breath and drove to the hospital for a planned C-section. Thirty minutes after prep, the medical team delivered a perfect, beautiful little girl. A minute or two later, another girl was pulled from Anna's womb.

Two girls! Two healthy, beautiful little girls!

In that instant, I felt like the richest man in

the world. "Did you see them, Anna? They're here! They made it! You did it!"

"*We* did it. *Together.*"

I took her hand in mine and watched as the doctors and nurses cared for the babies on the other side of the room. It was the happiest moment of my life.

But the moment was short-lived.

The first thing I noticed was that the nurses attending to the older infant were scurrying around, whispering things to each other. And they looked more serious than the crew with baby number two. I caught bits and pieces of the frantic whispers.

"*Heart rate spiking . . . lungs . . . oxygen . . . hurry!*"

Anna heard the whispers too, and tried to peek around the doctor who was still working on her uterus, but she couldn't get a good view.

"It's nothing," I said. "I'm sure they're just taking precautions."

But they weren't just taking precautions.

The baby's lungs were not as developed as everyone had hoped, and they were filled with fluid, which only complicated matters. As the whispers escalated, the lead pediatric doctor directed his team to wheel the baby to another room. As they left, he turned and glanced at me, just for a split second, and I could see in his eyes that the situation was grim.

"Ethan! Tell me what's the matter!"

At that point I still didn't know for sure what was wrong. I only knew that it wasn't good. "It's fine, sweetie," I lied. "Everything is going to be fine."

But it wouldn't be fine.

An advanced respiratory team got the baby breathing, but only with the help of machines. She spent the next twenty-four hours enclosed in a plastic bubble, under constant supervision in the pediatric ICU. I wasn't allowed anywhere near her.

The day after that, she passed away.

Anna's doctor had lots of medical mumbo-jumbo to describe our daughter's condition, but all I really heard were his parting words. "You know, even with all of our advances in medicine, sometimes these things just happen."

I could've punched him. Why did he have to say *that?* We knew perfectly well that things "just happen." How many times do you have to see things "just happen" before you're an expert on such things?

What we couldn't comprehend, and what no doctor could tell us, was why they kept happening to us.

Chapter 11

*T*he name we chose for our oldest daughter was Faith, owing to the fact that her unfortunate death was, if nothing else, another major test of ours. Anna was adamant that we name the younger one Hope, because that's what she felt when she looked into the infant's bright blue eyes. I agreed to the name, though I privately questioned the wisdom of it, since one can hardly have hope without faith.

Although my dream of writing songs for a living had come in fits and spurts over the years, often taking a backseat to the morose challenges of life, I'd still managed to accumulate a respectable assortment of music equipment to support the habit. At the time of Faith's death I owned two electric guitars, a twelve-string acoustic, an amplifier, a digital effects processor, an eight-channel mixer, a synthesizer for simulating percussion, and a tabletop recording machine so I could layer tracks together. And of course, I still had Grandpa Bright's old dreadnought in my possession.

Our savings account had enough in it to cover about half of the funeral expenses, including the tiniest casket I've ever seen. To pay for the rest of it I hocked all of the music equipment in the house, except for Karl, which wasn't mine to sell.

The extra cash not only saved us from incurring more debt, it allowed us to pay for an upgraded burial plot on a hill. We also splurged on an extra line of text on the grave marker.

Octavius and Lance Burke drove down from Idaho for the funeral. Stuart, Heather, and their kids came too. The Brights had smaller numbers in attendance, with Grandpa and Aunt Jo flying from Oregon. Outside of direct family, not many people even knew that it was going on. Mark Lloyd brought a couple of close friends from work, and that was it.

Before we left for the funeral home, Grandpa suggested that I bring his old guitar along and play a song during the service as a way to say goodbye to Faith. Not only did I decline, but I told him I'd had the instrument in my possession for too long, and that he should take it home with him when he went back to Oregon.

"Hogwash," he shot back. "Especially not if that's the only guitar you have left. Besides, my arthritis won't mind a bit if you hang onto Karl a little while longer. And I feel better knowing it's being played." He paused, studying my face. "It is getting played, isn't it?"

"Sometimes," I said.

Anna overheard both the question and my response as she was walking by. She slowed just enough to frown and say, "Not for at least three months."

"Oh," Grandpa intoned slowly. "I'm sorry to hear that." He put a hand on my shoulder. "Do you remember when you found me playing the guitar after your grandmother passed away?"

"How could I forget?"

"Then let me just say this: *It helped.* Of that I'm sure. And I'm willing to bet it would help you too." He patted me once on the arm, then turned and shuffled out to the car.

Forty minutes later, when I was sure that everyone who was coming to the funeral was already there, I told the pastor we were ready to begin. Then I took a seat next to Anna on the front pew of the funeral home's tiny chapel.

The pastor gave a little song and dance about not fully understanding the mysteries of God and how we can be comforted in the fact that life carries on, even beyond the grave. I'd always been taught that, and thought I even believed it. I certainly wanted it to be true, but as I stared at Faith's tiny casket, it felt more like wishing and less like believing.

Oh God, I prayed, *please let it be true.*

After the service we caravanned to the cemetery a few miles away. Anna held Hope tightly in her arms during the entire graveside ceremony, refusing to look at anything but the infant's bright blue eyes, especially when Faith was lowered into the ground. We both willed ourselves not to cry. As I studied Anna's pain-wracked face during the procession, I thought about how excited we'd been that she was carrying twins.

It felt beyond our capacity to accept that where there had been two precious little girls, now there was only one.

One heartbeat. One Hope.

Later that night, after everyone was gone, Anna and I lay awake in bed, too numb to talk or sleep. Too numb to even cry. For the Bright family, it had not been a good day.

Well past midnight I rolled over in bed and stared through the darkness at the bassinette in the corner of our bedroom. Near the bassinette I spotted the dark, shadowy form of a guitar case. It reminded me of what Grandpa had said about playing the same guitar in the aftermath of losing his wife: *"It helped."*

Even though I was only six at the time that she died, I remembered that day. I'd been living with Grandma and Grandpa Bright for a year and a half when the tumor in Grandma's abdomen was discovered. She knew she'd been putting on weight, but attributed it to stress, overeating, lack of exercise, hormones, turning fifty; anything but a cancerous mass that was doubling in size every few months inside her. By the time the diagnosis was confirmed, the tumor was already the size of a volleyball, with tentacles reaching into vital organs in her chest. Back then, none of the available treatments came with prognoses that were anything but dour. Doctors tried to help her but, for all their best efforts, the end result was a painful death in the middle of a warm summer night.

The funeral was a few days later. It was only the third time I'd seen my dad since he abandoned me. Grandpa went missing as soon as the family got home from the cemetery, but nobody at the post-funeral gathering seemed alarmed by his disappearance. Who wouldn't need a little time alone after closing the casket on a loving wife of thirty-plus years marriage? The adults just figured he'd wandered off by himself to collect his thoughts, and for the most part, they were right. What they didn't know was where he'd gone to collect them—or how.

My grandparents' stately brick home in Garibaldi had plenty of room to spare, even with a flood of guests. Unfortunately, it only had two bathrooms—the primary one on the main floor and a master bath upstairs. After an oversized helping of Aunt Ruth's cheesy funeral potatoes, followed by three cans of root beer and a ladle full of sparkling pineapple punch, my almost-seven-year-old digestive system needed a time-out. Much to my chagrin, the main bathroom was occupied, with two unfamiliar elderly women already waiting in line.

I silently slipped past them and went upstairs.

As a general rule, I wasn't supposed to go in

Grandma and Grandpa's bedroom. They'd instigated that rule when Grandma got sick, to make sure I wasn't always coming in and out when she needed to rest. But this was an emergency, and Grandma was "gone." I twisted the bedroom doorknob, gently pushed on the door, and then, seeing that the coast was clear, tiptoed across the spacious room to the bathroom door on the opposite wall. I was reaching for the handle when I heard a sound from within that stopped me short.

Someone inside the bathroom was playing a guitar and humming an unfamiliar tune. It was beautiful and vibrant and sad, all at the same time. I knew it must be Grandpa, but I didn't recognize the song. My stomach pains seemed to disappear as I stood there, eavesdropping. With one ear pinned against the door, all of my attention was focused on the sound of the music.

After a minute I got curious. *Why is he playing in the bathroom? Is he watching himself play the guitar in the mirror?* I wanted to see for myself. I suppose it would have been appropriate to knock before entering an occupied bathroom, but I was afraid that doing so would put an abrupt end to the concert. Without a noise, I squeezed the handle and opened the door just far enough to peek with one eye through the crack.

What I saw I will never forget.

Herbert Raymond Bright, the great patriarch of the Bright clan and the only licensed psychologist in Garibaldi, lay sprawled out in the bathtub, still wearing his black shoes and charcoal suit from the funeral. His shirt was untucked and his tie had been loosened a bit around the neck, but otherwise his outfit was just as it had been an hour earlier at the graveside ceremony. I didn't see any water in the tub, just a man in his fifties and a guitar that looked equally aged. With his eyes closed and his head tilted back against the cold porcelain tile, he seemed to be smiling as he hummed and plucked the nylon strings. While I continued to watch, the humming changed to words.

It didn't take a genius to deduce that the song was about Grandma.

> They tell me that you're gone,
> But I know it won't be long,
> Until I hold you once more,
> And we finish the stor-y . . . of love.

Part of me wanted to turn and leave. I should have. Even my boyhood brain knew that I wasn't meant to hear—*or see*—what was going on inside the master bath. But as much as I knew that walking away was the right thing to do, my feet remained drilled to the floor. Something about the way he sang was oddly comforting; it held me captive. I'd watched Grandpa's expression earlier as they lowered Grandma into the ground; he looked tired and broken then, like he might never be happy again. But now? There was an undeniable sense of peace about him.

The singing stopped and the humming resumed, and I continued to spy, watching each strum of the guitar with a careful eye. Soon the singing started up again, the words flowing effortlessly to the same, somber melody.

Last I checked the door was closed,
But now I see a little nose,
Just poking through.
Ethan, is that you?

By the time it registered that Grandpa had just embedded my name in the middle of the song, both of his eyes shot open and he sat straight up in the bathtub. With a giant grin he stared back at me through the crack in the door, catching me totally off guard. I gasped at being discovered, then spun on my heels and ran.

"Ethan!" he shouted before I reached the other side of the bedroom.

I heard the guitar bang against the tub with a loud thud.

"It's okay!" he called again. "Don't go! Come back!"

I stopped just short of the hallway to hear what he had to say.

"Please, Ethan. I don't mind you watching me play. It's nice to have an audience."

After briefly weighing my options, I tiptoed carefully back to the bathroom door, which remained open just far enough for me to see in. Then I put my eye up to the crack again and exhaled loudly through my nose to announce my return.

"Hi there," Grandpa said with a wink. "Come on in. I won't bite." He adjusted his glasses, tilted his graying head to one side, and smiled warmly. "I might pinch or tickle you some, but I definitely won't bite."

I shoved my nose deeper into the crack and the door swung open a hair further. "I needed to use the toilet."

"Oh, I see. I'm so sorry. Let me just crawl out of the tub then, so you can have some privacy." He picked up the guitar and began to stand.

Leaning in, I pushed the door open far enough with my forehead to expose my entire face. "I needed to before, but now I don't have to. It went away when I was listening to you."

Grandpa laughed. "Poor kid. Here I am hogging the bathroom while you're standing out there, quiet as a church mouse, with important business to take care of." He walked toward me, guitar in hand, and gave me a little hug. "Go ahead, Ethan. Do your thing. I'll just wait in the bedroom until you're done." He gave me a nudge toward the toilet and then closed the door behind him.

When I was finished, Grandpa was sitting on his bed, propped up against the headboard, still humming the tune from before.

"I like your new song," I said.

He nodded. "Just started it today, when we got home."

"Is it about Grandma?"

"Yes. I'm trying to let music work its magic."

"Magic?"

"Haven't I told you that music is magical? Oh yes, pure magic, Ethan. Music can do things that nothing else can."

"Like what?"

"Well, take your grandmother, for instance. I miss her like crazy, and I always will. After all she's endured in this life, it kills me that she had to go the way she did. But somehow when I play and sing, the words and music speak right to my heart, and I feel like maybe everything is going to be okay, and that I'll be with her again someday. Kind of like we're still connected." He exhaled slowly and placed a hand on my shoulder, then smiled softly and added, "Through a lifetime of experiences—some good, and some as downright miserable as any you can imagine, I've learned that the right words with the right music at the right time can heal the soul like nothing else. Doesn't that sound like magic to you?"

I nodded eagerly. "I want to be a magician just like you, Grandpa."

Since I still couldn't sleep, I pulled back the covers and got out of bed. Using the moonlight from the window, I made my way to the guitar case. It had been months since I'd bothered opening the thing. In the strings was a pink envelope. I slipped out of the room to the hallway, where I could turn on a light without waking Anna or Hope. The note was dated twelve weeks earlier, long before the birth of the twins. It was short, but welcome.

Ethan,

Thank you for playing a song for me tonight. This bed-rest stuff is no fun, but listening to you play made me forget the discomfort, if only for a few minutes.

I wish you played more!!

Which reminds me, how's my song coming along? Don't worry, I know you're busy. And soon, when the twins are here, you'll be even busier: changing diapers, making bottles, burping the kids—all the things that parents do! Yay!!

Given the frequency of your guitar-playing lately, I know it may be a while before you get this note. When you do, will you do me a favor? Come play me a quick song! No matter what I'm doing, I'm sure it will brighten my day.

I love you so much, Ethan Bright. I know we've had our trials, but together we can get through anything.

XOXOXO
Anna

I wasn't sure if Anna was still awake, but I crept back into the room and took the guitar to the bed. Sitting up against the headboard I played a soft, slow rendition of Pachelbel's "Canon in D." Whereas the music had once served us well as a wedding hymn, now it sounded more like a funeral march. By the time I was done, tears were rolling down my face. Anna was crying too, and trembling uncontrollably. The floodgates of her emotions, which had been locked tight all day long, were suddenly flowing without resistance. Every tear that should have been released during the funeral now poured down her face all at once.

Eventually she looked up at me and smiled. "Thank you," she whispered, "that's just what I needed tonight."

THIRD VERSE:
Trio, *ACCELERANDO STACCATO*

Chapter 12

I won't say that the sting of losing Faith went away quickly, but to my surprise it did subside sooner than Anna or I expected. Not that we weren't still sad when we thought about her; only that we were so wrapped up in taking care of baby Hope that there wasn't much time to continue dwelling on the loss. We cried our tears, made our peace, and then did our best to focus all of our love and attention on the baby we still had.

At Anna's urging I dutifully played the guitar more regularly than I had been, not only for her but for Hope as well. Having read somewhere that listening to Beethoven and Mozart can help stimulate brain development, I frequently played classical selections when Hope was little, though occasionally I splurged and threw in a good country song or rock anthem just to make sure she was well-rounded. And her eyes lit up every time I sang "Puff the Magic Dragon." That became her bedtime song, and by the time she was two and a half she knew every word by heart.

On her third birthday, after blowing out the candles, Hope announced that she was now "a big person . . . like Mommy." We warned her not to grow up too fast and told her she was still our little girl, and would always be our little girl, no matter how big she got. She looked at us both very sternly and held up three little fingers. "No, I'm big *now*. See, I'm dis many . . . one, two, free!"

Yes, Hope was "free"—free to do just about anything that her little mind could dream up. Between her third birthday and the time she turned four, we were constantly reminding her about all of the things that "big people" *don't* do. For instance, big people don't run off and hide under the racks of clothes at JC Penney, concealing themselves quietly for half an hour while their mom is calling their name in a panic. They also don't flush stuffed animals down the toilet, cut their bangs to the scalp with kitchen shears, or sneak out of the house while Mom is napping, to chase a stray cat down the street. One night, when I was frustrated about how little sleep I was getting with a bony little knee in my back, I had to remind her that "big people" don't typically sleep in their parents' bed.

Even though her three-year-old antics were sometimes exhausting, there wasn't a single moment that we didn't love having Hope around. In fact, looking back, those were some of the best times of our life. In the evenings after work we would walk to the park and push Hope on the swings, or watch as she screamed with delight going down the slide. Then we'd go home and sing songs or read stories. On weekends we'd go downtown and ride the trolleys, window-shop at the stores, or just hang out at the house and play on the living room floor. None of us really cared what we were doing, as long as we were together.

All things considered, we had everything we needed in life back then, and just enough time together as a family to enjoy it. But in the back of my mind (and often right at the forefront of my thoughts) I felt like I was still far short of the kind of success I'd always envisioned for myself. On top of that, I worried that I still wasn't doing enough to adequately provide for my family. We were doing okay from month to month, but wasn't there a better life I should be giving my wife and daughter? Was our home big enough? Was the condominium the right place to raise a child in? And what about saving for the future? Was I earning enough to put Hope through college? Our bank account wasn't growing fast enough to support that kind of expense, and I feared it never would.

To fuel my financial worries, I couldn't help feeling a little inadequate every time I thought of Stuart. He'd already tucked away enough money for both of his boys to go to college. His estate was completely paid off, along with his cars, his boat, and his motor home. And after all of that, he was still earning more *per month* in interest on his holdings than I earned annually as a salary. Somehow it didn't seem fair. I tried hard to hide my jealousy, but it wasn't easy, especially during our monthly visits to their place in Fresno for Sunday dinner. Walking through their manicured gardens or dipping my feet in their pool, it was easy to see that I was still a long way from what anyone would call successful.

"We're doing fine," Anna once told me when I was griping about my salary on the ride home from her brother's. "We're happy, and money can't buy that." She was saying the right words, but I detected that she might also be trying to convince herself.

"Your brother is happy too, and he's loaded."

"He doesn't care about the money, you know that."

"Because he has more than he could ever spend! After hanging out at their McMansion, don't you think our place is feeling a little crowded? If I could just afford to upgrade us to a house, things would be a lot better. If we had another bedroom, we could turn it into a home office. Plus Hope will be starting school soon, and I think we could be in a better school district."

Anna thought about that for a moment. "A bigger house *would* be nice." The way she said it, I could tell she'd thought about this before. She paused, then added, "And maybe a newer car. I feel like yours is in the shop more than not, and mine isn't much better. The ABS light blinked on again yesterday, but then it went off."

My feelings of inadequacy mushroomed, and I went on the defensive. "Yeah, well, we'll have to get it looked at, again," I mumbled.

"I'm sure it's fine," she assured me.

"Maybe, but I don't want you and Hope in a car that might have a problem with the brakes. What if something happened? We just can't afford a new car, but I'm doing the best I can."

She patted my leg. "I know you are, and I appreciate it."

I didn't say much for the rest of the ride home. Instead, I sat thinking about how hard it is to get ahead in this world on a single income. When Hope was born, Anna and I had jointly decided that she should wait to reenter the work force until Hope was in school. Given the amount of effort it took to have a baby, we didn't like the idea of a stranger raising our daughter for eight hours a day. Of course that meant that all of our expenses rested squarely on my shoulders. It was a burden I gladly bore, but one that suddenly felt heavier, knowing that Anna privately hoped for some lifestyle enhancements that I just couldn't afford.

The reality was that I saw no path to making more money. I'd tried over and over to shop my songs to agents and producers, but it just wasn't happening. And while my day job offered the word "manager" in its title, that didn't mean it came with a salary that could outpace San Francisco's steep cost of living. It paid the bills and put food on the table, but not much more.

We didn't bring up the topic of finances for several months after that. I tried not to think about the pile of dough my brother-in-law was swimming in, because there seemed little I could do to compete. And Anna mercifully avoided mentioning the single-family home and pristine backyard that she was no doubt still dreaming of.

During those same few months, the economy hit some unexpected bumps in the road. While politicians in Washington and investment bankers on Wall Street were busy trying to find someone to blame, my friends and colleagues at work were fretting about layoffs. It didn't take long for the rumor mill to conclude that a RIF—*reduction in force*—was in the works. Most people were predicting cuts of anywhere from ten to thirty percent. As a first-level manager, I thought I'd know for sure if something like that was coming, but if there was concrete information to be had, then I was out of the loop. Given all the rumors, the fact that I wasn't being told *anything* by upper management had me more than a little worried.

I didn't want Anna to stress over it though, so I never mentioned the rumors to her. When she asked if the economic turmoil was impacting my firm, I downplayed what I knew. "Things may have slowed a little, but we're still hanging in there."

Six months after the first rumors started, a company-wide memo was distributed from the board of directors, explaining that, as part of a restructuring, they had "regrettably released" several prominent executives at our headquarters in New York City. In their place, a woman named Jessica Hocker had been brought in from the outside to serve as the new vice president of sales and operations.

Within a month of joining the company, the new VP began laying people off. In conversations between cubicles she quickly earned the name "The Hatchet" on account of how deftly she was lopping off employees at our sister offices all over the country.

Early in the third month of her tenure, the Hatchet showed up unannounced in San Francisco. When I arrived just after 7 in the morning she was already there, flanked by a rent-a-cop. She'd staked out the general manager's office as her home for the day, and she remained sequestered in there until 9:30, ostensibly to review employee records with our Human Resources manager, Miriam Scott. When she was ready, Jessica had Miriam gather all employees for a brief meeting in the large open area on the second floor.

It was a meeting I'll never forget.

The first ten words that came out of Jessica's mouth were, "Good morning, it's a pleasure to be here with you." It was a benign introduction, but it was so obvious by the way she spoke that she despised being there—no, *despised us*—that I almost laughed out loud. The Hatchet was a short, plumpish woman, and much younger than I'd pictured in my head—maybe a year or two older than me. Her physical features weren't entirely unattractive, but she came across so pompous and arrogant that it was hard to look at her, much less listen to her. All I needed was those ten words to know that this woman was trouble. Her next ten words validated my assessment. "My objective today is to implement some much-needed changes."

Her introduction went downhill from there. "As a result of economic pressures, combined with reasonable expectations from shareholders, local restructuring is needed to better align our operating expenses with revenues." We were informed that those who were being let go would be called in to her office individually to hear the terms of the separation, and then they'd be escorted out of the building by security.

After concluding her remarks, I swear the woman looked like she was smiling, enjoying the control she had over our fates. She walked assertively to the GM's office and closed the door behind her. A few minutes later, the first victim's name was called.

"Dana," said Miriam as she approached the crowd of folks still sitting in the open area. "Come with me please."

Dana Abbot was a young gal from accounting who'd only been with the firm for about a year.

She stood nervously and followed Miriam to the corner office. Five minutes later Dana emerged with blotches all over her face. The security guard walked her to her desk to gather her personal items and then escorted her out. She kept her head up and tried hard to smile as she passed the group, even while tears ran down her face. I'd only spoken to Dana a few times, but I knew she was the mother of two young children, and I doubted this would be easy on her family.

While Dana was heading to the exit, Miriam found the next person on the chopping block. To everyone's surprise, it was Frank Dane, the general manager. He'd been running the entire San Francisco office for fifteen years, and he reported directly to Jessica. By the look on his face when his name was called, he was just as shocked as everyone else. A short while later, Frank walked out of his old office, looking as mad as I'd ever seen him, and marched to the front door without saying a word.

It soon became obvious that Jessica's list of cuts was itemized alphabetically. As a B, this was a huge relief. My own boss, Mark Lloyd, had to sweat it out until almost noon, when they finally moved on to the M's. By then I'd already stopped watching the parade. It was more than I could stand to see so many of my associates being kicked out on their ear. I sat in my office trying to get work done until it was all over. At two o'clock,

Brock White, the last name on the company directory, was shown the door. The poor guy had been sitting on pins and needles all day, and when his number finally came up he vented with a string of profanities that made my hair curl. Hearing his outburst, I stepped out of my office to see what was going on and caught the tail end of a hand gesture before the security guard grabbed his arm and "helped" him the rest of the way to the exit.

With the alphabet complete, those of us that remained breathed one more huge sigh of relief, though the moment was bittersweet. Part of me wished I'd been let go. The guilt over being left behind was almost as debilitating as the fear of being fired had been. Across the building, several people who still had their jobs were crying. As a manager, I felt it my duty to give them some encouragement, so I made my way through the cubicles and offered whatever words of advice I could think of.

While I was busy talking to people, Miriam Scott came back out of Jessica's office and called for Mark Lloyd. When I heard the name, I forgot what I was saying and watched in horror as Mark stoically crossed the floor to Jessica's office. It felt like he was in there forever, but the clock on the wall said only twenty minutes had passed when the door opened again and Mark came out.

I thought the smile on his face was a good sign, but it didn't explain why the security officer was walking along beside him. Together they marched back to Mark's office. A few minutes later, when they reappeared, Mark was holding a small box of his things.

Whispers began erupting all around. "They're still not done with the layoffs!" I heard one woman gasp.

"Not *Mark!*" railed another.

As he passed nearby, Mark—the man who'd been impressed enough by my talent to hire me in the first place—gave me a courteous smile and a nod, and then he was gone.

Thirty seconds later, with my heart still racing, Miriam left the confines of Jessica's office and made her way to where I was standing. I tried not to make eye contact, but eventually she was standing right in front of me and couldn't be ignored. My heart sank. She could have been coming for anyone, but somehow I knew she was here for me. If Frank and Mark had both been axed, then surely I was next. "Mr. Bright," the woman said without emotion, "Ms. Hocker would like to speak with you."

It was a long ride home that day. The longest of my life. I honestly didn't know how I was going to explain everything to Anna. I practiced a hundred different ways to break the news, but nothing felt quite right.

"You're home early," Anna said when I walked

into the kitchen. "To what do I owe the pleasure?" She was busy tidying a few dishes in the sink. When I didn't respond, she stopped scrubbing the pot she was working on and stared at me. "Everything okay, hon?"

"It was a tough day at work. They . . . A woman from corporate was there."

"Oh?" She dried her hands on a dish towel without taking her eyes off of me.

"They call her the Hatchet, because she's got a knack for carving up businesses, streamlining, that sort of thing."

"This doesn't sound good."

My mouth was dry, like I was sucking on sand. "No. They—*she*—cut our workforce by nearly fifty percent."

"Oh my gosh . . ."

"Yeah, it was a real butcher job."

"So you . . . were part of the fifty percent?"

"Umm . . . no. But thanks to some last-minute shuffling, my fate may actually be worse."

"Huh?"

"They fired Frank Dane," I explained. "They were going to move Mark into his spot as GM, but Mark decided he wanted the severance instead. Apparently he's been looking for a way to move back to where he grew up in Pennsylvania, and this seemed like a good time to make a clean break."

"Oh my gosh," she said, obviously stunned by

the news that my mentor and friend had jumped ship. We'd had Mark and his wife to our house several times and felt as close to them as anyone. "So who's going to replace Frank?"

I took a deep breath. *"Me."*

She let out a muffled laugh. "You?"

"Crazy, right?"

"No, I'm sure you'll do great. It's just . . . to me you're still that starry-eyed kid playing music on the street, not a—what are you now? A business executive? Who'd have thought?" She paused. "Will your schedule change much?"

"Yeah, that's the big downside. It will mean quite a bit of travel. Many of our key clients are down in L.A. and San Diego, but there's a bunch in Seattle too. And Denver. And of course I'll have to stop in New York now and then to meet with Jessica."

"Who is Jessica?"

"My new boss, the Hatchet. I now report straight to the VP."

"Wow." She sounded genuinely impressed. "Look at you. From first-line manager straight to corporate bigwig."

"I promise, there won't be any glamour in it. After losing all those people we're going to be very shorthanded. I'm going to have to work my tail off just to keep things afloat."

She gave me a long hug and whispered, "I know you can do it."

"Thanks for the vote of confidence," I replied. Sadly, I knew that my new boss did not share the same confidence. She'd only plugged me in the position because Mark told her I was the best man for the job, and since there were very few people left, she really didn't have much of a choice.

"Consider this a temp position, if you will," Jessica had said to me during our conversation. "At the end of the day, if you're successful at it, then it could become permanent. If not, well . . . I think you know what's at stake."

Yeah . . . my job. I assured her that I would exceed all of her expectations.

"I have no expectations," she replied smoothly, "because I don't think you're ready for this position. But I'll give you a fair chance to prove me wrong."

I didn't share any of that conversation with Anna. Maybe I should have, but she seemed to like the idea of me being the new general manager. She put her arms around me and gave me a playful little squeeze. "Dare I ask if your new job comes with a pay increase?"

Jessica didn't think I deserved more money, since the promotion was a spur-of-the-moment decision, but Miriam advised that, legally, everyone must be compensated based on the documented pay band of their position. When they told me what the band was for a GM, I nearly choked.

Staring into Anna's eyes, with her arms still around me, I allowed myself to smile for the first time. "That, my dear, is the only good news in all of this. I think we'll be able to get out of this condo and move into something a little bigger, in the neighborhood of your choice."

I knew I was jumping way ahead of myself, mentally spending paychecks that hadn't even come in yet, banking on a job and a salary that could just as easily be yanked away the very next day. But I didn't care. I'd seen so many people lose their jobs that day that I knew nothing is permanent. So why not enjoy the moment? If only for a while, I was going to take advantage of my newfound success.

Her eyes lit up like I knew they would. "Really!"

"Yes. But remember, this new job is going to take a lot of work. If I want to keep the inflated salary, it'll take a lot of sacrifice on everyone's part."

She pulled back just a little. "What kind of sacrifice?"

"Time, mostly. I won't be around as much. Are you going to be okay with that?"

"How much more will you be making, exactly?"

I reeled her back in so I could whisper it in her ear. *"A little more than twice as much."*

She let out a little shriek and hugged me as hard as she could. "Then that's a sacrifice I think I can live with!"

Chapter 13

*I*n retrospect, maybe Mark Lloyd was wise to take the money and run, rather than trying to live up to Jessica's expectations. As time wore on, she proved to be just as shrewd and cutthroat as everyone made her out to be. I knew I walked a very thin line with her, and that knowledge was what pushed me to perform. Not only was I desperate to keep my salary, but I didn't want to give Jessica the satisfaction of saying something like, "See, Ethan, I knew you weren't good enough."

Anna and I had acknowledged right from the beginning that the GM position would be a sacrifice, and it was. For starters, I traveled almost every other week. When I wasn't on the road Jessica liked to hold frequent t-cons, but on east-coast hours, so I was often at the office by six in the morning. That became an even bigger burden once Anna found a house she liked in an upscale neighborhood thirty minutes further from the office. With a one-hour commute each way to work, long days of meetings, and a boss like Hitler, my entire existence became one large sacrifice.

The next couple of years passed by in an instant. Hope was suddenly almost five and attending preschool. Every time I came home from a business trip it seemed she'd gained half an inch in height. And every day she was looking more and more like her mother—tall, a natural beauty, with a disarming smile. On the nights when I was home to tuck her in, she no longer asked me to sing to her. Somehow in the blur of our existence I think she'd forgotten how I used to play the guitar for her before bed. Perhaps she'd forgotten that I played at all.

There were certainly times when I wondered if all the work was worth it. But the size of my paychecks helped shove such thoughts aside. *This is the only way to get ahead,* I told myself. *And it won't be forever. Eventually things at work will slow down.*

But things didn't slow down.

Shortly after Hope turned five, Jessica took me out to lunch during one of my New York visits and surprised me with the first quasi-compliment I'd ever heard pass through her lips. "I'm seldom wrong about people. I had you pegged as a creative type, a flake who could never cut it in a senior level position. But you proved me wrong."

"Thanks," I said, "I think."

"You're welcome. You've really shown yourself to be a team player, Ethan. I know I can count on you to do *whatever* it takes to get things done, which is why I'm making you my new Vice President of Operations, Western States."

While that might sound like a promotion, it was

really just an enhanced GM position to accommodate yet another restructuring. Sadly, more layoffs were coming in several offices, including San Francisco, so they'd decided to make me manager for all of the markets west of the Mississippi. That allowed them to cut GMs at other locations and dump their work onto me. But with that added responsibility came things that didn't show up in the job description. Like more meetings with customers. And more early-morning teleconferences with the executives in New York. And more expenses to approve. And more, and more, and more . . .

As time wore on, Anna grew less and less supportive of the demands on my time, even though we both enjoyed the financial rewards of my hard work. She also seemed less secure. "I don't understand why you have to be gone all the time," she would say. "You're working too hard. Do they really expect this much out of you, or are you just happier when you're at work?" That last comment stung. I hated being tied to my work. The only reason I continued to do it was for her and Hope. And now that we'd locked ourselves into a huge mortgage and two car payments, the need to maintain my job was all the more important.

"It'll ease up soon," I would assure her. "Just a little while longer, until the economy bounces back. Then I'll be able to delegate more." But that "little while longer" never ended. The long hours continued, along with Anna's periodic complaints about my availability.

The year that Hope was seven was the most stressful of all. Most of the companies we dealt with had drastically cut their marketing budgets as a way to trim expenses during the downturn, so we were having to fight for every single "win" with customers. That meant more planning, more meetings, more customer visits, and more calls from Jessica pressuring me to pick up the pace of my teams.

But it wasn't only work that was stressful. Being at home was hard at times too. Mentally, I was so consumed with business that even when I had a free Saturday to spend with the family, it was tainted by thoughts about clients, my employees, and rumors circulating throughout the office that another round of layoffs was in the works.

On multiple occasions that year, Anna and I got into heated arguments over the silliest things, probably because one or the other of us felt overstressed. The stupidest was a spat over redecorating.

It started on a Thursday night when she asked my opinion about what color to paint our master bedroom. "Paint it whatever color you want," I told her. "It doesn't matter to me. I only sleep there half the time anyway."

She bristled at the remark, but let it go. The next evening, however, she brought several paint chips into my study while I was working and asked, "Can I interrupt?"

I was right in the middle of rank-ordering everyone who worked for me. The rumor mills were spot on; there were going to be more layoffs, and I had the dirty job of deciding who would stay and who would go. "You just did," I said.

"It'll only take a minute." She handed me two paint samples. "For the walls, do you want *Sackcloth* or *Burnt cherry?*"

I couldn't have cared less, but not providing an opinion would have only lengthened the interruption. "The reddish one." I hoped that was the one she liked too so there wouldn't be a negotiation.

"Good," she chirped. "Me too. Now how about for the ceiling?" She handed me two more paint chips. "*Apple blossom* or *Whimsical linen?*"

My head was still wrapped up in the names of the people I was about to send to the unemployment line, so I was already hugely bothered that we were even having this conversation. And when I saw the colors she handed me, and held them up to the light, I lost my cool. "Are you serious? You're asking me to choose between white and white."

"No, the apple blossom is more of a true white, the linen is richer, and a little more warm."

"They're exactly the same. You really want my opinion? Go with either one, and I'll never know the difference."

Her voice became as short as mine. "Oh yeah? Well do you want *my* opinion? My opinion is that your opinion is . . . is *completely lame*. Kind of like you, lately."

"Is that right?" I tossed the paint chips on the ground at her feet. "*I'm lame?* How lame is it that you have time to worry about imperceptible differences in a stupid color sample? White is white, dear, whether you like it or not."

"And how lame is it that you don't care about the things that I care about? You used to. Or how lame is it that you're gone so much that I don't have anyone to talk to about *anything?*"

"I don't have time for this," I said flippantly, then spun back to face my computer. "This is the dumbest argument ever. Oh sorry, the *lamest.*"

"You don't have time for anything anymore. How lame is it that we're even married?"

Her comment sent a chill down my spine. I spun back around. "What's that supposed to mean?"

She shrugged. "When your schedule frees up and you have time to give it some thought, I'm sure you'll figure it out."

That was the first time she'd ever suggested that there were holes in the armor of our marriage that had the potential of being breached.

It wouldn't be the last.

• • •

Three weeks before Hope's eighth birthday, Anna called me on my cell phone while I was having dinner with several hotel executives in Las Vegas who'd seen their profits steadily decline and were looking for a marketing overhaul to help get things back on track. It was the type of deal that couldn't be interrupted by a spouse, so I put the phone on silent and let it go to voice mail. When I got back to my hotel later that night, I returned the call.

"It's almost midnight," she said coolly.

"I know. Sorry. These guys really wanted to talk."

"You sure you're not . . . getting into trouble? It is Vegas, after all."

"Anna, I hope you don't really think that. This is me we're talking about."

She let the phone go quiet for several seconds. "Lately, I'm not sure I even know who you are." She paused again, waiting to see if I would respond. When I didn't, she said, "You do know that our daughter's birthday is approaching, right?"

"Yes, I got your e-mail about the party. Why is it on a Friday, a full week before her actual birthday?"

She sighed. "I guess you didn't have time to read the whole e-mail. Three of Hope's little friends from school are busy on her birthday, but they all want to celebrate with her, so we picked an earlier date."

"Oh, that's right," I lied. "I remember reading that now."

"Uh huh. Anyway, you need to make sure you have that afternoon free. Have you scheduled the time off yet?"

"I'll have my assistant take care of that first thing in the morning."

"Please don't forget. You already missed her school play, a dance recital, and a dozen other things she wanted you to see. You absolutely can't miss her birthday party."

"I know. I'll be there. I promise."

Anna let my words hang there. How many things had I promised to do over the years? And how many of those promises had I fulfilled? I tried not to think about it. But regardless, even if I failed on some of those little things, I was faithfully fulfilling a more important promise to take care of my family and provide for their needs. Didn't that balance everything out?

"You better," she said, with just a hint of doubt.

Two days later, once I was back in town, Anna and I were talking on the patio late at night, trying to catch up on our parallel lives. She filled me in on what Hope had been up to, and I offered bits and pieces of where I'd been and the deals I'd closed.

Eventually she asked if I'd booked the time on my calendar for Hope's birthday party. I hadn't, but lied and said I had, making a mental note to do it the next morning at work.

"Thanks." She sounded relieved. "You also need to make time to get her a present between now and then. Don't take this the wrong way, but I'm tired of picking things out and saying they're from you. I think she's catching on. She needs to know that her father cares."

"You're right. What is she into these days? Dolls, bikes?"

"Ethan, you really need to spend more time with your daughter. I shouldn't have to tell you things like that."

It must have been too late at night, because I let her comment annoy me more than usual. "Oh, don't give me that," I shot back. "I would love to spend more time with Hope, but instead I'm working my tail off so you can enjoy this life that you've grown so accustomed to."

She sat up in her lounge chair, her eyes narrowing on mine. "What is that supposed to mean?"

"You heard me. While I'm killing myself every day, you get to hang out at home, have lunch with your friends, take a nap, whatever you want—no responsibilities whatsoever."

Anna's face turned bright red, though in the glow of the patio lamp it looked kind of orange. I think if she were a cartoon, I'd have seen steam shooting out of her ears. "Well *someone* has to raise our child! How is that not a responsibility?"

"Oh, sure," I said, mocking, "that's very important after the bus drops her off from school. But what about the rest of the day? What happened to you going back to work when Hope started kindergarten, Anna? She's in *third grade!* Don't complain about me not being around unless you're willing to help make that possible. Because I can guarantee, the first moment I start to let off the gas at work, the Hatchet will have someone there to fill my shoes, and in this economy there isn't a lot else out there. And I highly doubt unemployment will pay for all of *this*." I waved my hands at the house and yard. "Is that what you want?"

"Of course not!" she hissed. "I just want . . . I want . . ." She let the words drift. The anger in her countenance suddenly melted into sadness.

I couldn't tell if she didn't know what she wanted to say, or if she knew but didn't want to say it. "You just want what, Anna? The house, the manicured lawn, the new cars, *and* me around all the time? That's called having your cake and eating it too, and I'm afraid it's just not possible."

The sadness that had started to swell evaporated instantly, replaced once more by fiery contempt. She clenched her fists menacingly, then got out of her chair. "I was going to say, 'I just want my husband back,'" she spat through clenched teeth. "But now I'm not so sure."

Anna turned and stormed into the house.

Thirty minutes later I figured I should go inside

and try to sort things out. I had another business trip the next day, and I didn't want to go away on a sour note. I found Anna lying on our bed, staring up at the ceiling.

"I'm sorry," I said.

"Me too," she replied without diverting her gaze from the spot directly above her. Her voice was still tense.

I lay down next to her and stared in the same general direction. "Anything interesting up there?"

"Where?"

"On the ceiling."

"No. I just see lots and lots of chaotic white space. It reminds me of our marriage."

"Ah, but that's not white," I corrected, gently poking her in the ribs. "It's *Whimsical linen*. Nine months ago the artist in you assured me it was much more warm and rich than plain white."

Her voice softened unexpectedly. "I don't know if the artist is there anymore. It just looks white to me now."

"That's okay, the musician in me seems to have faded as well."

She finally turned to look at me. "That's *so* sad. What happened to our dreams, Ethan? We should be sharing those things with Hope, and instead we've just given up on them. I feel like we've given up so much in the last few years."

I didn't have a response. At least nothing came to mind that didn't have better than an outside chance of leading us right back to the conversation we'd had on the patio, so I kept my mouth shut.

She went back to staring at the Whimsical linen above her. "You asked what Hope is into these days. Do you really want to know?"

"Yes."

"*Music,* Ethan. She loves music. It's her favorite part of school."

"So what, you think I should buy her an iPod?"

With a little groan she replied, "I was thinking now might be a good time for you to get her a guitar. One that's just her size."

I loved the idea as soon as she said it. "Ah, it's perfect."

"But Ethan," she cautioned, "a guitar is just a thing. She won't know what to do with it, and it certainly won't play itself. If you're getting her a guitar, you also need to give her some lessons. Teach her. Share your talent with her. She needs that from you."

The thought that crossed my mind was that with my current travel schedule, Hope would have to start stowing away in my luggage in order to have time for lessons, but I knew better than to say that right then. "I will," I pledged. "Absolutely."

She turned and examined me with a look that said, "I've heard that line before," but the only thing that came out of her mouth was, "Good."

Without another word she rolled over and went to sleep.

Chapter 14

The following afternoon, I flew back to Vegas to spend another three days pitching ideas to the hotel chain. Then I went to Portland for two nights, followed by a day in Seattle to review a presentation one of my teams was preparing for a large coffee company. From there I hopped a flight across the country for a three-day strategy session in New York. When I finally got back to San Francisco, there were just four days remaining before Hope's birthday party.

The first of those was spent in long meetings with the local creative team, helping them understand the direction the hotel chiefs wanted us to go with their upcoming marketing blitz. Anna called me at lunch to see if I'd found time to buy the guitar. "Tomorrow," I told her. "Things around here should be a little quieter by then."

The next day I received a similar phone call.

And the day after that.

When I came home that night, two days before the birthday party, Hope was already asleep. Anna was sitting on the sofa watching a show. Her face had the telltale signs of fresh tears.

"Chick flick?" I asked, knowing full well her crying had nothing to do with what she was watching. Anna was stoic, sometimes to a fault.

Short of losing a child, usually the only thing with the capacity to make her cry was me.

"Huh?"

"Your face . . . it looks like you've been . . ."

She shot me an annoyed glance. "It's not the movie."

"What's going on then? Everything okay?" I took a seat next to her on the couch.

"No," she labored to say. "Everything is *not* okay. I . . . you . . . me . . . us—we're not okay anymore, Ethan. I feel like I'm just barely holding on. I can't take it anymore. Something has to give."

"What can't you take anymore?"

"For starters, constantly feeling like everything is on my shoulders. I feel like a single parent! You're never around. *Ever*. And Hope and I end up sitting here alone, just wishing we were as important as your work. You know what we'd give just to spend a little quality time with you?"

"Haven't we already had this conversation, like a hundred times? The only thing I love about my job is that it provides for our family, and I think it would be hard to just give that up. So unless you're saying that you're ready to get a job again and help pay the bills, then I don't know what you're crying about."

She sat up on the couch and wiped her face, then dropped a bomb. "I'm ready."

"What?"

"I don't want any more excuses from you as to why you're always so busy. So I'm ready to get a job, if that's what it takes."

"You're serious?"

"I'm glad you have a good job. It's been great. And I'm so thankful that you support us like you do. But money is only part of the equation, and we could get by on a lot less than you're making. When I married you, I married *you,* not your income." Anna paused long enough to grab a familiar white vomit-bag from the coffee table and tossed it on my lap. "You'd be surprised at how often I pull this out and read it, Ethan. For richer or for poorer, remember? If richer means that I have your money, but I don't have you, then from here on out I choose poorer."

I wasn't sure what to say. I'd come to believe that Anna was so tied to all the nice things we had that she would never willingly give them up. Yet here she was, willing to sacrifice it all. We'd once agreed to trade time for money, and now she was ready to make the same trade in reverse.

"Ethan, do you understand what I'm saying?"

"That I need to cut back my hours at work a little bit?"

She shifted her shoulders to face me squarely. "No, not a little bit. I'm saying that I can't take this anymore. It's like we're not even married. For the past few years we've been like two bullet trains—

maybe we're on the same set of tracks, but it feels like we're quickly going in opposite directions. I need a husband. And Hope needs a father. Life is slipping away, and I can't just sit idly by and wait for some magical time in the future when all of a sudden we'll be a happy family again. I need you, and I need you now." She pointed at the list of wedding vows I'd jotted down years before on the bag. "If you're not willing to live up to those things . . . well, then . . ."

"Then what?" I pressed. The hint at divorce was obvious; I wanted her to come right out and say it.

Anna stared at me, forcing back a wave of tears that I could see were on the verge of rolling past her eyelids. "Please don't let it come to that, Ethan. I can't imagine how much that would hurt. I want our marriage to last. I really do. But honestly, for that to happen I need you to be the man who wrote down all those wonderful things on the day we got married. I know I haven't been perfect either, but I'm trying, and I need you to try too. I'm tired of broken promises."

I kind of nodded and shook my head at the same time. I understood what she was saying, but the consequences of carrying it out were sobering. "I want what you want, Anna. But that's one heck of an ultimatum: *Give up your job or lose your family*. I kind of feel like giving up my job would sink our family too. It's a catch twenty-two."

"I'm not asking you to stop working. There are other jobs out there."

"Not like this one."

"Exactly! Find a job with a boss who isn't a dictator."

"But those kinds of jobs won't pay like this one."

"Didn't you hear me? I don't care about the money. Maybe I did before, but not anymore. It's just not worth it."

I leaned back on the couch, letting the plush leather cushions absorb my weight, and let out a long deep breath. It felt like all of the successes I'd worked so hard for were being exhaled right along with the air. My mind was grasping at straws. "Maybe," I said slowly, "I can talk to Jessica about working remotely from home once in a while. Or perhaps she'd allow a flex schedule, so I have more down time to compensate for some of the longer days."

"And if that doesn't work?"

I knew what she wanted me to say, but the concept of walking away from a perfectly good job seemed so backward to me. I'd seen Mark Lloyd do it, but that involved a nice severance package. What Anna was asking of me equated to professional suicide, and I wasn't sure I could pull the trigger. What would I do then? If I couldn't find another job, where would we go once we defaulted on our mortgage? Back to live with Anna's father like we'd done when our apartment burned down? That was okay when we were newlyweds, but what about now that we were in our thirties with a child of our own? It all felt so irresponsible.

There's got to be another way, I told myself.

"I'll figure something out," I told Anna.

Hope and Anna were both still sound asleep the next morning when I left for the office. I kissed Anna gently on the forehead, then slipped out the door. Like most days, my schedule at work was packed full of meetings. The only break I had between 7 a.m. and 7 p.m. was the ninety-minute gap I'd carved out during lunch so I could go buy a guitar for Hope.

At noon, as I was putting on a jacket to leave, Jessica called from New York. "Ethan," she said without saying hello. "I just e-mailed you a file. It's a mock-up for a movie house that's looking for a little pizzazz promoting a new indy film. The producer put the package together to give your creative team an idea of what he's after. He wants to see you today to go over it. I double-checked with Lisa and she said you're only available until 1:30, so he's on his way there now."

"Umm . . ."

"Something the matter?"

My mouth went dry. "No," I said hoarsely. "I'll take a peek at the file and be ready when he arrives."

"Good," she said flatly, then clicked off.

Twenty seconds later I was on the phone with Anna, swearing up and down that there was nothing I could do about the situation and that I needed a solid career strategy before I did anything too drastic. "Can you *please* bail me out on the birthday present? Maybe run out and pick up a guitar this afternoon? I simply don't have time. The guitar store closes at eight, and I'm not sure I can make it across town by then."

It was a long time before she responded. Her voice splintered with emotion when she finally spoke. "You never have time. You can't even keep your promises for a single day. Just last night you swore that you would do better, that you would start putting your family first again. And on your very first opportunity, you've once again shown me exactly where your priorities lie."

"Anna, I have to do my job."

"You can't even take a lunch break? You're the general manager, doesn't that hold some sway? Stop cowering to your boss! Because I can't live like this anymore, Ethan. I just can't. Something's got to change or our family—*our marriage*—isn't going to survive."

"Listen, Anna, it's going to be different. I swear. This won't happen again. Let's talk about this more tonight, but . . . can you just get the guitar for Hope this afternoon? I don't want to disappoint her. Then after today I'll talk to my boss about changing my hours—or shifting my responsibilities around—something to allow me more time to spend at home."

"It sounds like another hollow promise, Ethan."

"It's not. Trust me. I love you, and after today things are going to change."

"Sure they are."

"They are!"

"And what about tomorrow afternoon?"

"What do you mean?"

"It's Hope's party. Have you taken the time off?"

Dang it! I'd been meaning to schedule a half-day vacation for weeks, but I kept getting distracted by more pressing things. I didn't want to be dishonest with Anna, but, as upset as she was about the guitar, it seemed prudent not to stoke the fire any further. "Of course, I told you before it's all taken care of. I had my assistant block it out."

Anna started crying openly into the phone. "I spoke with her earlier today . . . I could tell she doesn't know a thing about it. *You're lying to me, Ethan! Flat out lying!* There are a lot of things I'll put up with, but that's not one of them." She paused to catch her breath. "I don't know if I can get the guitar for you. I don't know that I want to. I just . . . I need a little time to think about things. I need to decide if my love for you is enough to keep trying to make this work. Maybe I'm being selfish for wanting to have my husband around once in a while, but I'm not asking for anything more than this family deserves." She hung up before I could respond.

The only thing I could think after the phone went dead was that she was right. I had failed miserably in so many ways. I'd been so focused on financially providing for my family that I had lost sight of their other needs. And worse, I'd allowed myself to be bullied by Jessica. Granted, she was the meanest woman on the planet, but I'd let her walk all over me without putting up even an ounce of resistance. But I was ready to change—I had to.

Lisa, my assistant, popped her head in the office while I was debating how best to confront my boss on the importance of work–life balance. "The producer is here. Can I send him in?"

"Yes, thank you. Oh . . . and Lisa, would you mind blocking out tomorrow on my calendar? I'm going to be taking a little vacation time."

"Will do, Mr. Bright." She turned to leave.

"Wait!" I called out before the door closed behind her. "Scratch that. I don't just want tomorrow off. I want tomorrow and the next two weeks."

"And your travel reservations?"

"Cancel them, please. I'll send Jessica an e-mail advising her of my absence. If she calls for me, she can reach me on my cell phone." I paused, then added, mostly to myself, "I haven't taken time off in over a year. I'm long overdue."

Chapter 15

*A*t six o'clock in the evening, while sitting in my next-to-last meeting of the day, I received an unexpected text message from Anna.

"I will get Hope's guitar. Please come home quickly and pay sitter. Put Hope to bed. Give her a kiss from me and tell her I love her."

It didn't surprise me there was no *XOXO* or *Love Ya!* at the end of the message. But at least she'd consented to get the guitar. For now, that was enough. The rest of the mess I'd made could be fixed later.

My final meeting of the day ran over, so I didn't get out of the office until nearly 7:45. By then the city traffic was light enough to make the commute home a breeze.

"Dad?" Hope said as I walked in the door at 8:30. "You're home?"

Since when did she drop "Daddy" from her vocabulary? I wondered. I was exhausted from work, but managed a smile. "Were you expecting someone else?"

"No," she replied casually. "But it seems like you're always at work."

I ruffled her hair. "I know . . . and I'm sorry. But right now it's bedtime. You got to stay up a little later than normal tonight because Mom's out, but she gave me strict orders to put you to bed when I got home." The babysitter, a ponytailed teen who lived a few houses down, was folding up a blanket on the couch. "How much do I owe you?" I asked her. "I have no clue what the going rate is these days."

In perfect teenage prose she replied, "Whatev."

I pulled a wad of cash from my pocket. "Forty okay?"

She nodded, trying to suppress a grin, then let herself out.

After tucking Hope in bed, I went to wait for Anna in the living room.

At nine o'clock I began to get worried. If the store closed at eight, she should have been home already. I left her a voice mail, telling her to call me immediately. There was no reply.

By nine-thirty a steady uneasiness settled into my gut. *Where was she?* It wasn't like her to be out so late, especially without checking in. I tried her cell phone again, but it still went straight to voice mail.

In my mind I rehearsed all the things she'd said during our earlier conversation. *You never have time . . . Something's got to change or our marriage isn't going to survive . . . I need to decide if my love for you is enough to keep trying to make this work.* The more I thought, the more I wanted to find my old list of wedding-day vows just so I could puke in the bag.

"That's it," I said glumly to myself as I paced

the floor, stealing glances out the window every few seconds for any sign of her. "She's given up. I've let her down one too many times, and now . . . what? She's ignoring me? Teaching me a lesson? Or . . ." I didn't even want to think it, but I couldn't stop my mind from going there. "Oh crap . . . she's actually leaving me." My stomach lurched at the thought.

Just then the phone rang a few feet away, and I pounced on it. "Anna?"

"Hello?" The deep voice was definitely not my wife's. "Is this Mr. Ethan Bright?"

A telemarketer, I told myself, trying to relax. "Yes. Who is this?"

"Hello, sir. This is Reggie Wilson, a social worker with San Francisco General Hospital." He paused just long enough to clear his throat. "Mr. Bright, there's been an accident."

As soon as he said it, all the blood rushed from my face.

"I hate calling out of the blue like this," he continued, "but your wife is in pretty serious condition, and we'd like you to come as quickly as you can."

I couldn't breathe. God's metronome stopped abruptly; time stood still.

"Mr. Bright? Hello?"

"I'm here," I whispered numbly. "How serious . . . ?"

"I think it's best if you come to the hospital and

we can give you more details here. Are you able to drive?"

"Yes," I said hoarsely. "I'm on my way. I can be there in fifteen minutes."

"Perfect. I'll wait for you in the ER lobby."

"I have a young daughter. Can she come too? I can't leave her here alone."

"Of course. See you in a little bit."

As if on cue, a tiny voice behind me said, "Dad, is Mommy home yet?"

I hung up the phone and turned slowly, wanting to cry when I saw her. I knew I had to tell her what was going on, but at the same time I wanted to shield her and protect her from the tragedies of life. I motioned for her to come closer, then knelt down and wrapped my arms around her. "No, pumpkin. But we're going to see her right now."

"I'm sure everything is fine," I kept telling Hope as we drove to San Francisco General. "It's just a little car accident. Nothing to worry about."

She nodded every time I said it, but didn't say much.

When we entered the ER lobby, it was packed with people. Some were sleeping in seats, others were complaining about the wait, and a few were moaning in pain. Off to the side, leaning against a wall about thirty feet from the entrance, I spotted a well-dressed African–American man with a hospital badge clipped to his shirt. Maybe it was the frantic look on my face or the fact that I was towing Hope along behind me, but he seemed to recognize me when our eyes met, even though I was sure I'd never seen him before in my life. He waved us over with a subtle hand motion, then finished scribbling something on a notepad.

"Are you Reggie Wilson?" I asked as I approached.

He capped his pen and slid it into the spiral binding of his pad and lifted his hand in greeting. "Call me Reg; all my friends do. You must be Ethan Bright."

I had to let go of Hope's hand to shake. Then I got right down to business. "Where is Anna?"

"In surgery. That's about all I know at this point. By the time they gave me your number she was already in the operating room."

"So we can't . . . ?"

"See her? No, not until the surgery is complete. I told the nurses you were on your way, but they warned it could still be a while." He shifted his weight to his other leg.

It wasn't that I doubted the social worker, but my chief concern was seeing my wife and finding out how she was doing, and I wasn't sure he was the right guy to make that happen. I nodded politely. "Well, I should probably tell the nurses that I'm here anyway." For Hope's sake, I wanted to stay as calm as possible—even if just on the outside. I excused myself for a moment and approached the intake desk. "We're here to see Annaliese Bright," I told the first attendant who looked up. "Can you point us in the right direction?"

She smiled and typed a few things into her computer. Then her smile faltered. "Are you family?"

"I'm her husband, Ethan Bright."

"I see."

She typed some more. "Mr. Bright, your wife is still in surgery. Once they're done, it looks like they've arranged to put her in the Intensive Care Unit. The ICU has its own waiting area. I suggest you go wait there. I'll notify the ICU staff that you're waiting to hear news, so if you're there it'll be easy for them to find you."

"So you can't tell me anything?"

"I work in admitting, Mr. Bright. This is a big hospital, and they don't keep me posted on everything. But if you'll go to the ICU, I'm sure they'll have some information for you."

I nodded impatiently. "Fine." With Hope in tow, I quickly returned to Reg on the far wall and told him about the ICU.

He nodded like he already knew. "I have some paperwork I need to finish filling out," he said. "Can I bring you anything when I'm done?"

"Thanks, but we're fine." I shook his hand once more and took off down the hallway.

When I got to the ICU, I ran into another brick

wall. "Until the surgery is over," explained a doctor, "there isn't really anything we can report. I do know that your wife was rushed to the OR as soon as she arrived, and she's getting the best attention possible. But right now I think it best if you just hold tight until we have something concrete to share."

"So we still can't see Mommy?" asked Hope, who was looking more tired every minute.

"Sorry, pumpkin. It looks like we'll have to wait a little longer."

The doctor crouched down to look at Hope. "But I promise we'll take good care of your mom, okay? And we'll let you see her as soon as we can."

Thirty minutes later, Reg popped into the ICU waiting room, carrying a small stuffed bear. Hope was already sound asleep. "Oh, looks like I'm too late. She's already out." He handed me the toy instead.

"She'll appreciate it when she wakes up. Are you all done with your paperwork?"

He nodded. "It never really ends. But I've done all I can for now."

"Was it something to do with Anna?"

He nodded again. "I wanted to pull as many details as I could from the police report so we have them for her medical record. You never know what little tidbit of information might help the doctors later on."

"Nobody has told us *anything*," I said, not hiding my frustration. "Can you at least explain what happened?"

A soft, sympathetic tenderness settled into the features of Reg's face. This obviously wasn't his first go-round with a frazzled spouse, and his patience seemed equal to the task. "Of course, Ethan. I only know what's in the report, mind you, but I'm happy to share it with you." He flipped through some papers. "Let's see . . . at approximately 8:30, at the corner of Market and Guerrero, your wife, Anna, was struck by another vehicle while making a left turn."

My stomach churned uneasily. "Is the other guy in the hospital too?"

"It's not a guy. The other driver was a female college student. She was driving her parents' Escalade, which is big and safe to begin with, plus she had the vehicle's big block engine between her and the point of impact to offer added protection. Last I heard they were checking her out for a possible concussion and whiplash, but otherwise she came out with just a few bumps and bruises."

The word "college" immediately made me think "alcohol."

"Was she drunk?"

He grimaced as he shook his head. "Worse."

"Drugs?"

"Nope. *Texting* while driving. I swear I'd rather

hand these kids a beer than a cell phone when they get behind the wheel. Texting is almost an addiction to some people, especially the younger generation. It's like they can't *not* reply to a message the moment their phone vibrates, no matter what they're doing at the time."

"Texting . . . ," I said numbly, trying to imagine someone driving at full speed with their eyes and thumbs focused on a two-inch screen rather than the road ahead. "So you never got a chance to see Anna when she arrived in the ambulance?"

Reg shook his head. "No. Like I said, she was rushed off to surgery before I was made aware. But I did get a chance to speak briefly with one of the EMTs who'd treated her."

"And?"

It was clear he didn't like this part of his job. He took a deep breath, then let it out in a long sigh. "I won't lie to you. He said it couldn't have been much worse. I know that's probably not the easiest thing to hear, but part of my role in all of this as a medical social worker—in fact probably my biggest role—is to make sure that you have the best information possible, and then help you deal with the situation in an appropriate manner. I'm here to help you, Ethan, above all else, and in my view part of helping is to avoid sugar-coating anything. Your wife was T-boned—hit right on her door with that same big-block engine that was keeping the other driver safe. Her little Saab was no match for the SUV. Based on what I heard, she took a pretty good hit. The EMT's exact words were that he was surprised she was still alive when they pulled up to the ER."

It was hard to breathe with a giant lump in my throat, let alone speak, but I needed more information. "Do you know much about her injuries?"

"I know she was alive, but unconscious, when they loaded her in the ambulance, and that's about all."

I swallowed another lump, then whispered, "I understand."

Reg answered a few more clarifying questions before his pager started beeping, at which point he excused himself to go work on another case. The only sound in the ICU waiting room was Jerry Springer, who was playing on low-volume on a flat-screen directly opposite from the door. I turned him off and sat in silence.

Hope was sleeping peacefully with her head on my lap. When I tried to get out from beneath her so she could stretch out more on the couch, she lifted her head briefly and said, "I'm not going to sleep, Dad. I'm staying awake to see Mommy."

Ten seconds later she was conked out again, this time with a small cushion to support her neck, instead of my leg.

I couldn't help but marvel at how much she reminded me of her mother. The same beautiful hair. The same long eyelashes and large round eyes. And definitely the same mouth. I wondered if I would ever see Anna's mouth smiling at me again. Reg's words echoed in my head. *I won't lie to you, it couldn't have been much worse.*

For the first hour sitting there I expected some-body—a doctor, nurse, anyone—would be coming in at any second to give me an update. Nobody came. By then I felt like I should be making calls to let our families know what had happened, but I hoped to have some concrete details to share before doing so. At 11:30, still without any updates on Anna's status, I bit the bullet and dialed Anna's father.

"Hello?"

By the sound of the voice on the other end of the line, he'd been asleep. "Hi, Octavius. It's Ethan."

"Oh. Awfully late to be calling, isn't it? Is everything okay?"

"I know. I'm sorry . . . and no, things could be better. Octavius . . . there's been an accident."

I heard a little gasp through the line. "Is it Hope?"

Looking down at the face of my sleeping daughter, I was at least grateful that she'd not been involved. How hard would it be to hear that something awful had happened to my little Hope? Realizing that I was about to share bad news about another father's daughter—*his little girl!*—tore me to pieces. To help keep my emotions in check,

197

I gave him the condensed, Reader's Digest version of what I knew. When I was done he was full of questions.

"Where are you right now? Is she there? Can I talk to her?"

I quickly explained that Anna was still in surgery and that I hadn't talked to doctors yet. "But an EMT on the scene said she was unconscious, so who knows when she'll be up to talking. I'm so sorry, Octavius. I wanted you to know as soon as possible. I'll definitely keep you posted as I learn more details."

"Oh my . . . Do you think there's a chance that she might . . . I mean . . . Should I come down there? Would that help?"

"That's up to you. But given how little we know, I think the best thing might be just to wait until there's more news."

"I understand." He thanked me for letting him know, adding that he'd let the family know what was going on, starting with Stuart and his wife Heather in case they wanted to drive up.

After talking with Octavius I made a quick call to Grandpa, asking him to keep Anna in his prayers and to spread the word among the rest of the family.

A gray-haired doctor entered the waiting room about half an hour later, tailed by two younger doctors and one of the ICU nurses. Each of them wore faded blue scrubs and a look of exhaustion.

"Mr. Bright?" asked the eldest of the bunch.

"Yes," I replied nervously.

"I'm Dr. Rasmussen, one of the neurosurgeons here. I've been with your wife for the last couple of hours. We all have." He glanced at Hope, asleep beside me. "Let's go down the hall to my office."

"It's that bad?"

"We'll have one of the nurses keep an eye on your daughter for a few minutes."

He led me to his office, and the nurse went in the opposite direction to find someone to sit with Hope. The younger doctors pulled chairs closer in while Dr. Rasmussen closed the door behind us, then sat in his chair across the desk from me. "Mr. Bright, this is Dr. Schafer, an orthopedist, and Dr. Gooding, from internal medicine. We worked collaboratively tonight on your wife, along with a team of other folks who I'm sure you'll have a chance to meet over the next few days." Both doctors nodded when he said their names.

"Good to meet you all," I said. "And thanks for what you've done. But I don't think you brought me into your office for introductions."

"No," said Dr. Rasmussen softly, looking suddenly very tired. He tapped his lips thoughtfully before continuing. "We know you're anxious to hear how your wife is doing, and that's why we're here." He took another long breath. "The good news is that she's alive. I know how that must sound, but given how she looked when she first arrived, the fact that she's still with us is a small miracle. Usually, when individuals have sustained as much trauma as she did, this conversation would be the sort that I hate to have with spouses."

The younger men in blue solemnly nodded their approval.

I appreciated the "good news," yet he seemed to be holding something back. "But . . . ?"

Dr. Rasmussen's chest swelled in a giant sigh. "But there are some very serious complications that we're trying our best to manage. For starters, one of your wife's lungs collapsed. Tracheal intubation was performed at the crash scene for ventilation, and she still needs mechanical assistance to get oxygen. We have her hooked up to a machine right now that's doing the breathing for her. Also, in the ambulance her heart stopped beating and—."

"Her *what?*" I gasped.

Dr. Gooding piped up for the first time. "Her heart stopped. Defib paddles got it going again, but it took some doing."

I ran a panicked hand through my hair. "Will she be okay?"

"In time," the younger doctor continued, "the lungs and heart should mend. Unfortunately, those are the lesser of Anna's injuries. One of her kidneys received direct trauma in the accident. As a result, we had to remove it."

"But people can function with one kidney, right?"

Now Dr. Schafer joined in, though with slightly less sympathy in his voice than the other two. "Yes, they can. But when your wife's heart stopped, the other kidney went without blood for a long enough period of time that it, too, was damaged. It's too early to tell how that will impact it, but we're guessing it will only have about half its normal function. Which means even if your wife recovers from everything else, she'll still require regular dialysis to clean out the toxins in her blood, or they would kill her."

The nurse who'd gone hunting for a babysitter slipped into the room while Dr. Schafer was speaking. She took up a post just inside the door, leaning against the wall.

I glanced around at the other three, studying their faces. Dr. Rasmussen looked like he had more to say, and my intuition told me that the worst was yet to come. "What else?" I demanded.

"As I said before," he replied, "I'm a neurosurgeon. They only call me if there's—. Let me back up. Your wife's head sustained very serious trauma from the force of the impact. We've already performed a craniotomy to—."

"A what?"

"Craniotomy," he repeated. "Her brain has a significant amount of swelling. We opened up a hole in her skull—her cranium—to relieve the pressure. But . . ."

The tears I'd been resisting finally let loose. My emotions felt like they couldn't take any more bad news. "There can't possibly be another 'but'!" I lifted my shoulder to wipe my face on the sleeve of my shirt. "Just . . . stop it, already! How can it be worse than what you've already said?"

He let me take a moment to gather myself before saying, "I'm sorry, Mr. Bright. I know this is a lot to digest all at once, but you need to understand the full reality of your wife's condition. The biggest concern is that she currently lacks all perceptivity and receptivity."

"Which means what, exactly?"

"Perceptivity is a response of the nervous system to learned stimuli. Think of it as the act of thinking, or consciously perceiving the world around you. Receptivity is more of an innate response of the brain; things like turning to find the source of a loud sound or recoiling from a sharp pain."

Frustrated, I repeated my question. "Which means *what*, exactly?"

"Which means, she's literally not responding to *anything*. She's in a coma, Mr. Bright, and even if the rest of her heals, there's a decent chance that she won't come out of it, no matter what we do."

Again, the other two doctors nodded their agreement, this time joined by the nurse too.

It took a moment for what he'd just said—and what they were all nodding about—to fully sink in. By the time it did I was in complete shambles. I felt almost numb, like I wanted to keep crying, but was so far beyond that that the tears would be wasted effort. The only thing I sensed was a giant ache in my chest, which made me wonder how long it would be before they were using the defibrillator on *me*.

"So Anna will never wake up . . ." The words dropped from my mouth like cold stones on a grave. I was defeated, and I knew it.

With a shake of his head, Dr. Rasmussen said, "Not exactly. She's not really asleep. Even when we're asleep, our brains respond to outside stimuli. It's more like her brain has gone into hibernation, kind of like what a computer does when we're not using it. It's not really on and not really off. But in this case, there's no way of knowing if it will ever turn on again."

"So she's just not responding." I was still unsure how that differed from sleeping and never waking up.

"That's correct. There's a standard we use, called the Glasgow Coma Scale, to measure basic reactivity to a stimulus. On each of the measures—eye response, verbal response, and motor response, she scored a one, for a total of three. That's the lowest possible score, meaning there was no detectable response."

"But . . . she could improve, right?"

"Yes. And we'll take frequent measurements to

monitor her progress. If her Glasgow score goes up, that's certainly positive. But her score is so low that . . . Mr. Bright, I've had patients with higher scores than hers who have remained in comas for a very long time."

My mouth was so dry I could hardly speak. "How long?"

"Years," he replied softly. "Until they finally passed away."

I wanted to cry again, but willed myself to be angry instead. "Then how in the hell is this conversation *easier* than telling someone their loved one didn't make it? *'Hello, Mr. Bright. Good news, your wife's not dead! Bad news, she might as well be!'*"

Dr. Rasmussen was more patient in his response than I might have been if the roles were reversed. He just sighed softly without saying a word.

The nurse, however, who'd joined the conversation late, thought my outburst deserved a response. "You have to understand, these situations aren't easy for us, no matter what the outcome. We know how difficult this is for you. Unfortunately, sometimes these things just—"

"No!" I snapped, catching her by surprise. "Don't you dare say 'these things just happen.' *Don't* say it. These things don't *'just happen.'* They just happen to happen to Anna and to me, and I'm tired of it! I'm tired of things just happening."

The doctors waited until I'd had a moment to

cool down. Then Dr. Rasmussen cleared his throat and addressed me by name, speaking in smooth, measured tones. "Ethan, none of us would pretend to know what you're going through—or what you've been through in the past, for that matter—but I can tell you there is a big difference between telling someone their loved one is gone, versus the situation you find yourself in right now."

"Oh really?" I snarled. "And what is that?"

He stood slowly and paced around his desk, then placed a hand gently on my shoulder. It was something my grandfather might have done to calm me down had he been there. "As I see it," he said, "even though the odds aren't good, at least you still have a little hope to hold onto." He paused. "Ethan, there's not much you can do here tonight. I suggest you go home. Your wife is still in post-op, and it won't be until tomorrow sometime that you can be with her in the ICU. You should go get some rest."

I nodded absently.

The other doctors stood as well and shook my hand; then the nurse led me back to the waiting area where Hope was still fast asleep.

Even though they wouldn't let me be with Anna, I wanted to be as close to her as I could, so I sat in the waiting room all night. Hope slept comfortably with my jacket over her, while I stayed awake, worrying about what misery lay ahead for our little family.

Even when things in our life—and our marriage—weren't brilliant, I'd always assumed that, eventually, our future together would be full of light, but with Anna on life support, I could feel the darkness settling in.

Chapter 16

I don't mind admitting that I always thought Anna's brother Stuart was quirky. For that matter, I doubt he would disagree with my assessment, much less be offended by it. He was a computer nerd to the core, and I think he secretly enjoyed living up to the stereotype, in both appearance and demeanor. No matter how many times we all told him that socks, especially dark socks, and sandals are a lousy combination, he refused to make a change (he apparently had cold feet year round). Socially, the word that describes him best is "awkward."

It was easy to distinguish between him and the other Burke son, Lance, a rugged outdoorsy type who taught middle school woodshop in Pocatello, Idaho. Whereas Stuart was a rich homebody, Lance didn't mind being dirt poor, choosing to skimp on material things during the school year so he could blow his savings during the summer months on exotic adventures around the globe.

Hope overheard me use the term "the rich one" once when talking about her uncle, and decided that if Stuart was "the rich one," then Uncle Lance was "the cool one." On the few occasions that we saw Lance, he had never-ending stories to tell from his escapades climbing mountains, backpacking in the Amazon, or bicycling across China.

"Gosh," I replied to Hope, "I think having millions in the bank would be pretty darn cool."

"Oh, Dad," she said, sounding as though she were suddenly a teacher and I was the silly student who didn't understand anything. "It's *just* money. There are things that money can't buy, you know."

"Oh? Name one."

With that she stretched out her arms as wide as they would go and, with a smile that was wider still, she announced, "Ta da!"

Smart kid.

At seven in the morning, "the rich one" showed up at the hospital with his wife, Heather, and their two kids, Devin and Jordan, ages ten and twelve. I'd just barely drifted off when Jordan plopped down loudly on a nearby seat and blurted out, "Oh man, Uncle Ethan snores like a bear. Can we watch TV until he wakes up?"

"I'm awake," I mumbled groggily. "And I don't snore." I glanced at Hope, still asleep beside me; then I stretched my neck from side to side to get the kinks out.

"Sorry to wake you," said Stuart.

"It's fine. I can't believe you made it here as early as you did. What time did you leave? Like four o'clock?"

"Four thirty. There was zip-o traffic, so we breezed up the interstate faster than Amazon spitting e-books from the Whispernet."

There was an awkward pause. Like I said, he's quirky.

Heather rolled her eyes, then got very serious and asked how Anna was doing.

I glanced quickly at Hope again to make sure she was still sleeping soundly. "I haven't seen her. But it doesn't sound good. They came in late last night and warned me that she could very well—." I stopped short and stared at the boys. Something about their eager attentiveness unnerved me; maybe I just didn't want them to know how bad it really was.

Stuart recognized my hesitation. He quickly pulled out his wallet and handed each of them a ten-dollar bill. "Boys, go find a snack machine or something. Bring me back Pop-Tarts if you can find them." They both seemed to catch on that they were being uninvited from the adult conversation. With some reluctance, they took the money and left. "You were saying?" Stuart asked once they were out of sight.

I shrugged. "Honestly, I don't have a lot of details yet. She's in a coma, though. I do know that much." My eyes danced very quickly between their horrified stares. "And even if the rest of her gets put back together," I added soberly, "it's possible that she won't come out of it."

Heather put a hand over her mouth. It covered up her gasp, but it didn't stop her eyes from watering.

"Good Lord," said Stuart. The news shook him enough that he needed to sit down. "Do you know how it happened?"

For the next fifteen minutes, while the boys were still scouring the hospital for snack food, I shared what I knew about the circumstances of the collision. Then I gave them all a thorough rundown of the previous night, starting with the phone call from Reggie Wilson and ending with Jerry Springer. Hope woke up near the end of the discourse and cuddled up next to me. With her awake, I was careful to avoid saying anything that would give clues about the seriousness of her mother's condition.

Jordan and Devin returned a few minutes later, much to Hope's delight. The boys were trailed closely by a nurse who called my name as she entered the waiting area.

"I'm Ethan Bright," I replied, jumping to my feet.

"I know you've been waiting a long time. Thank you for your patience. The attending doctor says that you can see your wife now. Would you like to follow me?"

Everyone in the room stirred excitedly.

"Is she awake?" I asked.

The woman responded with a slow shake of the head. "I think for starters you should probably come alone. The room isn't very big, and there's a lot of equipment in there. And . . . given the shape she's in, I'm not sure—"

"I understand," I said, cutting her off before she said too much in front of Hope. Then I reached down and gave my daughter a squeeze. "Sweetie, do you mind hanging out here with *cool* Uncle Stuart and Aunt Heather so I can check on Mommy?"

She lifted her head to look at me. "He's the rich one, Dad, not the cool one."

Stuart just chuckled.

"Yes, pumpkin, that too. Is it okay if I go for a while?"

Hope nodded and smiled in a way that said, "I'll be fine, Dad."

I followed the nurse down a long hallway, through a set of double doors that opened automatically, past a group of ICU nurses who were huddled behind a desk, and then tiptoed into Anna's dimly lit room.

The first thing that caught my attention was the mountain of devices surrounding the bed. There were monitors of all shapes and sizes, each of them beeping and blinking sporadically; there were respirators, oxygen tubes, miscellaneous wires and cables, graphs, and more IVs than I'd ever seen.

At the center of it all was something that gave me chills: the body of a person I didn't recognize.

"That's not my wife," I whispered.

The nurse flipped a chart. "Anna-lies Bright?"

"Anna*liese*," I corrected. "But that's not her."

"Well, you have to understand, she's in very serious condition. There's a lot of swelling right now. But it *is* her."

I just shook my head. The person lying on the bed didn't look anything like Anna. The face was engorged, especially the left side, where the eye was swollen completely shut. The head was wrapped in thick, sterile bandages, and the parts of her scalp that were exposed looked like they'd been shorn right down to the skin. The nose and lips were all black and blue and disfigured from swelling. A jagged line of sutures ran from just below the earlobe to the center of the cheek. One forearm was heavily wrapped, and the other arm had bright gashes just below the shoulder.

I took a couple steps forward. "No. I don't think so." I was secretly praying that I was right, and that this was all just some big hospital screwup. Maybe Anna was at home, wondering where in the world her daughter and husband had been all night. "I don't see a ring on her finger."

"They had to cut it off," the nurse explained. "With all the swelling in her hand, it had to go. It's in a plastic bag on the dresser."

Looking quickly at the dresser to my right, my heart sank when I spotted Anna's ring, just where she'd said. Inching closer to the bed, I kept my eyes trained on the swollen face lying on the pillow. I kept moving forward until my thigh brushed the bed's metal rail. As I stared down at her from above, I could just make out the distinctive shape of my wife's mouth, hidden there beneath all of the cuts, scrapes, and swelling. "Oh, Anna," I whispered.

The nurse scooted a chair over next to the bed so I could sit down; then she left abruptly. When she returned thirty minutes later, she was followed by Reg, the medical social worker, and two men I didn't recognize. The taller of the two wore scrubs; the other, a suit.

"Mr. Bright," the nurse began, "this is Dr. Knight, the attending physician in the ICU today, along with Nathan Birch from our legal department. And I think you've already met Mr. Wilson. There are a few things they'd like to go over with you."

"Legal?" I asked warily as I shook their hands.

Reg gave the nurse a look that said he would handle it from here. "Standard operating procedure," he assured. "Can we sit?" There were only three chairs. The nurse and the guy in the suit remained standing while the rest of us sat and faced each other. "How you holding up?" Reg asked with a crooked but compassionate smile.

"Fair . . . I guess, under the circumstances."

His eyes said he understood what I was going through. "Get much sleep last night?"

"Not a wink."

He looked around the room. "It's a little tight in here, but there's definitely enough room for a recliner. I'll make sure they bring one in so you can rest up."

"Thank you." I briefly traded glances with the other three faces in the room. "But I bet that's not what everyone came to talk to me about."

"No," he said softly. "Ethan, I don't think I took the time last night to fully explain my role here at the hospital. Sometimes, when families like yours have particularly difficult medical issues to deal with, the hospital assigns me to help out—to sort of look out for you and help you get through the ordeal. Emotionally, physically, psychologically, what you're going through right now can be very difficult, but I want you to know I'm here to help, no matter what. And if you want, I can help be an advocate for you and guide you through some of the medical complexities of caring for patients in your wife's condition."

"I appreciate it."

His compassionate smile was still there, but a distinct sadness washed over his face. I guessed he was about to broach whatever subject had warranted the presence of legal counsel. "Unfortunately," he continued, more slowly, "another aspect of my job is to help prepare individuals and families for the eventuality that their loved ones might not make it, no matter how much we wish it weren't so. As I said, above all else I'm here to help you, and part of helping is making sure you are well informed about the situation. To that end, I want to impress upon you just how serious your wife's situation is. I believe Dr. Rasmussen and the others filled you in last night on the extent of her injuries. Is that right?"

I nodded. "I really couldn't comprehend it . . . until I came in here and saw her."

Mr. Birch was standing directly behind Reg, rifling through papers attached to a clipboard. He pulled a yellow sheet from the stack and handed it to Reg. "Mr. Bright, I think what Mr. Wilson is getting at," the attorney said abruptly, "is that, given your wife's current state, some important decisions are going to need to be made on her behalf. To that end, we need to establish whether or not she made legal plans for medical crises of this nature. I know you probably don't want to be thinking about this right now, but given your wife's condition, and her inability to make decisions concerning her own care, we need to know if she has a living will."

I didn't respond. Not because I couldn't, but because I didn't want to.

"Ethan?" Reg asked. "Do you know what that is?"

I nodded.

"And?"

During our first year of marriage, after losing everything we owned in the apartment fire, Anna made it a goal to have every possible eventuality nailed down. Even before the very first miscarriage, she'd made me sit down with her and an attorney to fill out several legal documents, one of which was a living will. I'd thought it was the right thing to do at the time. Now I was absolutely sure it wasn't, because I knew what her wishes were.

"If something should ever happen to me," she'd said, "I don't want you to have to worry about what decision to make. And I don't want to live on life-support forever. Pull the plug, Ethan, and let me go peacefully."

Pull the plug? Just like that? It sounded sensible at the time, when the likelihood of something like that ever happening to either of us seemed so remote as to be laughable. Now that it was actually happening, the thought made me sick.

"Ethan?" Reg asked again.

"What? Oh, sorry. Like I said, I uhh . . . didn't sleep much last night. I'm not sure if she has a living will or not. I'll have to look around at home . . . I guess." Even to me it sounded like a bad lie, but I didn't dare tell them the truth, for fear they'd stand up right then and turn everything off. "But . . . what if she *doesn't* have one?"

The lawyer leaned closer. "Then as her husband, you would be her legal proxy. Should she not show signs of improvement, you would need to make some very important decisions for her."

Reg sat up in his chair and handed me the yellow paper Nathan Birch had given him. "If she doesn't have a living will, you'll need to fill this out, attesting to that fact. You would then be solely responsible for how we, the hospital, proceed."

I glanced at Anna once more. "But we're not . . . I mean . . . the accident just happened yesterday, so . . . we're not talking about making major decisions *now*, right? I mean, not *that* decision."

Dr. Knight scooted forward in his chair. "Mr. Bright, I reviewed your wife's case with Dr. Rasmussen and the other surgeons who operated on her last night, along with a team of some of the best doctors on our staff. Based on the severity of the trauma, the types of injuries she's sustained, and her general lack of responsiveness, we're all in agreement that the likelihood of your wife recovering from this is not good. That's not to say there's no chance. It's still early yet, so things could improve. At this moment, however, based on both statistical data and expert opinion, she might have a five percent chance of recovery. But recovery from things like this can be a long process, and we're only at the beginning, so let's give it some time. I just want you to be prepared for the possibility that, at some point down the road, you may need to think about whether or not your wife would want to remain like this, or whether she'd prefer that you . . . let her go." He paused, allowing me time to digest. "As you say, though, the accident just occurred. We'd certainly like to see how things go over the next couple weeks. Hopefully the brain swelling will go down, and that may give us a little better read on things. In the meantime, however, I'd ask you to give some thought to the possibility that things might not go the way you want."

My vision bounced from the doctor, to Reg, to Mr. Birch, to the nurse, and back to Dr. Knight. Not wanting to look any of them directly in the eyes, I turned away altogether and let my eyes crash-land on Anna's distorted face. "I understand," I whispered.

After watching a machine force air into Anna's lungs for another hour, I went out to the waiting room. Heather was reading a book. Everyone else was watching an old episode of *The Smurfs* on the television. They all looked up when I shuffled into the room.

"Is it my turn to see Mommy now?" Hope asked excitedly, as she leapt from the couch into my arms.

"I'm sorry, sweetheart. The doctor says right now only Daddy can see her." I didn't like lying to her. But what's worse, telling an eight-year-old that a doctor won't allow her to see her mother, or giving the child the memory of seeing a lump of broken flesh that looks nothing like Mommy? I turned to face Stuart and Heather. "Would you mind taking Hope back to our house? I'm not sure how long it'll be, but you'd be doing me a huge favor if you could just watch out for her for a little while."

"Of course," said Heather.

"Abso-*smurfly*," added Stuart, attempting to lighten the mood for the kids' sake.

After they were gone, I grabbed a bite at the cafeteria, then went back to Anna's room, where I watched the rise and fall of her chest for five straight hours. Periodically I would say things to test her reaction, like, "Anna, I'm here," or "Can you hear me? Please, just try to hear me." Once I even shouted, which brought two nurses running into the room to see what was the matter. But through it all she never moved an inch. Aside from the systematic expansion of her lungs, she lay completely still.

At three o'clock the new shift supervisor came to inform me that I had a visitor in the waiting room.

"Who?"

"She didn't leave a name."

I walked around the corner and back down the hallway to the waiting area. A woman in her early twenties looked up. She had a nick on her chin, a fat lip, and dark blue rings under both eyes, but still she had a pretty face. On a different day I'd have guessed her to be bubbly and confident, but at the moment she had the look of a frightened kitten.

She swallowed hard, then stood and said, "Oh . . . are you . . . ?"

"Ethan Bright."

Before she said another word, the girl's hands began trembling and her eyes filled with deep pools of moisture. "Please . . . *please* tell me you're not related to Hope Bright."

"I'm her father. How do you know Hope?"

She covered her mouth and nose with both hands as the water in her eyes spilled onto her cheeks. *"Oh . . . noooo,"* the girl whimpered sadly. She struggled to maintain her breathing for several seconds. When the heaving abated, she lowered her hands, and when the sniffling finally concluded, she collected herself enough to say, "I'm Ashley . . . Ashley Moore. I was a student teacher in Hope's class. I'm . . . the one . . . who . . ."

I tried to remain calm. "Who crashed into my wife?"

The girl nodded remorsefully, after which a long, awkward silence ensued. I wasn't prepared to be talking to my wife's assailant, so I just stood staring, waiting for her to say something.

She stared back, but remained mute.

Finally I couldn't take it anymore. "I have to get back to my wife. Was there something you wanted?"

More tears started pooling above her rosy cheeks. When she nodded, they all rolled down. "I wanted . . . to say I'm . . . *really* sorry about what happened."

The way she was crying again, I was surprised she got the words out at all.

"Is that it?"

Ashley nodded again. By now her mascara was vacating her eyelids in wide swaths. She carefully blotted tears with the back of her hand, trying to preserve what was left of her makeup.

For reasons I can't explain, hearing the young woman use the word "sorry" for the harm she'd caused seemed absurdly inadequate to me. No amount of sorrow was ever going to make up for what she'd done to our family, and I wanted her to know it. So I cleared my throat, and in the nicest, calmest voice I could find, I said, "Honestly, I don't want to hear it. And I don't care that you know my daughter. I really don't." I reached methodically for my wallet in my back pocket, then flipped it open to a picture of Anna and held it up to Ashley's face. "Do you know who this is?" I could feel my temperature rising. "Did you ever talk to her when she picked up Hope from school? Do you remember her face? Well, I can promise you, if you were to go to her room right now, you wouldn't recognize her. After what you did to her, *I* don't even recognize her."

Ashley's face was as white as a sheet; she stared at the picture like she was seeing a ghost.

"Tell me," I said, now fighting to keep the vitriol

from my voice, "what was so important that you couldn't wait to send that last text message? *OMG, was it your BFF?* Well guess what, because of your stupidity, *my* BFF is in a coma at the end of the hall. Why don't you text your phone pals and tell them that!"

"It was my boyfriend," she stammered. "He sent me a note . . ."

"And he's so important that you couldn't wait five minutes to send a reply?"

At that, Ashley gave up trying to have a conversation with me. The frightened kitten had been cornered by a Rottweiler, and she was ready to bolt. In one quick movement, she grabbed her purse from the couch, slung it over her shoulder, and dashed out of the room in a flood of tears. But she didn't get two steps down the hallway before she ran into someone else who was coming in the opposite direction.

There was a loud *thwap!* followed by another mournful, "I'm so sorry," from Ashley.

"That's quite all right, young lady," came the reply.

My heart skipped a beat.

I knew that voice all too well, and I was slightly embarrassed by the thought that he might have overheard my little tirade. When I turned around, he was standing just inside the room, hunched over from age and relying on a cane to support his weight. He looked somehow smaller than the last time I'd seen him, like gravity was finally bringing him down.

He didn't say a word.

He didn't have to. I could read Grandpa Bright like I was reading a book.

Chapter 17

*F*rom the look of disappointment on my grandfather's face, I guessed he'd heard the tail end of my conversation with Ashley Moore. I'd seen that particular look plenty of times before. Like when he was summoned to the high school my freshman year because I'd thrown a plate of ketchup-laden Tater Tots at a senior jock, in response to what he'd called one of my band friends. Or the time he caught me reading the private clinical file he kept on the paranoid schizophrenic guy who was always at the library telling patrons that the Tillamook Cheese Factory was actually a covert nuclear facility. "Don't eat the pepper jack," the man would whisper in all seriousness. "It's radioactive!"

Grandpa waited in the doorway until I spoke.

"You came," I ventured.

The disappointment in his eyes quickly gave way to the gentle tenderness he was so famous for with his patients. "I caught the first flight out. I hope you don't mind." He hobbled over and gave me a one-armed hug. The other arm held fast to his cane. The way he was stooped, his head only reached my chest. "I expected to find you in a state of sadness, and instead I happen upon you in a fit of . . . what was that? Infuriation?"

"Yeah, I lost my temper a bit. That was the gal that ran into Anna."

"Ah," he said knowingly, then added, "You should be careful not to let your anger taint your heart. You have a kind heart. No matter what happens to Anna, it would be sad to see you lose that."

"I don't think you understand. That girl . . . she . . . If Anna dies, I swear I'll . . ."

"You'll what?"

"Well for starters, I'll push as hard as I can for criminal charges. I bet we can get her for vehicular manslaughter."

He just shook his head.

I shook my head too, if only to shake off unpleasant thoughts of Ashley and get my head back on Anna. "The doctors are pretty sure she's going to die," I continued as I took a seat on the couch. "It's just . . . unthinkable. Last night, when I first found out how bad it was, I cried my heart out. Now that I've seen her and I fully understand the gravity of it, part of me just wants to curl up in a ball and stop existing." I paused, searching his wise eyes for any hint of a look that might legitimize my feelings. There was love there, and deep compassion, but nothing to suggest he would accept it if I just gave up. "Haven't you ever felt like that?" I pressed.

"You'll find a way to get through this," he replied, carefully dodging my question. "In time."

For the next couple of hours Grandpa and I stayed at the hospital. I hoped when he saw how bad Anna looked that he would validate my feelings of anger toward Ashley Moore. But even when he was standing right next to her bed, examining her injured body, all he would say was, "You'll get through this. I promise."

By three o'clock in the afternoon I'd made up my mind that I was going to stay overnight again at the hospital. "I need to run home to gather a few things," I told Grandpa. "Did you catch a cab here from the airport?"

"I rented a car. Why? You need a lift?"

"They actually rent to guys your age? No wonder insurance premiums keep going up."

In response to that, he "accidentally" stepped on my foot with the full weight of his cane as he shuffled toward the door.

Same old Grandpa, I thought.

Grandpa followed me home in his rental. I had to keep my foot on the brake most of the time to keep from losing him, but eventually we made it.

The first words I heard when I walked in the door were, "Is Mommy coming home tonight?"

"Oh, pumpkin. Mommy's accident was . . . a little more serious than I first thought, and she's . . . ummm . . . not up to it just yet."

Hope was crushed. "So no party?"

The birthday party!

I'd completely forgotten. A handful of kids were scheduled to arrive in less than an hour, expecting to play games and eat cake. If everything had gone as planned, they would also get to see Hope unwrap a brand-new guitar. There was obviously no way I could host a party. Not only did I not have the slightest inkling what Anna had planned for the kids to do, but I couldn't just throw a party while my wife was dying at the hospital. Hope didn't realize how serious the situation was with her mom, so I wasn't surprised that she was still thinking about her birthday, but the only thing on my mind was getting back to Anna. "Oh, honey," I said, squatting down to look her in the eyes. "I know how much you were looking forward to a party, but, I'm afraid—"

"Ethan," interrupted Stuart. "I . . . I hope I didn't overstep my bounds, but I saw the RSVP cards on the counter and . . . well, since I wasn't sure when—or if—you were coming home today, I sort of made some arrangements."

"Arrangements?"

"We planned a party," said Heather. "Is that okay?"

"Nothing fancy," Stuart added. "It's tough to get stuff for day-of, you know. All we could book was a bounce house and Presto the Magician."

"Presto the . . . ? A bounce house? Stuart, that's . . ." I was about to say *way too much to spend on a child's party,* but Hope was standing

227

right there, and I didn't want her to think she wasn't worth it. "That's . . . very kind of you. What do you think about that, Hope? Will your friends like a bounce house and magician birthday party?"

She gave an eight-year-old shrug, one that included not only her shoulders, but her arms, hands, and most of her face. "It's great, but . . . what about Mommy? Will she be sad that she missed the party? Maybe we shouldn't do it without her."

"Oh no, honey. It's fine. Mom will be happy that you and your friends are having fun."

"Even without her there?"

"You know what? We'll have Stuart and Heather take lots of pictures. Then you can show Mom everything that happened at the party when she gets out of the hospital. How about that?"

"That's right," piped Stuart while pulling his cell phone from his pocket. "I've got my camera right here. What do you say we go get ready and make this the best birthday ever?"

The best birthday ever? I froze when Stuart said it. His words jolted me back to the reality of the situation. Here we were, trying to coerce a little girl to have a wonderful, carefree party, while unbeknownst to her, her mother lay dying in the hospital.

Hope thought about Stu's question for a moment too. Her response surprised me. "If I have a choice, I'd rather go see Mommy."

I pulled her close and gave her a big hug. "I know, sweetie. And you will. But right now you've got a lot of friends who are probably already on their way. I need to go be with your mom at the hospital, so I need to know that I can count on you to have a good time while I'm gone. Can I count on you for that?"

She looked up at me and smiled courageously. "Okay, Dad." Then she ran off to get ready for her friends' arrival.

"Thank you, Stuart," I said as soon as she was gone. "How much do I owe you for this?"

"Nah, forget about it. This one's on me. You go be with Anna and we'll take care of everything here."

"You sure?"

"My little sister needs you there. Of course I'm sure."

He may have been a rich, quirky little guy, but at that moment I was very glad to have him around. "Thanks, Stu."

While I was stuffing toiletries and several changes of clothes into a duffle bag, Presto showed up at the house and began setting up in the living room. Grandpa found himself a comfortable seat on the couch and watched the preparations. I passed through the room several times in a five-minute span, but Grandpa didn't say a word to me until I was headed out the front door.

"Ethan, aren't you forgetting something?"

"I already said goodbye to Hope," I replied.

"That's not what I was thinking of."

"Oh. Uh . . . do you need help getting your suitcase and things situated? You're welcome to have the guest room at the end of the hall. I told Stuart and Heather they could sleep in my bed, and I think their boys are going to be on the futon in the basement."

"I meant Karl."

I stared blankly at him for several seconds. "Why would I need the guitar?"

"Why else, but to play it? To play it for her, and to play it for *you*. Don't you think it will help?"

"No," I replied honestly. "I don't."

He studied my face just long enough to make me feel like I was being psychoanalyzed again. "I miss that old guitar," he said with a sigh. "It's been through a lot. Too bad I can't play it anymore. These old fingers just aren't up to it."

"Neither are mine."

"Come again?"

"Grandpa, I haven't played that thing in months. There just are more important things."

"Nonsense."

"After this whole thing with Anna, I don't think I could pick up a guitar even if I wanted to."

He tilted his head ever so slightly, and in his best therapist's tone he asked, "Really? Why is that?"

I knew full well that I hadn't told him

everything about the night of the accident during our conversation at the hospital. I'd purposely evaded his inquiries about Anna's whereabouts when it all went down, but I no longer saw the value in keeping it a secret. "Well, if you must know, Anna was on her way home from a guitar store when she was hit. She was picking one up for Hope's birthday."

"And that's enough for you to give up on one of your greatest talents?"

"Not just that. When I was a kid and you told me music was magical—"

"Oh right. You said you wanted to be a *magician*."

I turned around to make sure Presto wasn't within earshot. "Yeah, well, I don't believe in that sort of magic anymore. Look at me—I wound up dedicating half my life to music, but what's come of it? I'm *not* a musician—or a magician. I can play the guitar, but the career it led me to leaves no time for anything else. And although I dreamed of being a songwriter, I couldn't sell a song to save my life. Anna's accident is just another way that playing the guitar has let me down. It's not worth it anymore. I'm done."

"Hmm," he responded, drawing it out thoughtfully.

"Hmm? That's all you have to say?"

"What do you want me to say?"

"I dunno. Something besides 'Hmm.'"

"That's all I've got."

I was growing more frustrated by the second. "Fine. You know what? I think it's time Karl was back in your possession. For good. I really am tired of having it around. I'll put it in your room and you can take it with you when you leave."

"But I don't want it," he said calmly.

"That makes two of us."

I stormed off down the hallway toward my room. There, leaning against the wall in the same exact place it had been for months, was Grandpa's old guitar case. I picked it up and marched it to the guest room and stowed it against another wall.

"It's all yours," I told Grandpa when I got back to the living room. "Enjoy."

"Are you sure about this?"

"As sure as Stuart is rich."

"Oh. How rich is he?"

"*Very.*"

"I see."

Just then I noticed he had something on his lap that hadn't been there when I left the room. It was an old wooden box, not much wider than a laptop, though maybe twice as thick. It had a brass lock on the front and two leather straps for hinges on the back. He was tapping his fingers rhythmically on the wood. I thought to ask about it, but I was already tired of the conversation and anxious to get back to my wife's side. "Sorry," I said. "It's your guitar, and I no longer have a use for it."

"Well, if you're adamant . . ." He let out a disappointed sigh. "But would you consider a trade?"

"Huh?"

"A trade. If I'm to take Karl, would you mind taking something in return?"

"What?" I asked skeptically, suspecting trickery from the master magician.

Grandpa lifted the box. "Just a little history. Something for you to read while you're sitting there at the hospital."

"A history of . . . ?"

"Me," he chirped. "I was planning on bequeathing copies of this to everyone after I'm gone, but I think now is a better time. I hope all of the Brights will find value in it, but I think you'll find it particularly interesting."

"Why now?" I asked. "And why me? I bet your kids will be mad that you shared this with me first."

A distinct weariness settled into his aged eyes, like years of sadness had suddenly taken up residence in his retinas. "Looking back, I wish I'd shared this with your father a long time ago. But that's neither here nor there. As for the others, they'll get their turns. Besides, you're like one of my own too, and you're the one who deserves to read this the most, because it will mean the most to you. Of that I'm sure."

"Why?"

He held up a bony hand to underscore the import of what he was saying. "Because, having had my guitar in your possession since you went off to college, you, of all people, deserve to know the truth."

"The truth?"

With a solemn nod he said, "Indeed. The truth about Karl."

I must admit, that last bit intrigued me. But my mind was already made up, and it was long past time for me to leave. "Sorry, Grandpa. Another time."

He favored me with another look of extreme disappointment. But then he started smiling, like he'd just thought of something. With a twinkle in his eye he muttered, "Yes . . . another time." Then he dismissed me with a quick wave.

I loaded the rest of my effects in the trunk of the car, but before I left, I remembered there was one more thing I needed to have with me at the hospital.

"Miss me, did you?" chuckled Grandpa as I came back through the door.

"Like an ex-con misses jail," I mumbled.

My briefcase was right where I expected it to be, in the den. I made sure its contents were still there, then turned to go. As I walked toward the door, I noticed Anna's corkboard hanging on the wall. I hardly ever bothered to look at the things she pinned up there, but on this occasion, one picture on the board grabbed my attention. It was Hope's class picture from school. In the picture, standing in the back row, was a very familiar looking student teacher. The photo was paperclipped to a sheet of paper. I yanked them both down together, staring first at Ashley Moore and then at the attached note. It was a letter from the teacher, summarizing a few of the highlights from the year and encouraging the students and families to have a wonderful summer. But it was the postscript that really mattered.

P.S.—Ms. Moore and I would love to hear from you over the summer! Please write to us at the following addresses . . .

It was like a gift from God. The address of the college student I'd met earlier in the day! All of my anger came flooding back. There were so many things I still wanted to say to her—so many ways I wanted her to suffer for what she'd done. With briefcase in hand, I took the address, plugged it into my GPS navigator, and paid the Moores an unexpected visit.

What happened next was, in a word, regrettable. Understandable (I think), but regrettable. I drove to the Moores' home, screamed at the house until they came outside, and drilled into Ashley until she was shaking with fear. Then I flipped open my briefcase, which they thought concealed a gun, and showed the young woman what *real* notes were. And only then, realizing that I was pushing the boundaries of rational behavior, I drove back to the hospital to be with Anna.

When I got to her room, the machines that kept her alive were still cranking. The obvious extent of trauma to her body brought me again to tears. But I wanted to help, so I sat at her side and talked to her for hours, telling her how much I loved her and how sorry I was for what had happened. Then I began reading aloud some of the notes she'd written to me over the years, hoping that might spark something in her brain. I begged her to respond, but nothing I said or did brought her back from wherever she was.

By ten o'clock I was feeling the physical effects of the past forty-eight hours, during which time I'd hardly slept. It made me wonder if Anna was tired too since, according to the doctor, a coma is not really sleeping. I did a final check to make sure her chest was still going up and down with the influx of air from the respirator. Then I told her goodnight, curled up with a blanket on the recliner that had been delivered to the room while I was away, and turned out the light.

Ten minutes later, just as I was nodding off, I heard an unfamiliar sound coming from the hallway. I remained motionless and listened.

Shuffle-shuffle-thump. Shuffle-shuffle-thump.

The sound grew steadily louder, then stopped

abruptly right outside the room. I remained perfectly still when the door opened and the sound entered.

Shuffle-shuffle-thump. Shuffle-shuffle-thump.

Doctors and nurses had been coming and going all day, and I'd spent enough time in hospitals during all of Anna's pregnancies to know that they would be coming all night too. I'd learned that the best thing to do in the middle of the night was just ignore them; otherwise, they sometimes wanted to stay and talk. So when the shuffling stopped right next to me, I carefully pretended that I was still asleep in the chair, suspecting that I was being watched. When the shuffling and thumping started towards Anna, I squinted with one eye to see if I could make out who it was.

If I hadn't already been lying down, the surprise at seeing Grandpa standing right there in the room might have knocked me clean over.

The source of the rhythmic *thump* was his trusty old cane. I couldn't begin to fathom how he'd gotten into the ICU after visiting hours, yet there he was, his dark, slouched form heading toward the empty chair next to Anna's bed. Tucked under one arm was the old wooden box.

Part of me wanted to flip on the light and tell him where he could go. I hadn't invited him and, even if I had, he was clearly breaking hospital rules. But this was Grandpa Bright, the man who'd raised me, who'd taken me in as a kid, and who would never in my wildest dreams do anything malicious or hurtful. If he thought it was important to make a late-night visit to Anna's darkened hospital room, then I wanted to know why.

And the easiest way to do that was by simply "sleeping" in my chair and watching things unfold.

INTERLUDE

Chapter 18

Grandpa crossed the room and sat down on the chair next to Anna, then bent over and set the wooden box at his feet.

"Hello, young lady," he said softly, speaking to her as though she could actually hear him. "Bet you didn't expect to see me here tonight, now did you? Looks like your husband is out cold. You should have seen him as a teenager. That boy could sleep through just about anything. Even school, as I recall."

He craned his neck slowly in my direction.

I quickly closed my eyes before he saw me watching.

"Too bad," Grandpa continued. "I really wanted to talk to him." He turned around once more, and I again opened my eyes.

Shifting in his chair, Grandpa grabbed the top bed rail with one hand to steady himself. "Anna, did Ethan ever mention that I fought in the Second World War? When he was younger, he used to ask about it all the time. I never gave out many details, though. All in all, I was probably more tight-lipped about my time in the service than I should have been. Everyone in the family has inquired about my experience at one time or another. There were things I would have loved to share, and probably should have, but those things might have led to other questions that I didn't want to delve into. So I remained mum about the whole ordeal.

"The thing is . . . I'm getting old." He snickered softly. "No, I *am* old, and have been for a while now. I won't be around forever. Before I go, I want my family to know . . . about me. Me and the war. I no longer want to wait until I'm gone to tell them what I went through, because then it's too late for those difficult questions. That's partly why I came down here to California. Ethan and I are a lot alike, and I think, out of all my children and grandchildren, right now he could benefit most from my experiences. But you know your husband—he's as stubborn as a mule. He wouldn't accept it when I offered it to him." He tapped the wooden box lightly with the heel of his shoe.

"I know the timing is bad, with you in the hospital and all, but I wish he'd have just taken the darned thing and read it. You wouldn't have minded, right? Heck, he could have read it out loud to you. I came here tonight to see if he'd reconsider, but alas . . . he's out."

Grandpa paused and turned around again. I could feel his eyes on me. I didn't move a muscle.

"But here's the thing," Grandpa continued, "I sort of need to get this story off my chest. I've kept it locked up—in the box, in my heart—for a long, long time. So since he's asleep, and you're such a captive audience, do you mind if I just tell it to you? It'll be good practice for me when I share it with the rest of the family. How does that sound, Anna? I think you'll find it entertaining. Believe it or not, though it's been more than six decades since it all happened, I remember it as clearly as yesterday. Some things in life you just can't forget, I suppose."

He waited briefly for a response that would never come, and then cheerfully said, "Well, thank you for indulging me. You know, I haven't shared most of this with anyone, not even my wife. You're the first, Anna. Ethan would have been, but his mind is on other things right now, as you can imagine. I don't blame him for that. I don't imagine you do either."

He paused again. "Ethan said he'd take the box some other time. This just happens to be another time, and since he's asleep over there, he can't really argue, now can he? So when I'm done, I'll just leave the journals here. That's why I brought the box."

I knew nobody would see me, but I rolled my eyes anyway.

Grandpa cleared his throat and then started up again. "Now, let's see . . . where should I begin? The very beginning seems appropriate, but pinning down exactly when that was is more complicated. I don't want to go back too far and burden you with unnecessary history, but neither do I want to give you too little and not have it make any sense."

I watched as he raised his old hand to his face and tapped his lips with a calloused finger. "Okay, I know the spot."

He filled his lungs with a long breath and started into his tale . . .

"Interpreter," he began. "That's what they called me. That's what they told me to tell people, if ever I was asked. That's what my parents thought I was doing; interpreting messages, translating intelligence, reading things on maps or in newspapers from the relative safety of a military base. Even my girlfriend thought that's what I was up to. And I suppose I did do a fair amount of that sort of thing, when there was a particular need, but most of my time was spent in much less favorable circumstances, trudging around the countryside in a German uniform, trying to blend in, pretending to be something I wasn't, hoping to not get killed.

"I was a rare breed in the U.S. Army, if I do say so myself. Born in Germany, raised in the states by parents who spoke German in the home, and willing to fight tooth and nail against the Nazi regime in my birthland. That made me somewhat of an exception. It also made my service exceptionally dangerous.

"When I enlisted, shortly after the attack on Pearl Harbor, my slight German accent raised some eyebrows at the local recruiting office. But after a thorough background check, including an inspection of my home, plus interviews with everyone who knew me, they decided that my language skills could be put to good use. Once I was properly trained and transported to Europe, it became clear that interpreting things was only a small part of what they needed me for. 'You have the potential,' one senior officer explained, 'nay, the talent, to operate behind enemy lines with less risk of them knowing you're with the good guys. With you navigating hostile territory, our boys have a much better shot of not getting dead.'"

Letting go of the bed, Grandpa leaned back in his chair and made himself comfortable. He seemed to be settling in for the long haul. "Anna," he said softly after a minute, "I hope I'm not boring you. You've always been exceptionally good to my Ethan. I couldn't have asked for a better companion for him. I hope you know that. He was blessed the day he met you. I am praying that you'll recover from this. I just wanted you to know. But, truly, if you don't find my yammering of any interest, just stop me anytime." He waited there momentarily in the darkness, then leaned back further in his chair and continued with his story.

"On a Sunday morning in November of 1944, I was operating by myself in a small town in northwestern Austria called Windhaag bei Freistadt. It was within a few kilometers of the rest of my reconnaissance squad, who were camped just over the Czechoslovakian border in a thick grove of trees. My objective was simple: find out if there were any straggling Nazis from the caravan we'd spotted driving through town two days earlier. If the coast was clear, my team could advance more easily toward several work camps to the south, near Linz, that were receiving—and likely killing—trainloads of prisoners.

"I circled the entire town twice. Finding no signs that enemy soldiers were in the area, I approached an old, secluded home off the main road. There was smoke curling from the stone chimney, a sure sign that someone was home. I hoped whoever was there could offer more concrete details about the troops who'd come through. The trick, as always, was probing for details without letting them know that I was probing. I said a little prayer and then knocked until I knew I'd been heard.

"The first thing I saw was a pair of small eyes peeking out through the dirty front window. They darted away as soon as they knew they'd been spotted. That was typical. Often the people that I spoke to, believing me to be a German soldier, were as afraid of me as they would have been had they known I was American. A few moments later, a nervous-looking woman opened the door.

"I'd learned that the sterner I sounded, the more

they believed I was who I claimed to be, so I put a scowl on my face and barked at her in German. 'State your name! I'm on official business.'

"She called herself Elizabeth Richter. There was fear in her eyes, which I knew would help me get the information I needed. Elizabeth became even more nervous when two scrawny children, maybe three or four years old, appeared from behind a door. They were twin girls, both with long dark hair and dark eyes. I noted how different they looked from their blonde-haired, blue-eyed mother. Elizabeth barely looked at me when she told me their names, Aloisa and Arla."

Lying in the hospital room, I was already listening closely, but the words "twin girls" perked my ears up even further. In the darkness of the room, my mind filled with images of my own twin girls in the hectic moments after they were born. I still had a perfect remembrance of the sound of Faith's cry when she came into the world. It was one of the few sounds I ever heard her make.

I let the images dissipate as Grandpa continued speaking.

" 'Where is the man of the house?' I demanded. 'I must speak with him immediately.' Of course I didn't really need to speak with 'the man'—I didn't even know for sure she had a husband. But if she did, and if he was around, it was better to know upfront than to be surprised later by his unexpected arrival. Especially if he had a gun.

"'*Nicht zu Hause*,' she stammered, still refusing to make eye contact. Not at home.

"One of the little girls started saying something, but Elizabeth quickly clasped a hand over her mouth.

"I explained that I'd received word that several families of Jews were suspected of hiding out in the surrounding area, and I'd been sent back to seek them out. 'Do you know of such filth infesting this town?' I pressed. I always hated saying things like that, but I knew very well that a true SS man would speak in exactly the same manner.

"The woman looked like a scared rabbit. But she pulled back her shoulders and assured me that there were no such people in Windhaag bei Freistadt. 'Now,' she said, 'will you kindly leave us? We have much work to do.'

"She tried closing the door, but I stuck my foot in the jamb, hoping to buy more time to seek out some shred of information that might help my team. I told her I was hungry. 'Would you turn away a faithful servant of der Führer so quickly?' I asked.

"She grimaced, like I knew she would. 'Oh . . . of course,' she replied. 'Come in. I have soup and bread in the kitchen.'

"I'd not yet been seated for two minutes when I heard a sound that made me jump. A deep, painful cough echoed from the other room, and then it was gone. I leaped from my chair instinctively, with both hands on my gun. As I got up, one of the girls squealed, 'Papa!' before her mother could stifle the sound.

"I moved quickly into the living room, where everything was now quiet. Elizabeth and the girls were deathly still in the kitchen too. Then I heard something else. A faint wheezing. I couldn't be sure, but I thought it came from the floor. Kneeling down, I felt around and discovered two loose boards. Elizabeth entered the room and watched with horror as I lifted the boards to find a man in his forties lying on the damp earth below.

"I smiled at the man and told him not to worry. I extended a hand to him and pulled him up as gently as I could. He was very weak. By the sound of his cough, I guessed he had pneumonia. Probably too many nights under the floorboards. As quickly as I could, I explained who I was, and what my true purpose was for visiting.

"They didn't believe me until I showed them my dog tags and spoke to them in English.

"Once everyone settled down, the father, Abel, wrapped a wool blanket around himself and we sat again to eat. And that's when things went terribly wrong. There was another loud sound from the other room; the sound of a door cracking. Then there were voices shouting, and a moment later the house was filled with soldiers.

"Somehow I'd been spotted by a small patrol of Germans who had taken up residence on the other side of town. When they saw me sneaking around by myself, obviously not as stealthily as I'd thought, they followed. One of them had been peering in through a window when I pulled Abel from the floor.

"'Explain yourself!' their leader yelled at gunpoint. 'Who are you, and why are you helping these *verdammt* Jews?'

"Abel and Elizabeth tried to say they weren't Jewish. Of the two of them, I figured Elizabeth was probably telling the truth.

"Hoping to avoid complete catastrophe, I said something like, 'I'm on special assignment, scouring the area for Jews believed to be hiding in the area. I came to this house on a good tip, and since they were preparing food, I sat down to eat. I told them if they fed me I might make arrangements to keep them out of the gas chamber.' I laughed as callously as I could. 'The fools, they actually believed me.'

"Everyone except the Richters laughed.

"But as the laughter subsided, one of the girls, who was just beyond the reach of her mother's silencing hand, blurted out, 'You said you're American.'

"I tried to laugh it off, but this time nobody laughed with me. Half a dozen rifles pointed straight at my head. Their captain lifted his pistol to my face and asked if that was true. I swore up and down that the child was making it up. Then he turned the gun to Elizabeth, pressing the muzzle to her temple. He told me if I was lying, he'd kill her.

"I figured the whole family was going to die anyway if they were sent to a concentration camp, but I couldn't stand there and watch them murder Elizabeth, especially in front of the girls, just to maintain my lie. Standing as tall as I could, I told them in plain English that I was proud to be an American soldier.

"From time to time I've heard stories of American soldiers being caught by Germans, only to find out that their captors hated Hitler as much as they did and were sympathetic to the liberating Allied forces. I'd have given anything to have such luck. They all laughed and called me a pig, then took turns spitting in my face.

"When they'd had their fill insulting me, they searched Herr Richter for identification. It took thirty minutes or more to properly sort through his papers and make calls to their superiors in Linz, but eventually they confirmed that the Richter family was not only Jewish, but that Abel was a former professor in Vienna who'd been on the run since the start of the war. What's more, their little home in Windhaag bei Freistadt was not theirs at all, but was part of a network of safe houses established to protect the so-called enemies of the Nazi regime.

"Capturing someone of Abel's stature, along with an American posing as a Nazi officer, was a small coup for the German patrol unit. Elizabeth, who wasn't Jewish by birth, was not much of a threat, but she'd married Abel and borne his children so it didn't matter—her fate would be the same as her husband's. After stripping me of my German uniform, they loaded me and the entire Richter family in a truck and started driving.

"We went southeast for an hour to what they jokingly said was our 'new vacation home,' Mauthausen—one of Europe's largest and most notorious death camps.

"The first thing that grabbed my attention, even before I entered the compound, was the smell. Mauthausen reeked of death. Inside the tall stone walls was a sight equally as haunting—*the living,* stumbling around in rail-thin bodies. They were skeletons with skin. I found it hard to look at them and, at the same time, difficult to look away.

"Mauthausen was not an ordinary concentration camp. It was one of a small handful of Grade III compounds, which meant it was not only more brutal than most camps, but was reserved primarily for the *intelligentsia*—those with high levels of education, the social elites, and the political enemies of the Reich. It was also massive. In addition to the main camp where I was, there were a series of smaller satellite locations scattered through the region. All of the

Mauthausen-run camps had the same common goal—namely, to work prisoners until they died.

"I was told later that the network of work camps under Mauthausen housed upwards of eighty-five thousand prisoners at any one time, making me just one face in a very hopeless crowd. With a life expectancy of only four to five months for new prisoners, the turnover rate at Mauthausen was high, the likelihood of survival low.

"The first part of my incarceration was spent in a windowless holding cell with the Richter family while camp directors decided what to do with us. When the cell door opened two hours later, a large uniformed man entered. He took a moment to shake everyone's hands, even the children's, and introduced himself as Oskar. He was maybe forty-five, with a thick mustache and bulky hands. Surprisingly, he was all smiles. I decided he was either the friendliest guy in the world, or he enjoyed his job way too much. Oskar also introduced us to a much younger man, no older than nineteen or twenty, named Karl, who was trying hard not to look at us. 'Karl is not just a new officer here,' he said proudly in German. 'He is also my son. This is his first week, and I'm trying to show him how best to deal with . . .' He paused, studying each of our faces. His jovial smile turned wicked as he finished his thought, '*special* guests.' He paused again and looked toward his son. 'Karl needs to become stronger,

253

braver, and you're going to help him.' Oskar motioned to a few of the guards in the hallway, who immediately escorted us out of the building and marched us to a large gravel courtyard, dusted with snow, at the end of a long line of barracks. Karl trudged slowly at the back of the parade.

"In the middle of the courtyard was a large barrel full of freezing cold water. Oskar explained that the children were dirty and needed a bath. One of the soldiers picked up Aloisa and plopped her in the makeshift tub, clothes and all. Then Oskar motioned for Karl to step forward. 'Karl,' he said, 'you *will* give the girls a bath.' His words were colder than the icy ground on which we stood.

"Everyone who wasn't a German soldier sensed that something was wrong. Aloisa was shaking from the cold, Elizabeth was whimpering, hoping beyond hope that her greatest fears were not about to be realized, and Abel was mumbling a little prayer. I just cried, partly out of sorrow for whatever was about to happen, and partly out of a sense of guilt that out of all the little homes in Windhaag bei Freistadt, I'd chosen to knock on the Richters' door.

"It was obvious that Karl was not a willing participant. He dragged his feet as he stepped slowly toward Aloisa and the makeshift tub. He was trembling as he placed a hand on her shoulder. Then he averted his eyes and pushed her under the water. Elizabeth, Abel, and Arla all shrieked. The guard nearest me shoved a gun in my face and warned that he'd love nothing more than to pull the trigger if I made a move. If I'd thought there was anything I could do to change the child's fate, I'd have gladly rushed forward. Maybe I was a coward, but offering my own silent prayer for the child seemed the only sensible thing. Karl's trembling turned to fits of weeping. After fifteen seconds he vomited all over himself, releasing his grip on the struggling child, who shot up out of the water, gasping for breath.

"Oskar, of course, was furious. He barked obscenities at Karl for being weak, then marched forward to the barrel while continuing to rail against his son. Standing in the middle of Karl's vomit, he grabbed Aloisa by the hair, and threw her back under the water; he kept his arm submerged until she stopped struggling. Then they dragged Arla to the barrel and did the same thing with her."

Grandpa Bright's voice was wavering. My own stomach was churning with disgust at what he'd seen. He breathed deeply through his nose, trying to calm his nerves.

I lay completely still, waiting to hear more.

Sniffling on what must surely have been tears, Grandpa pressed on with his narrative. "Most of the soldiers grinned as the last bubbles rose to the surface. Karl and I just watched in horror. By then,

Abel and Elizabeth were heaps of sorrow, flopped out on the ground, begging to be shot so they could join their children.

"Oskar told them they would have to wait to go to hell.

"In the next hour they shaved our heads and assigned us to barracks. Elizabeth went to a small contingent of women, Abel was put with a cadre of Austrian-born Jews, and I was assigned to a group composed of military and political dissidents from all over—mostly Spaniards, Hungarians, French, and Czechs, but also some Russians, Poles, Dutch, and two other Americans. A guard assigned me to a tiny bottom bunk that was already occupied by two Spaniards, both of them quite gaunt. I asked the guard how three grown men could be expected to share such a small bunk. He said that was our problem to sort out, but that I shouldn't worry too much about it, because one—or both—of them would likely die soon anyway. The two men didn't say a word. They just moved over to make room for me.

"As I said before, Mauthausen was designed as a work camp; a slave camp, really, aimed at extermination through labor. A few skilled prisoners, however, were occasionally assigned tasks to support the broader war effort, such as munitions and metal fabrication. Most of the women were rented out, at bargain prices, to neighboring communities, to do chores no one else wanted. But the rest of us spent our time hauling hundred-pound rocks out of the massive, on-site granite quarry.

"It was as miserable an existence as there can be, working twelve or more hours each day, walking up and down roughly hewn granite steps—one hundred eighty-six steps, to be exact. We called them the Stairs of Death. Within my first week there I saw at least fifty people collapse and die from fatigue going up and down those steps. One of them was Abel Richter, whose already weakened immune system couldn't keep up with the heavy physical demands. I wept for hours that night as I thought of Abel and his daughters, and how they were dead because of me. If I could have died in their stead, I would have done so gladly.

"Several others in camp were shot and killed for accidentally tripping over dead bodies on the stairs. Only when the stacks of bodies became impassable would the guards remove them by kicking the corpses unceremoniously over the side of the stairwell.

"During my second week, one of my bunkmates died on the high-voltage electric fence north of the quarry. Guards joked that it was suicide, but whispers among those who'd seen it said that he was thrown. Either way, the bunk felt oddly vacant without him.

"Two weeks before Christmas, we were

assigned a new night guard over our barracks. It was Karl, the weak-stomached young man who couldn't bring himself to drown the Richter girls. In his new assignment, Karl was expected to roam among a group of five contiguous buildings, including mine, from lights-out until dawn, exercising swift and severe punishment against anyone found out of their bunks.

"On his third night, sometime well after midnight, something woke me from a restless sleep. *Music,* coming from nearby. Though I knew it was foolish to get up, I couldn't remain in my bunk without discovering its source. Quietly, taking care not to stir the others, I tiptoed across the cold wood floor to a closed door in the middle of the building. On the other side of the door was the barracks' main entryway, which also served as a dividing space between two large bunk rooms. I dared not enter, but my curiosity pulled my eyes to a small crack between the poorly hinged door and its jamb. Much to my astonishment, Karl was there, sitting on a three-legged stool in the flickering light of a single candle, quietly playing a beautiful acoustic guitar. Behind him was the closed door to the other bunk room, and to his left was the main exit, which was also closed.

"After staring through the crack for several minutes, quietly enjoying the show, I decided I should return to my bunk. Unfortunately, as I lifted my foot to go, the floorboard upon which I was standing squeaked loudly. I froze, hoping Karl hadn't heard, but the music stopped abruptly and a split second later the door swung inward. He had a cocked pistol in his hand, pointed at my chest, but it wobbled in his trembling hand. Of the two of us, I think he was more scared. Not wanting to wake anyone else, he waved me into the breezeway at gunpoint and quickly shut the door behind us.

"Karl stared at me for what felt like an eternity, the gun still shaking in his hand. Finally, in what I considered remarkable English for someone who had not likely ever traveled to an English-speaking country, he said, 'You are the American, yes? The spy.'

"I assured him I was no spy. When he asked what I was doing out of my bed, I told him the truth—listening to beautiful music and remembering what it was like to hold a guitar in my hands.

"He raised an eyebrow. 'You play?'

"I nodded affirmatively, then asked him why he was playing the guitar in our barracks rather than at the guardhouse or the officers' complex.

"'The acoustics here are *wunderbar*,' he whispered. Then he added with a shrug, 'The bathroom would be better, but I can't stand the stink.' He paused to look me over once more; then he told me he should probably shoot me for being out of bed past curfew, and that his father would honor him for making an example of an American.

"In response, I told him he would be doing me a great favor by putting me out of my misery. It was a stupid thing to say, under the circumstances, but I sensed that he didn't want to harm me any more than he'd wanted to drown the girls. And what if I was wrong? Well, I knew death was coming for me anyway, sooner or later. It was only a matter of time before one of the SS or other guards decided I'd looked at him wrong and threw me off a cliff or hung me from the flagpole. Dying at gunpoint would be better.

"At first he tried to be brave, raising the wobbly pistol to my face. But, as I suspected, he couldn't go through with it. He lowered the gun and said he wouldn't kill me, on condition that I not tell anyone that he'd allowed me to be out of bed. It would be seen as weakness by his superiors and would likely come with severe consequences for him. By 'superiors,' I knew he meant his father.

" 'Thank you,' I whispered. 'I won't tell a living soul.' I quietly retreated to my bunk.

"The next night, at about the same time, I again heard the soft strumming of guitar strings. This time I'd purposely stayed awake, listening for it. After ten or fifteen minutes listening to it from my bunk, I decided to press my luck once more with Karl. I tiptoed to the door and knocked as quietly as I could. Again the door flew open, revealing a nerve-wracked young soldier holding a pistol and a guitar.

"'*Was machts du? Bist du blöd!*' he whispered sharply. '*What are you doing? Are you stupid?*' Then, perhaps to add another exclamation on the seriousness of the situation, he addressed me in English. 'You know the rules!'

"I told him I couldn't help it; the sound of the music was too tempting to stay away. I cautiously moved to a spot in the corner of the entryway and sat down on the floor. From there, no other guard would be able to see me through a window if he happened to pass by. He kept the gun trained on me while debating what to do. Finally he gave up pretending that he was serious about taking action. Looking slightly defeated, he holstered the weapon and went back to playing the guitar.

"For the next thirty minutes I sat quietly watching as his fingers plucked and strummed the instrument in the most amazing ways. I loved playing guitar and was decent in my own right, but I was a novice compared to Karl. He was a master. He could do things with the guitar that I'd never dreamed of."

Grandpa hesitated. "He was sort of like your Ethan in that respect, Miss Anna. Too bad he's given all that up. Anyway, after that, watching Karl's quiet practice sessions became a ritual. Each night, about an hour into his shift, he would come to the barracks and start playing; then I would sneak in to listen. It was my only enjoyment in life. During the daytime it helped divert my thoughts from the grueling task of hauling granite. It even gave me something positive to think about when people around me were falling over dead from exhaustion or when I heard guards bragging about how they'd squeezed more than a hundred prisoners into the gas chamber and then watched through a peephole as they all suffocated. Just having something to look forward to each day kept me from losing all hope.

"After a couple of nervous weeks, I got the sense that Karl was looking forward to our odd visits as well. Or at least he didn't mind them as much anymore. He stopped drawing his gun when I knocked, which was a good sign. Then he started opening up to me on a personal level, telling me about himself, where he was from, what his girlfriend was like, little things like that. It was strange for me to think of him as anything other than a Nazi soldier, bent on killing innocents. But it soon became apparent that he was no different than I; he was just a young soldier fighting for his country. He never came right out and said it, but he hinted a few times that he was not a supporter of Hitler.

"In addition to the guitar, Karl said he also played the piano, cello, and harp, and aspired to play in an orchestra. His dad hated the idea, but his mother had always been supportive. In fact, she'd been the one who'd bought him the new guitar when he was demoted to night guard, encouraging him to play it during his shift to help stay awake. While other guards played cards and smoked cigarettes to bide the time, Karl practiced music.

"It didn't take long for others in the barracks to notice the nightly acoustic serenades and the fact that I kept sneaking out of bed to listen. Everyone thought I was insane for trusting that the young Nazi wouldn't put a hole in my head. They chose to enjoy the quiet tunes from the safety of their bunks.

"A Hungarian man three bunks down from me was the official calendar of our barracks, having taken over the responsibility from a Russian who'd been thrown off the cliff shortly after my arrival. The Hungarian dutifully tracked the passing of time, informing us each morning which day of the week it was, and what date. When he announced it was December 24th, hardly anyone cared. Many of them didn't celebrate Christmas, so it was just another day to them. As the day wore on and the ache of hauling rocks set in, I too forgot that it was Christmas Eve. It wasn't until Karl's visit that I was reminded of the significance of the occasion. The first song he played was an Austrian original, 'Stille Nacht'—'Silent Night.' It was perfect. I don't think a song has ever warmed me more. On his second time through, Karl hummed the melody while he played. A few of us hummed along with him. In my mind, I sang the words loud enough for the whole world to hear.

"I waited until that song concluded, then I snuck over to the breezeway. Karl just smiled as I closed the door behind me. He continued to play, filling the dimly lit room with a string of well-known Christmas songs, including one or two from Handel's *Messiah*. After thirty minutes, I thanked him with a smile and a nod, then got up to return to my bunk. Before I got to the door he told me to stop. For a moment, I feared that maybe something was wrong. But as I watched him, he reached into his guitar case and withdrew a large loaf of fresh bread. 'From my mother,' he said. 'Merry Christmas.' I asked if she knew who it was for, and he nodded. I guess compassion in their family ran through her genes, because Karl certainly didn't come by it from his father.

"I thanked him for the kindness, then slipped back into the bunkroom and quietly divided the bread among the men.

"As I lay in bed that night, I thought about the gift I'd received from the 'enemy' guard who, by all rights, could have just as easily shot me. It wasn't just a loaf of bread I'd been given. He'd sacrificed beyond measure to bring that into the compound and hand it to a prisoner. He knew full well that the penalty for giving extra food to 'the slaves' was a quick trip to the firing squad. Yet he'd done so anyway.

"Never before, or ever since, have I received a Christmas gift that meant so much as that simple loaf of bread.

"The next night, on Christmas, Karl didn't show up, and I feared he'd been given a new assignment—or worse, that his generosity had somehow been discovered. Turns out, his father gave him the holiday off. The next night he was back in our barracks just before midnight, practicing the guitar. He stopped playing as soon as I came in. 'You're losing too much weight,' he said.

"He was right. I'd only been in Mauthausen for about five weeks, but the combination of exhausting labor and limited rations was taking its toll. I'd already shed at least thirty pounds and my skin was starting to feel loose on my bones. Granted, there were many others who were considerably thinner, but I was definitely looking gaunt.

" '*Ich weiß*,' I replied. *I know*.

"Karl opened his guitar case and produced a piece of cake, wrapped in paper. I felt guilty eating it all by myself, but he stipulated it was meant for me alone. 'I can't help everyone,' he explained. 'Doing so would be impossible, and would surely get all of us killed. But I can help you. Don't deny me this opportunity to help.'

"From then on, snacks came each night. Not enough to put meat on my bones, but enough to keep me from slipping further towards starvation.

"At the start of February 1945, nearly three months into my imprisonment, whispers started spreading throughout camp that the Germans were losing the war and that freedom was imminent. In response to the rumors, or perhaps out of desperation because the rumors were true, the SS guards and kapos at Mauthausen began killing inmates with increased frequency.

"When it came to brutality and death, nothing surprised me anymore. I'd seen it all: hangings, beatings, electrification, starvation, drowning, mass shootings, and lethal injections, just to name a few. On at least a daily basis I saw groups of the elderly and infirm being escorted to gas chambers. It was also widely known that medical experiments took place in the basement of the officer's building. I didn't see what they did to them, but I heard their screams from time to time, and that was enough. And of course there was 'parachuting'—shoving prisoners over the edge of the rock quarry to plummet to their deaths. Sometimes, just to be cruel, the guards would hold a gun to someone's head and ask them to make a choice: take the bullet, or pick another prisoner and push him over the edge. It was a horrible moral dilemma: self-preservation or murder. About fifty percent of the time they chose the latter, but either way someone died.

"On February 8th, according to our new Russian

calendar—our Hungarian calendar was beaten to death in the middle of January for not walking fast enough up the quarry stairs—Karl was a nervous wreck when he showed up for guard duty. He didn't bother getting out his guitar, but came straight to my bunk and pulled me out into the entry, where he explained that our barracks had been wagered as part of a sick poker bet among the SS, and as a result we were going to be gunned down at dawn.

"I think I probably shrugged. It was bound to happen sooner or later, and better to be shot than dropped over a cliff.

"It angered him that I wasn't more concerned about the situation. 'I haven't been your friend just to see you get killed!' he snapped.

"Thankfully, Karl had a plan. Inside his instrument case, stowed beneath the neck of the guitar, was a compass, a map, and a small package of food. These, he explained, were to help me reach the nearest U.S. Army platoon, which had recently made a temporary camp about thirty kilometers to the north. He showed me on the map where they'd last been seen.

"'What am I supposed to do?' I asked. 'Walk right out the front door?'

"He smiled warmly and said, 'Something like that.' He told me he'd be back right before his shift ended at five in the morning to give me the rest of the details. He patted me on the arm, as though trying to assure me that everything would be fine; then he left through the main door, leaving his guitar in its case, leaning against a wall.

"I went back to my bunk, but couldn't sleep a wink. At a quarter to five I heard the front door open again, followed by a soft, *'Pssst . . . Herb . . . come.'*

"In the entryway, Karl was sitting on the floor taking off his boots. I shuddered when he told me the rest of the so-called plan. He intended that I walk right out the front door of the camp. 'I am one of only a very few guards who do not live on-site, and only because my father has high rank and our home is nearby. Every morning I carry my guitar through the west gate without anyone saying a word. There is a guard on the wall, near the gate, but it is too dark right now to see faces, especially from his angle. He frequently waves at me, but nothing more. Take my clothes, my coat, my guitar, and my key for the gate, and everything will be fine.'

"As he began taking off his socks, it hit me that he was willingly risking everything—including his own life—for me. I couldn't let him do it. 'Keep your clothes on,' I said. 'Your idea will never work.'

He promised it would be fine.

"'No!' I charged, 'it won't! It might work for me, but it won't work for *you*. It puts you in too much danger.'

"Karl smiled and said he would claim that I'd attacked him and taken his things. Then he added, 'and even if nobody believes it, I'm sure my father won't let anything happen to me.'

"I told him that was a chance I wasn't willing to take, at which point he pulled out his pistol and told me I didn't have a choice. He was determined to save me, whether I liked it or not. I couldn't help but notice it was the first time the gun didn't wobble in his hand."

Grandpa let out an exhausted sigh, laden with obvious sadness. He sniffled softly, and I could only guess that his emotions were getting the best of him. He sighed once more, then pressed on.

"As much as I didn't like it, I put on the clothes. Five minutes later, bundled in Karl's thick overcoat, and with a cap pulled low to hide my face, I walked out of the barracks. Before I closed the door, he handed me his gun. 'Just in case,' he said.

"I thanked him, and that was that. Carrying the guitar case, I trudged down the middle of the empty courtyard toward the west gate, waved casually to the guard on the wall, then walked out of Mauthausen and never looked back.

"A day and a half later, having traversed the countryside with the aid of the map and compass, I allowed myself to be captured by a small group of Americans who were on patrol. They took all of my possessions and threw me in a makeshift holding cell at their camp. Two days later they drove me an hour north to their main command center, where they were able to verify that I was who I said I was.

"The next morning I was reunited with Karl's guitar.

"Having only been in Mauthausen about three months, and having received nightly snacks from Karl for half that time, my physical health wasn't nearly as bad as it could have been. I was skinny, but not to the point of being malnourished. As a result, I was given a choice: I could be discharged and return to the States, or I could join their battalion and continue fighting, albeit in a lesser role than I'd had before. I chose the latter. My new commanding officers allowed me to take it easy for several weeks while medics gradually increased my food intake. Once I put on fifteen pounds I was deemed fit enough to drive a vehicle, which I did gladly.

"I was assigned to drive a transport truck in their slow, calculated march through the countryside, stopping frequently in small villages to set up temporary command centers. Sometimes we stayed in one location for a couple of weeks, other times we moved on to the next location after two or three days. Karl's guitar stayed with me almost always, even while I was driving the truck. It made for a perfect stress relief following skirmishes with the increasingly disorganized

German army. The rest of my new platoon appreciated having the guitar around too. Everyone had a favorite song from back home, and with a little practice I could usually figure out how to play them. Often, when one of our guys was wounded in action, they would call me to the infirmary to play a little something. It reminded them of home, I suppose, putting their minds at ease and lifting their spirits. One doctor told me that although he could stop their bleeding, good music had a better chance of easing their pain.

"More than once I played for soldiers as they lay dying on their cots. One young man from Louisiana, whose shrapnel wounds were soaked in red, asked me to play his girlfriend's favorite song, 'Ferryboat Serenade,' by the Andrews sisters. Before the song ended, his own boat had sailed, but at least he went with a smile on his face.

"It was slow going, but by the end of April our unit rolled into Salzburg. By then there was very little resistance from enemy forces, and we all got the sense that the end of the war was close at hand. The locals sensed it too. More than a few of them thanked us for our efforts in bringing an end to Hitler's madness.

"Early in May—the fourth, to be exact—we drove out of Salzburg, crossed the border into Germany, and pressed on to a little town called Berchtesgaden at the base of the Bavarian Alps.

The next morning we plowed our way up a steep single-lane road to Kehlsteinhaus, Hitler's mountaintop hideout, otherwise known as the Eagle's Nest. It was largely a symbolic effort, since Hitler was nowhere to be found. But for us, capturing his private lair was cause for celebration. And for our unit, it marked the end of combat.

"My truck was near the rear of the convoy, so I was one of the last to enter the premises. Once I made it inside, I took myself on a self-guided tour. On the ground floor, at the end of one hallway, I found a bathroom. It was the first true indoor facility I'd seen in what seemed like forever. While sitting there, I decided I wanted a souvenir. Hitler had taken enough from me; I felt it only right that I take something from him. And so I whipped out my pocketknife and removed the bathroom door handle. It was narrow but ornate, and shaped like an elongated S. I tucked it in my pants pocket and continued my tour.

"Later that night word spread throughout our ranks that many of my peers had also taken souvenirs from Hitler's alpine mansion. My commanding officer made it very clear that we were not there to steal, and that he would be doing thorough checks of our gear to ensure nothing was absconded with. Privately, we all figured he wanted some of our goodies for himself.

"After what I'd endured at Mauthausen, I didn't think taking a door handle was a big deal, and I certainly didn't want Captain Reynolds taking it, so I hid it. The only place I could be sure he wouldn't look was inside the hollow body of Karl's guitar. I carefully unwound all of the strings from their tuners, taped Hitler's handle at the deepest part of the cavity, then restrung everything.

"As expected, no one ever found it."

Grandpa let a moment of silence fall on the room, perhaps to gather his thoughts. I pictured the old guitar in my mind, remembering every wear mark on its body, imagining how the strings felt beneath my fingers. I'd carried it as my own for years and years, never once suspecting what the thing had been through during its existence, much less considering that it might be hiding something inside it. I couldn't help wondering if it still concealed an old door handle.

Grandpa coughed a couple times to clear his throat, then finished recounting his experience.

"We stayed at the Eagle's Nest for the better part of a week. For many of us, it felt like a well-earned vacation. We were on top of the world, literally, with nothing to do but enjoy the view and write letters home. Near the end of that week we got word that Nazi strongholds were falling all across Germany and Austria. Mauthausen was on the list.

"My very first thoughts were of Karl. Though I hated the idea of returning to the place where I'd been held prisoner, I had to know what became of my friend. With the permission of a sympathetic lieutenant colonel, I was allowed to take a jeep and two other infantrymen for a quick jaunt back to Linz, but only on condition that we stick to the main roads, which were believed to be under the control of Allied forces.

"We were stopped for questioning by friendly troops half a dozen times along the way, which added a full day to what should have been a three- or four-hour drive.

"When we finally arrived at Mauthausen, I was thrilled to see the American flag flying overhead, but the compound was still a miserable place. I recognized a few of the former prisoners, who were milling around in their ragged jumpsuits, but I didn't see anyone from my old barracks. The newly freed prisoners were glad for their freedom, but their health was so poor that the moment was bittersweet. Some of their stomachs had shrunk so much that they could hardly eat, even though food was now plentiful.

"Most of the Nazi SS had fled before the U.S. troops arrived. Those who didn't were being detained in one of the barracks under constant watch. Among them was Karl's father, Oskar.

"'Ah, the American spy who escaped,' he said when he saw me. 'I never forget a face.'

"I wanted to punch him. 'Where is Karl?' I demanded. 'What happened to your son?'

"His face turned bright red. 'I have *no* son!' he hissed defiantly in German, then spat in my face. 'The coward boy named Karl must have been a bastard, for he could not have been mine. He was a pig, *like you.*'

"'Where is he?' I asked again, struggling to keep my emotions in check.

"Oskar grinned as wickedly as any man could, then let out a sick laugh. 'Probably hiding, like the coward he is.' He paused and spat at my feet. 'Leave me. I'm through speaking to swine.'

"Later that evening I stumbled across Elizabeth Richter while she was helping some young children who'd lost their parents. Elizabeth had fared better than most prisoners. She had been assigned to do housekeeping for a family in the town of Mauthausen, where, under less rigorous supervision, she was able to help herself each day to scraps of food they'd tossed in the waste.

"When she saw me she gave a little smile. 'You made it,' she whispered. 'Thank God, you made it!'

"It had been nearly four months since I'd last seen Elizabeth at camp, but the guilt over what had befallen her and her family on account of my actions was as fresh and real as the day I watched Oskar drown Arla and Aloisa. Upon seeing her, I . . ."

Grandpa was getting more choked up than I'd ever seen him. I couldn't see his face, but I could hear the weeping in his voice and guessed his cheeks were getting damp.

"I . . . burst into tears. I said, 'I'm so sorry, Elizabeth! If not for me, things would have been so different for you. I'm sorry . . . so sorry.'

"Stepping away from the children, she put a finger to her lips. '*Shhh,*' she said softly. 'You mustn't apologize for things beyond your control.'

" 'But I led them straight to you. *It was my fault!* I swear, though, if I'd known I was putting you in danger . . .'

"She smiled sympathetically. 'If you insist on feeling guilty, then I see only one course of action.'

"I asked what she meant, and she said, 'This.' Elizabeth stood tall, and in the softest voice possible she said, *'I forgive you.'*"

Grandpa was weeping unabashedly now. I pictured the tears rolling through the cracks and wrinkles on his weathered face, imagined them falling onto the wooden box at his feet.

" *'I forgive you,'* " he repeated, more forcefully. "To this day," he said, articulating every word with careful precision, as though commanding me to pay attention, "those remain the absolute sweetest words I've ever heard. In many ways, I think they saved my life just as much as Karl did.

"The following morning," Grandpa continued, sounding disheartened, "after breakfast, I was called to the barracks where the German soldiers were being held. The officer in charge informed me that Oskar wanted to speak to me again.

" 'Ah, the spy returns,' he said when I entered his room.

" 'What do you want?' I shot back, trying hard to remain unaffected by his wicked stare.

" 'Just to be heard, my young American friend,' he said.

"I told him we were anything but friends.

" 'No?' he asked. 'But you were Karl's friend, were you not?'

"I replied that I was, and proud of it.

" 'Good,' he said. 'Then you'll like what I have to say. As I was lying in bed last night I considered our conversation, and I realized I should have been more forthcoming yesterday. You, of all people, deserve to know what became of Karl.'

" 'Why the change of heart?' I asked.

"He chuckled again. I hated that awful laugh. 'Let's just say out of professional courtesy, eh? One morning we found Karl hiding in a cabin in his underwear. I think you know what morning that was, don't you? He had helped you escape. He didn't even deny it. As punishment for treason, we took him and everyone else in the barracks to the highest edge of the quarry.' "

Grandpa's words were drowning in his own emotions. He lowered his head and cried until the tears stopped flowing. Then he picked up right where he'd left off. " 'I told him,' " Grandpa said gruffly, taking on the tone of his former captor, "'if he shot the other prisoners I would spare his life, but if he jumped off the cliff of his own accord then the others would live. I knew he was too weak to hurt the prisoners. There was no hesitation. He jumped. Stupid pig, didn't even squeal on the way down.'"

Now I was wiping my own face. Karl had been a hero. I'd been playing a hero's guitar for as long as I could remember, and I never knew it.

"The soldiers with me didn't speak German," explained my grandfather, once more in his own, gentle voice, "so they had no idea what Oskar was saying. They asked if I was okay, and I nodded that everything was fine. 'And what about the other prisoners?' I asked Oskar. 'What was their fate?'

"He let out another vulgar laugh, as though he relished the memory. 'I shot them myself . . . one by one.' Then his face narrowed. I felt like he was staring right into my soul. 'But I wanted you to know Karl's fate,' he declared, 'because I want you to always remember that his death is on *your* head. Without your escape he would have persevered.' He paused, allowing enough time for my guilt to fully consume me, then added, 'Now, *spy,* you should go clean up. You've got a lot of blood on your hands.'

"That night I took Karl's guitar into the bathroom in the officers' building."

Grandpa Bright sniffled once more and wiped his nose. "Karl was right. The acoustics in there were good. I played the guitar . . . and wept for mercy."

With that, Grandpa got up slowly from his chair and stood beside Anna. "Thanks for listening to the ramblings of an old man," he said. "I apologize for not having better control of my emotions." He checked his watch. "I promised the old nurse out front that I wouldn't be more than an hour. Woops . . . blew right past that, didn't I? I guess I better get on my way. The folks back at your place are probably starting to worry. Rest well, Anna. We're all praying for you. And for your family."

He reached out and touched Anna's scarred arm, bowed his head solemnly, as if reverencing her, and then he picked up his cane and turned to go.

Shuffle-shuffle-thump. Shuffle-shuffle-thump.

I squeezed my eyes as tight as they would go. If there had been more light in the room, he surely would have seen the red blotches on my face. He passed by without saying a word.

He'd already said more than enough.

Shuffle-shuffle-thump. Shuffle-shuffle-thump . . .

FOURTH VERSE:

SOLO, *LENTO GRAVE*

Chapter 19

When the morning nurse came in to check Anna's vitals at a quarter to nine, she was whistling a cheery tune. I was still curled up on the recliner in the darkest corner of the room with a blanket covering most of me and was pretty sure she didn't see me. She seemed puzzled by the wooden box lying on the floor beside the bed; she picked it up, studied it briefly, then set it in on the small table in the corner opposite from me and began tending to my wife.

"Good morning, sunshine," she said. "Feeling any better today?"

Is that nurse humor? I wondered. *Talking to the dying about getting better?* I certainly didn't see any humor in it, much less any reason to sound so happy, but maybe that was my tiredness talking. "She can't hear you," I blurted out.

The poor lady was so startled that she practically jumped out of her white clogs. "Oh! Mr. Bright. I'm so sorry. I didn't realize you were there."

"Yeah, well . . . I am."

Frowning, she said, "You look terrible."

At least she was honest. "Thanks. I probably just need more sleep."

Her voice dropped to a whisper. "Sorry. I'll shut up so you can get some rest. I just need to take her blood pressure and temp. It should only be a minute or two."

I thanked her for the quiet and closed my eyes, though I doubted I would fall back asleep, because my mind was already rehashing Grandpa Bright's POW experience. I shuddered as a mental image formed in my head of twin girls in a barrel of water; then a faceless man jumping from a cliff and a soulless guard squeezing the trigger of a gun. I opened my eyes just a little and squinted at the still body of Anna in the bed; I imagined what it must have been like to have a giant SUV plow into you; I wondered if she'd felt any pain. Was her ordeal quick, like being shot in the head by a Nazi, or did she see the vehicle coming before impact, like a prisoner watching the ground approach after being shoved over the edge of a quarry?

"Why is the world so cruel?" I asked, completely out of the blue.

The nurse jumped again, but not as high. "Am I making too much noise?"

"No, you're fine. I'm just thinking out loud."

"I thought you were going back to sleep."

"Can't. Besides, she's sleeping enough for the both of us." Suddenly I was the one with the lousy humor.

The woman frowned once more. "You know she's not really—"

"Sleeping? Yes, I've been told. But that makes

my point, doesn't it? Only in a very cruel world would a woman like *her* have to lie there in limbo, just waiting."

She studied Anna for a moment. "What's she waiting for?"

I shook my head. "Only God knows. Waiting for her lungs to fail . . . ? Waiting for her heart to give out . . . ? Waiting for someone to pull the plug . . . ? I guess it doesn't really matter, the result is the same. And I don't understand it one bit."

"Eh hum," said a voice behind us. "Is now a bad time?" It was Stuart, poking his head in around the tall sliding curtain by the door. "Visiting hours haven't officially begun, but they said I could come in a little early, since you were already here."

"Yeah, they seem to make quite a few exceptions to the rules," I mumbled, thinking about Grandpa's late-night visit. "Are you alone?"

"Yep. Just me. I didn't think you were ready to have Hope come. But I wanted to see my little sister. You sure you don't mind?"

"Come on in, Stu."

The nurse smiled politely. "I'll get out of your hair. I'm all done."

Stuart took her spot near the bed. He remained there in silence for several minutes, taking it all in—the machines, the incisions, the bandages, the bruises, everything. Finally, without looking up, he said, "It really is bad, isn't it?"

"Yeah," I replied grimly. "It is."

"I overheard what you were saying to the nurse before I came in, about not understanding why things like this have to happen."

"And?"

"You ever watch *Babylon Five*?"

"Huh?"

"The show. It's sci-fi."

"Never heard of it."

"Hmm, that's weird. All my friends love it. You've seriously never even heard of—?"

"No, Stu. What's your point?"

He scrunched up his nose to adjust his glasses. "Well, it's a show that takes place on a space station, and some of its lines are just out of this world." He paused at the possibly unintentional double meaning. "So anyway, my all-time favorite quote from *Babylon Five* is this: 'I used to think it was awful that life was so unfair. Then I thought, wouldn't it be much worse if life *were* fair, and all the terrible things that happen to us come because we actually deserve them? So, now I take great comfort in the general hostility and unfairness of the universe.'" He paused again. "Makes you think, huh?"

I honestly wasn't sure whether the quote was supposed to make me feel better or worse about the present situation, but he was right about one thing—it did make me think.

Stuart stayed for another half hour. We mostly

just sat there and watched Anna. Not much was said, though periodically Stuart would make comments like, "Man, she's really hooked up to some serious bells and whistles," or, "It's amazing the technology they have these days . . . just amazing."

Maybe he was trying to get me to open up, but I didn't bite.

Eventually he announced that he was going back to check on the family. "You'll let me know if you need anything, right, Ethan?"

The only thing I needed was my wife back, but I told him I'd call if something came to mind.

The rest of that day I was in and out of sleep. Mostly out. Nurses came and went. A few doctors too. I didn't try keeping track of who they were, they all just sort of blended into one. Most of them hardly acknowledged me. I took that to mean none of them wanted to be the one to tell me that Anna wasn't showing any signs of improvement.

When I was awake, I just sat there, staring at Anna in the dimly lit room. Watching her breathe. Watching her do . . . nothing.

Grandpa and Octavius both called in the afternoon to see how things were going. Aunt Jo called once too, wanting to know if I'd gotten the flowers she sent. I had, along with similar bouquets from half the relatives on both sides of the family. "Are they pretty?" she asked.

"Sure," I replied halfheartedly. Okay, maybe

they *were* pretty. But I kept thinking about how all the roses in the vases had cut stems. They were nice enough to look at, but they weren't really alive. It was only a matter of time before they would wilt and be thrown away.

Just like Anna.

Later that evening Stuart called and put Hope on the line. "You doing okay, honey?"

"Yes. How is Mommy?"

"She's . . . doing better."

"Can I come see her?"

"Sorry, pumpkin. Not today. Mommy needs her rest."

There was a long pause. "Can I talk to her?"

"Hope . . . your Mom . . . well, she can't really talk right now. But she sends her love. Okay?"

More silence, then a quiet, "Okay, Dad. Tell her I love her too."

"I absolutely will." I hated the fact that my eyes were watering. I wiped the tears quickly away. "Are you having a good time with your cousins?"

She was.

"How about your aunt and uncle?"

"Yep. They're fun. I like them a lot." She went on to tell me all about her birthday party, and how Uncle Stuart surprised her with a brand-new bicycle. "Can I show it to you tomorrow?"

"Maybe. But probably not. It depends on how your mom is doing."

For a second I wasn't sure if she'd heard me.

Then she said, "Dad? Mommy is going to get better . . . isn't she?"

I glanced over at the tubes protruding from Anna's nose and mouth and watched as the ventilator compressed air with a soft wheeze. Wiping again at my eyes I said, "Of course. Don't you worry. Everything is going to be fine."

After hanging up I thought about what Stuart had said earlier. What if all the terrible things really *do* happen to us because we deserve them? And if so, what terrible things would be coming my way for lying to my daughter?

Chapter 20

The next few days were about as lonely as anyone could ever imagine. I stayed holed up at the hospital, hoping for any sign that Anna was getting better, but every time a doctor came in to check on her it was more of the same bad news. I wanted to plug my ears every time I heard someone say "Glasgow score," because Anna's was still at the bottom of the cellar.

The people who really cared what was going on with Anna checked in by phone at least once a day—Octavius, Grandpa Bright, Stuart, and of course, Hope.

Every time I spoke to my daughter she asked the same two questions: "Is Mommy better now?" and "Can I see her?"

It was obvious by the sound of her voice that the answers "not yet" and "sorry, no" were wearing thin.

Dr. Knight, the head of the ICU, came in every day before the close of his shift to give me the official update on Anna's status, though he rarely shared anything that I couldn't deduce on my own just by looking at her. Drs. Schafer and Gooding also stopped by in the afternoons to evaluate how her bones and organs were mending, while Dr. Rasmussen visited in the late mornings to check for neurological progress. Still, the face I saw the most was always Reg Wilson, who popped in at least three times a day just to see how I was holding up.

At the end of the week Reg brought a familiar yellow form with him. "Ethan, I know you've been pretty much camped out here, but I'll ask anyway: Have you had a chance to check if Anna has a living will? Because if she doesn't, we'd really like you to sign this so we've got the right paperwork in place before we begin thinking about next steps."

"I haven't really been home to look," I said.

"Have you thought about how you might like to proceed, in the event that she doesn't have one?"

"Not really." Sadly, I was getting very good at lying. I guess the more you do it, the easier it becomes. The truth, however, was that "how to proceed" was what I spent most of my time thinking about while I was sitting there memorizing the scars on Anna's broken face. "But is there anything wrong with how we're proceeding right now?"

"Not at all. Watching and waiting is the right thing to be doing right now. The doctors certainly don't want to jump in any one direction prematurely. From what Dr. Rasmussen has told me, and from past experience on similar cases, I know that most comas last from a couple of days to a few weeks. I'm sure he told you the same thing. Statistically speaking, the odds of recovery drop off fairly quickly after that, but we're only one week into this, so let's keep waiting before we cross that bridge. In the meantime, though, please take some time to look around at home. If there's any chance she has a living will, we really need to know. Legally and morally, I want to make sure everything we do for her is in accordance with her wishes."

"I'll poke around in our files," I mumbled.

"Hope? Hello?" It was early in the afternoon when I walked in the front door of my house. Grandpa's rental car was in the driveway, parked beside Stuart's Jaguar, but when I stepped into the entryway it was like everyone had disappeared. A radio in the kitchen was playing soft rock eighties tunes and the TV in the family room had a SpongeBob movie going, but there was nobody in sight. "Hello?" I called again, louder. "Is anyone home?"

There was still no response. I set my duffle bag down and went from room to room calling people's names, but nobody called back. Finally I poked my head out the patio door and yelled into the backyard. "Stuart! Hope! *Anybody?*"

"Dad?"

I heard Hope's voice, but I couldn't place her. "Hope?"

"Up here!"

Our backyard was fairly spacious, at least by

California standards. Most of it was filled up by four thousand square feet of manicured lawn, which was surrounded by undulating beds of shrubs and flowers. A row of four thick fruit trees ran along the west side, providing great shade when the summer sun was setting, and at the far corner of the lot was a stand of three tall pine trees, clustered in a triangle about fifteen feet apart. It was there, in the middle of the pines, that I located Hope's face, nestled among the branches about ten feet up, leaning out an open window—a window that hadn't been there when I was last at home.

"What in the world . . . ?"

"Hi, Ethan." Stuart's head popped into view directly above Hope's. "I hope you don't mind the tree house. I thought the kids needed a fun place to play."

"You . . . built a . . . ?" *A tree house.* Hope had been begging me to build one since she was old enough to say the words. It was her undying dream to have a private getaway in the yard where she and her Barbies could make-believe to their hearts' content. I'd told her time and time again that I would build one for her, but it never seemed to fit in my schedule. Now, thanks to "the rich one," she had exactly what she wanted.

"Hired it out, actually. I'm all thumbs with a hammer, and would lose my thumbs with a saw. The crew just left about thirty minutes ago, so this is our first time testing it out. You want to come up?"

Though it was partially covered by branches, it was obvious that the tree house was big. It filled the entire space between the tree trunks, and then some. From where I stood on the patio it looked like a mini-mansion hovering in the air, complete with a shake roof and cedar siding. "Where is everyone else? There's no one in the house."

"Up here, Dad," said Hope. "With us!"

"Everyone's up there?"

"Uh huh."

"What about Grandpa Bright?" I asked as I started walking across the yard toward the trees.

"Relaxing up here on one of the chairs," piped Stuart.

"Welcome home, Ethan," I heard Grandpa call from inside the raised abode.

Stuart recognized my consternation over how an old man with a cane made it ten feet up a tree. "He was the ultimate test of our elevator system," he said, beaming. "It's pretty simple really. A few well-placed pulleys and a winch from a Jeep Wrangler, and *voila!* He went right up."

One of her cousins called Hope's name, and like a flash she ducked out of view.

I stayed on the yard side of the trees and stared up at my brother-in-law, who was still hanging out the window. "This is crazy, Stuart. No, *insane*. How did you even have time for this?"

"There's lots of construction guys looking for

work these days, and this is really just four walls and a roof, with a few small upgrades thrown in for fun. I had five guys working on it, and it only took them two days."

"Do I dare ask how much you spent?"

He waved off the question. "It's just my way of helping your family get through a tough time."

I hoped the neighbors didn't complain—I was sure Stu hadn't bothered checking if a permit was needed to build something like this. I wanted to be mad, but it was hard to get mad at him for something that Hope clearly loved, especially when he framed it as "helping."

"Fine. But please, you're doing enough just by watching Hope. No more big surprises like this, okay? Between the tree house and the birthday party, I'm going to have a hard time competing."

"Understood," he said. "So what's the latest on Anna's recovery?"

I still didn't want Hope to hear about Anna's condition. "Is *she* close enough to hear?"

Stuart pulled his head into the tree house, then reappeared. "Heather has the kids decorating the walls. Hope is completely engrossed in her work."

"In that case," I said, "I'm not sure 'recovery' is the word I'd use. There's been no change whatsoever. It's not looking good."

"Still unresponsive?"

"Yes. All she does is breathe, and even that's a struggle."

Stuart held up a finger. "Just a sec." He disappeared briefly, then poked his head outside again. "Hope wants to give you the grand tour. You ready to come up?"

I nodded and went around to the "elevator," which functioned exactly as Stuart had described. To me it looked like an elongated crate with open sides. It was supported on top by thick cables and some cleverly placed pulleys attached to the tree above. I stepped into it, pushed a button on the winch, and slowly ascended to the front door.

The inside of the structure looked smaller than it had from ground level, especially with six other people in it.

"You need to shave," Hope observed as soon as I closed the door behind me.

I gave her a hug. "Thanks for noticing. I'll do that just as soon as you show me around."

She took me by the hand and led me all of fifteen feet to the designated sitting area, where Grandpa Bright was lounging in a soft chair that Heather found at a garage sale. Then she showed me where her kitchen set would eventually reside, and her doll collection, and her refrigerator—

"Whoa, hold on," I said. "Refrigerator?"

"Please," she begged.

"Sure, maybe when you're like twenty-five. This is a play house, not an apartment."

She folded her arms. "Fine. I can put a bookshelf there."

"Excellent idea."

And just like that we were back at the front door and the tour was over. We all stayed up in the tree house for another half hour, admiring the construction and enjoying the breeze. But eventually I started getting antsy again about Anna. "I need to get back to the hospital," I announced.

"I'm going with you," said Hope.

"No, sweetie. Not yet. I'll tell you when it's okay for you to see Mommy."

In a move that surprised me, Grandpa banged his cane twice on the tree house floor and said, "Oh, c'mon, Ethan. Let the poor girl see her mom. She's been begging for a full week."

"Excuse me?" The last thing I expected—or needed—was him questioning my parental decisions, and doing so right in front of Hope was completely out of line.

"You heard me. Let the girl go see her mom. She deserves it."

Everyone else was completely still.

I'm sure my face was bright red. I turned quickly to Hope. "Honey, why don't you run inside for a minute. Grandpa and I need to talk."

"Yeah," said Heather. "Kids, how about we all head into the house for a while? It's getting kind of stuffy in here. Stu, weren't there some things we wanted the kids to get done before dinner?"

"What . . . oh, right," Stuart replied. He seemed

disappointed that he wasn't going to get to hear what I was going to say to Grandpa. "Uh . . . c'mon guys."

I waited until everyone was out of the tree house and halfway across the yard before I lit into the old man. "What are you thinking? How dare you undermine my authority like that?"

He gripped the top of his cane with both hands. "Needed to be said."

"Why? What gives you the right to say something like that in front of Hope?"

He met my stare with a look that said he wasn't going to back down. "Why shouldn't she see her, Ethan? What gives you the right to keep her away?"

"Because I'm her father! And I know what's best for her!"

"Do you?"

"Of course!"

"Then when are you planning on telling Hope the truth? And when will she get to see her mom? Tomorrow? The next day? Next week? Or is that day never going to come?"

I leaned against a plywood wall and thought about what he was asking; I wanted to make sure I believed my own answer. "She will . . . ," I said at length, "once Anna wakes up."

He raised his eyebrows questioningly. Then in a much subdued voice he asked, "And what if that moment never arrives? What if tonight or tomorrow Anna suddenly slips away? What if her body decides just to give up the ghost? Hope already knows something is wrong, more than what you've told her. I can see it when she talks to you on the phone. Don't you think she deserves to know the truth, and deserves a chance to see her mom again while she's still alive? Would you really deny her that?"

I felt my face getting hot again, perhaps because I knew he was right. But I wasn't ready to concede just yet. "If it means saving her from a lifetime of nightmares that would come from seeing the patchwork quilt of her mom's body? *Absolutely!*"

"Very well," he sighed, making his disappointment known. "You're her father. If that's how you feel, then I'm sorry I spoke up the way I did. I disagree with how you're handling this, but I was out of line for speaking out like I did."

"Yes, you were. And now that we're in agreement, would you like help getting out of here? I really need to get going so I can get back to the hospital."

"Go on ahead," he said, sounding a little exasperated. "I'm not too old to push an elevator button."

I left Grandpa alone in the tree house and went inside to gather some things. One item I knew I needed to find was in the den, filed under "legal documents" in our metal cabinet. The third document in that folder was the one the hospital wanted: *Anna's living will.*

Before stuffing it in a manila envelope, I scanned through the legalese to confirm what I already knew. Anna had gone to great lengths to develop her position on dying. After studying all sorts of facts, figures, and medical journals dealing with recovery rates for patients on life-support, she'd settled on one month as the magical number for aborting life-support measures.

"I wouldn't want you holding out longer than that," she'd told me, "if there isn't a strong indication that I'll recover. Heaven forbid either of us ever have to face this, but if we do, let's not drag it out." And so I went along with her. My own living will said the same exact thing. Both of us had signed on the line that, in the event of certain medical conditions—one being terminal coma—we would allow life-support machines to be removed after four weeks. Four lousy weeks! Twenty-eight days! That's only six hundred seventy-two hours. With a quarter of that time already gone, it felt infinitely too short.

As much as I would have liked to run it through the nearest paper shredder, my conscience wouldn't let me. I stuffed the documents in my duffle bag along with a few fresh changes of clothes. Then I went searching for Stuart and Heather.

"I need to ask a favor," I told them. "I know you guys can't stay here indefinitely. It's not fair to you or your kids. But it may be a few more weeks before I'm really able to get away from the hospital. Would you mind watching Hope at your place for a while?"

"You mean take her back to Fresno?" Heather asked.

"Yes. It'll be a change of pace for her. Maybe it will help take her mind off of visiting Anna."

Stuart looked very concerned. "You sure it's wise taking her so far from home?"

"I'm not sure about anything anymore, Stu . . . except that I need to be with Anna. Will you help?"

"Of course."

Hope was playing in her room with Devin. Before I left for the hospital, I stopped in to tell her what was going on.

"Why can't I stay with you?" she asked. Her bottom lip was quivering, which only made it harder to respond.

"Sweetie, Mommy needs me right now. And I need to make sure you're safe while I'm with her. Going to stay with your aunt and uncle will be for the best."

"But . . ."

"No 'buts.' It's settled. Now give me a hug before I go."

"When will I see you again?"

"Soon," I said. "You'll hardly even miss me."

"You promise?"

"I promise," I said warily. "You, me, Mommy— we'll all be together again before you know it."

"When?"

"Oh . . . a few days probably. Maybe a week." *Maybe more.*

She finally relented. "Okay, a week. And then I get to see Mommy."

I gave her a very long hug goodbye and tried to pretend it would only be a week.

Chapter 21

Dr. Rasmussen made his daily visit shortly after dinner. "How are we doing?" he asked.

"We? Or her?"

"Both."

I glanced at Anna's body and wondered, for the umpteenth time, if she was even still in it. "It's safe to say we've been better."

He appeared to take that at face value. "Any luck at home looking through your legal documents?"

"No," I lied.

Or was it a lie? I was becoming exceptionally skilled at rationalizing things to fit my needs. In this case, he'd asked if I had "luck" looking for the will. No, I had *skill.* I had preexisting knowledge of where the thing was in the file cabinet. There wasn't an ounce of luck involved.

And the distorted truth shall set you free!

"Ah well. Maybe next time. There's no decisions to be made yet anyhow. And even if there is no will, I'm sure if it comes to making hard choices, you'll know what's best for your wife."

"Let's just hope it doesn't get to that," I mumbled.

Later that night, as I was reading True Love Notes aloud to Anna, I was interrupted by a familiar sound approaching in the hallway.

Shuffle-shuffle-thump. It gradually grew louder, and then came to an abrupt halt.

"May I come in?"

I'd already turned around to face the door in anticipation of his arrival. "What brings you here?"

Grandpa was holding the old guitar case in one hand and his cane in the other. "I'm reneging. I don't want Karl back."

"Neither do I."

"Tough luck. It's all yours now, free and clear. I'm too old to play it anyway, and it'd be too much work taking it back with me on the airplane." He shuffled further into the room and sat down in the vacant chair near the foot of the bed.

"You're flying back to Oregon?"

"It's time. I thought I could be of some help here, but . . . maybe I was wrong. Now that Hope is gone and you're here, there's not much point in me hanging around."

"Well, for what it's worth, I'm glad you came down. And I'm sorry you're going back so soon. But . . . I really don't want the guitar."

"Tough nuts. It's staying." He leaned it up against the small table near his chair. "You can do with it what you want after I'm gone. But it's not going with me." His old wooden box was on the same table. Grandpa caught me stealing a quick glance at it. "Oh, I was wondering where this old thing went to." He chuckled lightly. "Did you take it from the house?"

"Very funny."

"Well how did it get here? I thought you said you weren't interested in it."

"I said I didn't want it at the hospital. *And I didn't.*" I paused and stared at the old man, thinking about what he must have looked like when he was a soldier. The smile on his face softened my mood. "It's . . . true?" I finally asked. "What you told Anna the other night?"

His smile grew. "I thought you might be listening."

"Of course I was. How could anyone sleep through all that yammering?"

With a solemn nod he said, "It was all true. Every last word."

"You really took Hitler's bathroom door handle?"

"Darn straight."

"And you hid it inside the guitar?"

"Sure did."

I didn't want to seem too overly excited, but I couldn't help asking what I was dying to know. "It's not still there, is it?"

His smiled dimmed, just enough to notice. "No, it's gone. I got rid of it a long time ago. Before you were even born."

"Why?"

"Ah, now there's a question."

"And the answer is . . . ?"

With a patented sigh he said, "*Because.* Because I was tired of clinging to the past. What I saw

305

during the war—the things I endured, the things I *did*—it didn't just magically go away after we came back home. It hung around in my head . . . in my heart. At times I felt consumed with anger. Guilt too, because of how my actions destroyed that innocent little family, not to mention what happened to Karl. Eventually I decided I needed to let those feelings go."

"And?"

"And? And that's it."

"But what about the door handle?"

"Didn't I say I wanted to let go of the past? That door handle was just like the rest of the things I didn't want anymore. I was holding onto it as if it was important, when it wasn't. It was, after all, just a door handle—from the john of one of the most notorious men to ever walk the earth no less. What good was it doing me? None whatsoever, which is exactly what I was getting from all the emotional baggage I was carrying. And so one day I walked it down a long pier and threw it into the Tillamook Bay. Sounds silly, perhaps, but for me it was actually quite cathartic."

Grandpa let the room go quiet as his eyes wandered to Anna's face. My gaze followed close behind. For a moment, the only sounds were the beeps and wheezes of Anna's machines. Grandpa tipped his head in the direction I was looking, "Traumatic events can cripple you, Ethan, if you don't deal with them properly. That's something

I've learned through a lifetime of encounters with heartache. I've also learned that no matter how bad things seem in the moment, it's only a moment. 'This too shall pass,' as the saying goes. What I went through was awful, but I survived."

An unexpected rush of blood burned my cheeks. "Oh, I get it. *You* survived your ordeal, so I should be able to get through mine, is that it? That's why you decided to finally share your story with me? Like maybe if I heard what you went through, then perhaps watching my wife die won't seem quite so bad? It could be worse?"

"Ethan that's not—"

"Not what? Not why you brought down your wooden box and war story? Of course it is! Why else would you choose this moment to finally open up about the concentration camp? And don't say it's because I needed to learn why you named the guitar Karl. This goes well beyond that! This is probably just some sort of therapeutic experiment to you. *'Hmm . . . let's see if the old shrink still has it in him, eh?'* Does that about sum it up?"

I could tell by his expression that he was hurt. He pounded his cane on the floor defiantly. "Stop it right there, young man! That was *not* my intent. You're not my patient, you're my grandson, and that's the only thing you are to me. *A son.* And yes, I did share the story because I thought it might help with what you're going through right now, but not in the way you think. I had no intention of comparing our misfortunes. The night of the accident, when you called, I could tell right off this was going to be hard for you. I thought, perhaps, when you read . . . or if you heard how simple it can be to just . . ."

"To what?" I pressed.

Grandpa shook his head slowly. "No, I don't want to spoon-feed you, Ethan. If you *really* want to know how I thought my story could help, then just give some more thought to what I told Anna when you were eavesdropping. Or better yet, open the box and read the journals. It's all there in black and white. I know I'm not a particularly good writer, but I promise, the answer is sitting right there, plain as day. Don't dig too deep, though—it's not rocket science. Look for the low-hanging fruit, because the sweetest things in life are usually right there for us to grab."

I threw my arms up in the air. "You're seriously not going to tell me?"

"Of course not. What good would that do you?"

"It would save me reading your depressing tale, for one thing. I have enough to deal with right now."

Grandpa's smile returned. "Nobody's forcing you, Ethan. But it's there if you want it." He looked at his watch. "Wow, look at the time. I need to be heading out. I've got a plane to catch."

"You're really going?"

"Really." He stood, shuffled forward, and gave me a one-armed hug. "Oh, and Ethan? Play the guitar, won't you?"

"I don't think so, Grandpa."

"I really think you should. I dare say Anna would probably love to hear it. But more than anything, I think it would be good for *you*."

"I'll think about it," I lied.

Chapter 22

I was still sound asleep the next morning when my cell phone rang. I should have looked at the number before answering.

"Ethan, it's nice to know you're still among the living. How's your vacation?" Jessica's voice sent chills down my spine.

"Not great."

"Sorry to hear that." She said it with such detachment that I knew she couldn't care less. "Anyway, work is piling up left and right around here. What are the chances of you coming in for a few days—just to help with a couple big new accounts we're trying to land out west near you? I know you were planning on a few more days, but would you mind?"

I'd completely forgotten about work. With everything else that was going on, I hadn't even called in to tell them what had happened to Anna. Frankly, I was surprised that Jessica wasn't calling to inform me that I was being laid off for even thinking that I could spend time off with my family.

"Jessica, that's not going to be possible."

"Oh, c'mon. You're my number one guy."

"Out here I'm your *only* guy. But seriously, it's impossible."

"Well if you can't come into the office, how

about a t-con? Just a few hours tomorrow, and then three or four the following day. Oh, and if you have a laptop we could—"

With a single push of a button, I ended the call. The phone rang again ten seconds later.

"Hi, Jessica."

"Ethan? I guess we got disconnected."

"No," I stated matter-of-factly. "I hung up on you."

The phone went briefly silent. "I hope you're joking, or we have a serious problem."

"Yeah," I said, staring at Anna, who was in the same position she'd been in for most of the past seven days. The only times she moved was when the nurses lifted her limbs to change her dressings or adjust her monitoring devices. "We have a serious problem."

I could only imagine what was going through Jessica's head right then; I braced myself for the axe that was no doubt about to fall. But her response surprised me, because in my wildest dreams, I'd never imagined that she saw me as anything more than a warm body who was willing to get the job done. "Oh jeez . . . let me guess. You're not on vacation at all, are you? This is some sort of interviewing excursion, and you're getting offers from our competitors."

I was too shocked to speak. When I didn't say anything, she became desperate. "You haven't made any commitments, have you, Ethan? Oh please tell me you haven't. Just tell me what they offered you and I'll beat it by five percent."

"Jessica . . . I didn't. It's Annaliese."

"Is that a marketing firm?"

"My wife."

"She offered you a job?"

"Stop it!" I snapped. "Just listen for two seconds. My wife . . . was in an accident, seven days ago when I came home from work."

She let out a huge sigh of relief, like it was the best news in the world. "Oh thank heavens, because you're already paid top dollar, and another five percent in this economy would be a tough sell to the board of directors. How's your wife doing, by the way? You taking good care of her while she's on the mend? I've got to say, that doesn't sound like much of a vacation."

Just like that, I was as furious as I've ever been. In a few short minutes she'd managed to wake me up, ask me to cut my vacation short, bribe me to stay with the company, and then, to top it all off, act like my wife's health was a minor afterthought. I cleared my throat, to make sure what I was about to say came out crystal clear, because I was only going to say it once. "She's *dying*. And I quit."

I hung up for the second time and turned off my phone. Then I moved from the recliner to the hard chair next to Anna's bed. She looked so peaceful lying there, like there wasn't a care in the world.

"Good morning. Did you hear that, Anna?" I asked, knowing she hadn't heard a thing. That was the hardest part of "conversing" with my best friend. Even when I was just reading aloud to her, it was like I was talking to a door, and I desperately wanted access to the person on the other side. "I'm officially unemployed. Heck of a way to start the day, huh?" I waited, doubting that she would reply, but wanting to at least give her the opportunity. "Still tight-lipped I see. Bad night's sleep? Me too. I've got a kink in my neck from that stupid recliner. Do you think they'd rent out the bed in the next room to me? I don't think there's anyone in there at the moment. Maybe I should just sneak in at night when the nurses aren't looking so I can get a decent night's sleep. No, on second thought, I'd rather be here with you. Of course now that I quit my job, we can spend as much time together as you want. Do you hear that, Anna? I won't be working long hours anymore. It'll just be you and me and Hope, doing whatever you want. No more missed dinners, no more late meetings, no more traveling to heck and gone every other week." I reached out and took her hand in mine. "How does that sound? Anna? Anna . . . ? Anna! Please, sweetie, just give me any indication that you can hear me. Anything! Lift a finger or blink an eye. Wiggle a toe. Or smile. Can you do that for me? Don't be stubborn, okay? We both know how determined you can be

313

sometimes. If you're just holding out because you're mad at me . . . please don't. I'm serious, Anna. I need to know that you're still there. Are you there, sweetie? Can you hear me? Anna . . . ? I want to talk to *you*. I need *you*. Please, if you can hear me, just give me a little sign."

I'm a sane person . . . I think. But there are moments when I've teetered on the edge. Sometimes, when I realized how alone I was in that room, I felt precariously close to losing it. She didn't hear a thing I was saying. Not only was I talking to a door, but I guessed the room on the other side was empty.

Later that morning the nurses reconfirmed that Anna was still scoring at the very bottom of the coma scale. No eye response, no verbal response, and no motor response. But it didn't take a medical degree to know that.

Midmorning I caught sight of Grandpa's wooden box sitting on the table and decided to open it up, partly out of curiosity and partly out of a sense of guilt for how I'd treated my grandfather during his visit. He'd only come to help, and whether it was my tiredness or my overwhelming sense of helplessness, I'd unfairly taken out some of my frustrations on him. For the rest of the day I sat reading his journals to Anna, seeking for whatever nugget of wisdom Grandpa had been hinting at. It read pretty much like he'd told it a few nights earlier, though with some extra details of genocide that I'd have rather not known. Yet for all my effort, I didn't get anything more out of reading it than I had when he told it. Yes, I found his exploits to be moving and intriguing. But if his point wasn't to show me that everyone has trials to pass through, then I was still missing something.

I asked Anna what she thought, but she didn't know either.

Sometime after dinner I turned my cell phone back on. There were half a dozen new messages on it—a couple from my boss, wanting to know if I was serious about quitting, one from Grandpa informing me that he made it home safely, and the rest from Hope, wondering if she could come see Mommy now.

Hope was the only one I really felt like talking to, so I dialed Stu's number.

"Burke residence, this is Heather."

"Hi Heather. It's Ethan. How's Hope doing?"

"Oh, fine. She and the kids are sitting in the Jacuzzi right now. Hope really likes the bubbles."

"I bet. Should I call back later, after they're done?"

"Nope. The phone is portable. I'm walking there now. Just a sec . . . Hope, it's your father."

There was a muffled "Hooray!," followed by splashing. Then Hope picked up. "Dad?"

"Hey, how's my favorite little girl?"

"I'm your only little girl."

"Exactly, which means you'll always be my favorite."

"Dad?"

"Yeah?" I knew what was coming next.

"Can I see Mommy now?"

"No, pumpkin. The doctor says not yet. But maybe soon. A week . . . or so . . . maybe."

"But I *want to*." Every kid whines now and then, and this was sounding like one of those times for Hope.

"I know you do. But . . . the doctor says no."

"But I say yes!"

"Sorry, Hope."

"But *whyyyyy?*"

"Just . . . because."

"*It's not fair!* Why can you see her but I can't?"

"I know, sweetie, it's not. The thing is, it's very quiet here, and I don't think they want kids running around making noise. It's not good for the patients."

The whining stopped almost immediately. "I can be quiet."

"Hope, the answer is 'no.'"

She accepted that as my final answer and finally gave up arguing. "Okay, Dad."

"Are you having fun there in Fresno?" I asked, wanting to change the subject.

That perked her up more than I expected. Maybe

even a little more than I wanted. "Yes, I forgot all the cool things they have. Today we jumped on the trampoline and swam in the pool. And remember where they used to have just dirt in their yard? Now they have miniature golf. It's so much fun, Dad. I could stay here all the time."

I was happy for her . . . right up until that last sentence. *I could stay here all the time.* Would she really want to stay there? *Really?* Were all of those fun things making her so happy that she'd prefer staying with the Burkes over me? *Then again,* I told myself, *at least there she'd have a mother.* I wanted to put such thoughts out of my head, but with Anna showing no signs of improvement, it was looking more and more likely that Hope and I were about to lose the glue that held our family together. And then what would we do? What would *I* do?

"Well, don't have too much fun. I don't want my little girl getting spoiled. I miss you, Hope."

"I miss you too, Dad."

"Love you. See you soon."

I plugged the cell phone into its charger and then sidled up next to Anna's bed. "You hear that, honey? Hope's loving it at your brother's. Great, huh?"

Yeah, just great. "The rich one" has all the money he would ever need and a perfect little family to boot. And what do I have? A wife on death's door, no job, and a daughter who, though she might say otherwise, doesn't seem to miss me a bit.

It had been a long day, and I was exhausted, but my mind wouldn't slow down enough to let me sleep.

Why did I quit my job? Will I be able to find another one? What will I do if—or when—Anna dies? Will I just shut down and give up on life, like my father did when my mom passed away, or will I be strong enough to carry on without her? What about Hope? Would I be an adequate single parent? Would I be able to give her everything that she needs? Or would she be better off in a more stable home . . . like with the Burkes? Would they take her? Would I let them have her? Would Hope care?

To help focus my mind on something other than the myriad questions that I really didn't want to face, I opened up my briefcase and retrieved a few of Anna's True Love Notes that I hadn't yet read to her.

I opened the topmost envelope. It was from one of the less joyful days of our marriage—the day of Faith's funeral. The first line sent a chill through me. "Ethan, part of me died yesterday. I'm sure that part will never heal, never return." My eyes teared up instantly. I glanced at my wife on the bed. "Is this a coincidence, Anna, or are you trying to tell me something?"

She remained silent.

I started over from the beginning, trying hard to keep my tears at bay. " 'Ethan, part of me died yesterday. I'm sure that part will never heal, never return. Why is life so cruel? God takes some and leaves others with no apparent rhyme or reason.

" 'Yes, part of me died yesterday when I watched them lower Faith into the ground. When she died, I lost of piece of myself. And yet . . . we have Hope. Maybe that's how God compensates for the bad times, by making sure there is always a little hope to hold onto.

" 'Ethan, you have been my rock through all of this. I depend on you. I need you. I love you fiercely.

" 'Last night, as I was lying in bed, mourning the loss of our daughter, I admit I was beginning to question whether all of the pain we have endured is worth it. And then, like an answer to a prayer, you brought your guitar to bed and played me a song. Thank you for that. It was so beautiful. It reminded me of all the wonderful things we've shared together. It warmed my heart and made me feel loved. That's exactly what I needed.

" 'I know together we can endure all things, come what may. I love you!

" 'Forever yours, Annaliese.

" 'P. S. Please play for me more often. We both need more beautiful music in our lives.' "

Karl's guitar case was still leaning against the little rolling table on the other side of the room. If it had had eyes, I'd have sworn it was staring at me.

I stared right back. "I'm done with guitars," I said, mostly to Anna, but partly to Karl as well. "Where has playing the guitar gotten us? Look at yourself, Anna? If I didn't play, we'd have never wanted to teach Hope how to play; I'd have never asked you to pick one for her birthday, and you wouldn't be lying there not hearing me talking to you like a raving lunatic. Besides, didn't you hear Grandpa's story about his guitar? That thing's like a magnet for misery, and I've had quite enough of that already. I'm *not* playing it. I'm just . . . not."

I pulled a blanket up to my neck, leaned back in the recliner, and flipped off the light.

Chapter 23

*E*ven though I was young, I recall quite vividly how my father imploded after my mother "left." At first he tried to put on a courageous face, but that façade didn't last more than a few weeks. One day I came home from first grade and found him passed out on the couch when he should have been at work. I shook him but he didn't wake up. I shook harder and screamed, but that didn't do the trick either.

In a panic I dialed 911.

Dad was dazed, confused, and embarrassed when smelling salts awoke him to find the local volunteer rescue crew in our living room. Two of the rescuers were close personal friends of his. Everyone knew about my mom dying, so they brushed the incident off as a normal reaction to a traumatic loss.

After that, I found Dad passed out frequently when I came home. I never called 911 again. Instead, I learned to leave him alone and fend for myself. We only lived like that for a few months before Dad decided he lacked the skills and the emotional fortitude to be a widower–father. I didn't disagree, and neither did Grandma and Grandpa, who kindly offered to take me in.

As a kid I couldn't fathom how a father could just give up on life like my dad had. How could he stop going to work? How could he turn his own child over to someone else? How did he reach the point where his only solace was the bottom of a bottle?

I never understood it. At least not until my experience waiting for Anna to breathe her last breath.

I'd been trying so hard to stay optimistic as I sat there next to her bed day after day. I'd been telling myself that things would be okay. Either a miracle would happen and Anna would pull through or Hope and I would rise above the loss and carry on without her, with our chins held high. But no matter what, I would not end up like my dad.

However, on day ten at the hospital, while I was reading another stack of Anna's notes aloud, pretending she could actually hear me, something inside me changed. Grandpa might have called it depression, and maybe he'd be right. To me it felt like the tiny shreds of hope that I'd been clinging to just evaporated.

That was the day I began to *give up,* and I soon understood how my father had fallen to such a lowly state of wallowing when I was a boy. I never went completely over the edge like him, but I dangled my feet far enough over the precipice that I could see and feel what was waiting at the bottom, and it wasn't pretty.

In my emotional funk, I stopped doing the daily things that had kept me going up to that point, like trying to coax her out of the coma through one-sided conversations. Shaving and showering seemed like an utter waste of time too. Who was I trying to impress by grooming? Certainly not Anna. The easiest thing to do was just sit in the recliner and feel sorry for myself.

I continued on in that miserable state of mind for days on end, all the while still hiding Anna's living will from the hospital's legal and medical staff. The days blurred together. Most of my time was spent watching my wife's lungs go up and down, waiting to see if the next breath would be her last. While I watched, I also pondered things that probably added to the depression. Like how I should go about telling Octavius Burke that his daughter would still be alive if it weren't for me. Or how I could convince Stuart and Heather that they were much better suited to raising Hope than me. And how I would go about explaining to my daughter that, in the long run, she would see that my handing her over to the Burkes was an act of love, not cowardice and self-pity.

Like I said, I was coming to understand my father more and more each day.

Other than the length of my stubble, very little changed in my life for the next couple weeks. As time wore on I began loathing the nursing staff, because they persisted in giving me the same bad news over and over, like a scratched CD that won't stop skipping. Worse yet, Reg may have been the nicest guy in the world, yet for all his good intentions I simply didn't want to talk about the "eventualities" that he kept bringing up concerning Anna, especially since the existence of her living will was still my little secret.

I occasionally checked the date on my cell phone to see how close we were coming to the magical four-week mark of Anna's coma. As the month wound down, my anxiety over not disclosing the will ramped up, but I didn't care. I wasn't ready to let go, so I kept the document tucked away inside my briefcase.

Twenty-two days after the accident, Dr. Knight brought a larger-than-normal entourage with him when he made his daily visit, including Dr. Gooding and Reg Wilson. "Good news," he announced. "Dr. Gooding says your wife's internal injuries have healed nicely. Her lungs, especially, have come a long way, so it's time to see how they do without the ventilator."

"But the dialysis machine stays?"

"That's right," said Dr. Gooding. "It's sort of a permanent fixture. But assuming she doesn't need all the breathing apparatus, we should be able to get her out of the ICU and into a room that will be more comfortable for you."

I pulled the hand-lever on the recliner to put it in a sitting position. "Why all the extra staff?"

Dr. Knight spoke again. "Just to observe. But if your wife doesn't respond as we expect when we turn things off, then it's also nice to have a few extra hands on deck."

"Ah," I commented as I stood up and walked to the foot of the bed, where I would be out of the way. "Expect the best, but plan for the worst."

"Exactly right," chirped one of the interns.

"You'd be smart to expect the worst," I said under my breath.

The process of turning off equipment took about thirty minutes, but most of that was just cautionary waiting between each step to be sure everything was okay before moving on. When they were done, the only things still attached to Anna were the feeding tube, an IV for fluids, and the dialysis machine.

Assured that she wasn't going to suddenly crash, the interns and nurses wheeled Anna out to her new room. I stayed behind to gather my things. Reg stayed behind too.

"You're not looking so good lately," he said candidly when we were alone.

"Can't a guy grow a beard if he wants to?"

"Ethan, it's not just the beard. It's the whole package—the clothes, the hair, the bags under your eyes. You look tired. No . . . you look *defeated*."

I picked up my duffle bag and briefcase. "Aren't I? Your team of doctors just wheeled my wife out of a room she never saw and into a room she will never see. How is that anything but defeated?"

"I know this has been horrible for you. I don't envy what you're going through right now. And I'm not sure I wouldn't feel the same way in your position. But from where I sit right now, I have to believe that you hanging around here twenty-four seven is not doing you or your wife any favors. What about your daughter? When was the last time you saw her?"

"She's in good hands," I snapped. "I talk with her every day, not that it's any of your business."

"No, you're right. It isn't. I'm just concerned, that's all."

"Well I wish you'd show less concern for me and more for my wife. She's the one who needs the help."

"Ethan, that's—. With Anna, we've reached a point where there's little left for the doctors to do. They've patched up most of her purely physical injuries. But we both know the brain is more complex; less predictable. She's shown no progress responding to stimuli, and it's been more than three weeks. Usually by now, if a patient is going to recover, we would have seen some significant improvement."

"What are you saying?"

"I'm saying, it's time to start thinking about how long we're going to carry on like this. How long do you plan to leave your wife living on a feeding tube? And by extension, how long do you plan to sit by her side, waiting for something to happen?

I hate to say it, but Anna's not the only one in limbo right now. You really need to start thinking about letting go so that you and your daughter can move on."

Through clenched teeth I said, "What you're hinting at amounts to murder, and I won't murder my wife."

"No," he said calmly, "what I'm suggesting is that maybe she's *already gone*. Maybe she's been gone right from the start, and we just didn't know it. But now that her brain has had a chance to recuperate, and given her lack of progress, we need to think about what the most humane thing is for her. How long do we sustain her body in a vegetative state? Is it a matter of weeks? Months? Years?"

I thought of the living will hiding in my brief-case. My mind rehearsed the legal language that defined Anna's wishes for just such a scenario.

One month.

I quickly reminded myself that Anna didn't know what she was talking about. *One month is too short!*

"As long as it takes," I replied, then spun to go.

"Ethan," Reg called before I got very far. "You forgot your guitar."

I didn't even turn around. "You can have it."

Anna's new room was in the corner of the building, which meant it had windows on two walls, providing twice as much natural light during the day. It was nice for me, but Anna was oblivious. It also had two beds, which was another major perk. The nurses told me I could sleep on the vacant one until such time as the hospital became so full that they needed to start doubling up patients, but nobody believed that was going to happen.

On the morning after leaving the ICU, I awoke to find Karl's guitar case propped up in the corner of the room between the windows. I hated seeing it there. It reminded me of all of my failings: *never became the songwriter I'd dreamed of becoming; never wrote Anna the song I promised to write; stopped playing music for my wife and daughter because I was too busy with work; didn't take the time to pick out a guitar for Hope's birthday, which ultimately led Anna to her current state of semi-life.*

If I'd been more motivated, I might have walked Karl down to a Dumpster behind the hospital and been done with it. But somehow I knew I'd regret it later. After all, Grandpa had gone through hell to get it, so maybe it was best to just let it sit by itself in the corner.

The days leading up to the magical one-month anniversary of Anna's accident were some of the lowest of my life. The only thing I can compare it to is a movie my dad sent me for my thirteenth birthday, the 1968 zombie thriller, *Night of the*

Living Dead. He sent it along with a card explaining that it was the movie he'd taken my mom to see on their very first date (which probably explains a lot), and that he was sure I would love it.

I *didn't* love it. For weeks I had nightmares about zombies wandering around in a brainless stupor.

During those last few days at the hospital, *I* was the zombie moping around Anna's room, waiting for someone to pick up a club and put me out of my misery. About the only conscious thought I remember during that time was that the timer on Anna's life was rapidly winding down, and there was nothing anyone could do to stop it.

On day twenty-seven there was a flurry of activity after one of the nurses poked Anna's heel with a pin, causing a small flinch in her toe. It wasn't much, but it took her Glasgow score from a three to a six. At first, everyone was abuzz—especially me. I thought this was the turning point, where the injustices of the world would be corrected and I would have my Anna back. But when Dr. Rasmussen came in to verify the results, he put a heavy damper on the situation, sending my mood even lower than it had been before.

"I'm sorry," he explained, "but this doesn't mean much. The movements we're seeing are more indicative of muscular contraction than a response of the nervous system."

"So her brain isn't tied to the toe flinch?"

His eyes said he was sorry. "Not in my opinion."

"But you're not sure."

"Not one hundred percent, no. But reasonably confident."

"And what if you're wrong? Then this is a good indicator that she might recover?"

I could tell he hated to be the bearer of bad news. He pulled a chair next to me. "Ethan, in medicine, nothing is ever certain. We don't know everything. But we do know a lot, and what we know is that even if your wife has some minimal brain activity, her likelihood of recovering is very small."

"How small? I want numbers! There's got to be data on this that will support some other outcome."

"Okay," he replied calmly. "For starters, let's look at where your wife was twenty-four hours after the accident, which is the best predictor of outcome. She had the lowest score possible. Statistically, only about five percent of individuals with that score will make any kind of a recovery. The rest eventually die. Of those that recover, most start to show marked improvement within the first week. It has been almost four weeks for Anna, and this is the first bump we've seen in her score."

"What is the prognosis for a person with a score of six?" I already knew I was grasping at straws.

"Well these are rough numbers, but if a person scores anywhere from five to seven after twenty-four hours, more than half of them still die without any recovery. I don't have hard data on patients who jump from a three to a six after a month, but as far as I'm concerned, the most likely outcome is still that she will not recover."

The nurses seemed deflated by the news too. They finished whatever they were doing, then quickly vacated the room, leaving me alone again to wallow in what one male nurse had dubbed a "vinyl stupor," referring to my daytime residence in the recliner.

Then came day twenty-eight . . . and twenty-nine. Anna was still ingesting food through a tube and her toe still flinched when prodded, but that was the extent of her existence.

That evening after dinner I broke down again in tears, which I hadn't done since the first week of the accident. Mentally and emotionally, I was bankrupt. Life as I'd known it was officially over. Anna would never recover, of that I was now certain. My family was in ruins. And worst of all, I could no longer see myself functioning as a parent, much less a productive member of society.

"I'm sorry, Anna," I cried. "I didn't mean for any of this to happen."

My lonely pleading was interrupted by a phone call. Judging by the time of day, I correctly guessed it was Stuart's number on the screen, which meant Hope would be on the other end of the line. I didn't feel much like talking, mostly because I already knew exactly how the conversation would go. But I couldn't just ignore her, because that's something my own dad would have done.

I tried to sound happy when I picked up and said hello.

"Dad?"

"Hi, pumpkin."

"Please, please, please, *please* let me see Mommy now."

"You know I can't do that." I waited for an objection. "Are you still doing okay at the Burkes?"

"I'm fine."

"Any new news?"

She thought out loud with a very long *ummmm,* then said, "Oh yeah, I'm getting to be a really good swimmer. Their pool is so warm I don't even know why they have a Jacuzzi. And Aunt Heather bought me two new swimsuits today, and some really nice clothes. I'll show them to you sometime."

"Sounds good."

"Ummm, Dad? *When* can I show them to you?"

"How about the next time I see you?"

"When?" she repeated.

I glanced at Anna as I spoke. "I honestly don't know."

"How about when I come see Mommy?"

"That sounds good."

"I miss her, Dad. I want to see her."

"I know, pumpkin. And you will . . . in time."

"But I want to see her *now*."

"Hope, I'm sorry," I said quickly. "I have to go. I'll talk to you tomorrow."

I clicked off. *What kind of a parent intentionally hangs up on their own kid?* I asked myself. But the answer was becoming clearer to me every day: *The kind who shouldn't be a parent.*

I went to the spare bed on the other side of the curtain and tried to cry myself to sleep, but the only thing that came of it was a wet pillow. Three hours later, at eleven thirty, I was still wide awake. I got up and went back to Anna's bed. Standing beside her in the darkness, I took her hand in mine and caressed it softly. "Why won't you just wake up?" I asked. "And don't say because you're not really asleep. I hear that enough already from the doctors. I don't care where you're at or what you're doing, I just want you *here*. I've been trying to keep it together, but I can't. I can't do it any—"

My pining was cut off once more by my cell phone. When I saw the number on the caller ID, I hesitated answering—Hope should have long since been asleep, and I wasn't in the mood to talk to my brother-in-law. After five rings I answered.

"Hello?"

"Ethan, it's Stuart."

As soon as I heard his voice, alarms started going off in my head. He was panicky, and not just his normal social jitters. "What's up?"

"Ethan, you need to come down here. *Right now.*"

"Why? What's going on?"

There are a handful of words and phrases from my life I'll never forget. Things like *"I burned the chicken!"* or *"We're having twins!"* And who could forget *"Sometimes these things just happen"* and *"I'm sorry, Mr. Bright, Faith didn't make it."* Each of these is indelibly etched in the sinews of my memory. But no combination of words will ever be remembered more clearly by me than the ones "the rich one" said in the waning minutes of day twenty-nine.

"Hope is gone."

Chapter 24

Maybe it's just me, because I've experienced it so many times, but I swear there's nothing like a good calamity to pull your head out of the last calamity.

As soon as Stu said "Hope is gone," it was as if somebody flipped a switch on inside me. No longer was I the moping, wallowing, unshaven, lethargic victim of poor choices who was waiting helplessly for the death of his wife to put the final nail in the coffin of his life. Okay, maybe I was still unshaven, but I definitely wasn't a zombie, and that was an excellent start. I was *alive;* fully in the moment. I was a dad whose only concern was the welfare of his daughter.

I was *me* again.

"What do you mean, 'She's gone!' Gone where?"

"If we knew, I wouldn't have called. She said she was going to her room after she got off the phone with you." The panic in his voice was growing by the second. "It was already her bedtime, and she looked tired, so we figured she was going to sleep. Heather and I watched a movie. We went to check on her about thirty minutes ago, just to make sure she was okay before we went to bed, but she wasn't there."

"You sure she's not just hiding? Or asleep in the closet or something?"

"We've flipped the whole house upside down. She's not here, Ethan. The window in her room is wide open and the screen is popped out."

Add *"the screen is popped out"* to the list of phrases I'll never forget.

I felt sick. My first thought was about another little girl in the national news who'd been snatched from her own room in the middle of the night by a random psycho some years earlier. How could that possibly happen to *my* daughter? The Burkes lived on acreage with a fence around the property; didn't they have safeguards against strangers lurking around at night? "Have you checked everywhere outside? The pool house? The gazebo?"

"Ethan, we've checked everywhere! She's gone. We called the police ten minutes ago and they're already issuing an Amber Alert. Heather's trying to answer their questions on the other line, but I wanted you to know what's going on. I think you need to be here."

"Of course." My head was still spinning, trying to find other reasons for her disappearance. "Stu, is anything else gone from her room?"

"Not that we know of."

"No clothes or anything?"

"I don't think so."

"And she didn't have any money, right?"

There was a noticeable pause. "Well . . . she might have had some cash. I'll go right now while we're talking and look for her purse."

"Since when does she have a purse?"

"Heather found some Coach handbags on discount—like a hundred bucks—so she picked her up a couple."

"And how did she get money?"

"Allowance. I couldn't not give her an allowance, since the boys were getting one."

I wanted to scream at him for spoiling my daughter, but it wouldn't have helped. I calmly asked, "How much?"

"Well," he stammered, "the boys get fifty dollars a week, and I didn't want her to feel slighted, so maybe a hundred and fifty or so."

Now I honestly wanted to wring his neck. "Are you *insane?* She's eight! That's more money than she needs in an entire year! How could you possibly—? You know what, never mind. Did you find the purse?"

"I'm looking . . . I'm in her room now . . . just a second . . . no . . . wait . . . okay. I found one, but it doesn't have any money in it. I'll have the kids look in the other rooms, see if it's lying around somewhere."

While Stuart was hunting for the purse, I was grabbing my keys, throwing on shoes, and heading for the door. By the time he found the other empty purse, I was halfway down the hallway. "Stuart, listen to me. The Amber Alert was the right thing to do. Thank you for being so decisive. But I have a feeling I know where Hope is. You're not far from one of the Fresno Amtrak stations, right?"

"Well, technically we live in Madera, not Fresno. But close enough."

"Stuart! Your whole family says you live in Fresno! Get over it! Isn't there a little station near your home?"

"It's a of couple miles, yes. But we can see the trains just half a mile away when they pass by. The kids like to watch from our tree house when they hear the horn."

"Go there!" I said as I reached the hospital's main lobby. "Tell the police to go there. And if she's not there, check the bus station. Check all the public transportation in town. Call the cab companies too, see if anyone picked up a little girl asking for a ride to San Francisco."

"You think—?"

"Yes. I think she's got a ridiculous wad of cash burning a hole in her pocket, and she's going to spend it to get exactly what she wants. *To see her mother.*"

Twenty minutes later, shortly after midnight, as I was speeding through Oakland along Interstate 580, my cell phone rang for the third time that night.

"Stu?"

"We got her!" he screamed. "And she's okay. You were right, she went straight for the tracks and followed them to the station."

Earlier in the evening I'd cried over what

happened to Anna—painful cries of sorrow and anger and guilt over her fate. Sitting there in my car, with the accelerator pushing the limits of local speed traps, I cried the first tears of joy in as long as I could remember—maybe the first ones ever. "Oh . . . my . . . gosh," I gushed. "Thank you, Stuart. Thank *God*."

"It was you who knew where to look. But we'd have found her eventually too, because the lady working the night shift at Amtrak made a call to the police shortly after you and I talked. She told them she was keeping her eye on an obvious stray until they could get there."

"I'm just glad she's safe. Are you taking her back to your place?"

"Well . . ." he drawled. "Not exactly. She . . . um . . . doesn't want to go."

"She thinks she has a choice?"

"She says she already bought a train ticket to San Fran, and she's waiting for the train to pick her up."

"Stubborn little . . ."

"Just like Anna," he quipped.

Surprisingly, the reference to my comatose wife, and his younger sister, didn't sting like I thought it should. "Yeah," I sighed reverently. "Just like Anna."

"So, what should I do?"

"Do you mind hanging out at the train station for a while? I can be there in two hours."

"Take your time. Her train doesn't come through until five in the morning."

"Can I talk to her?"

He chuckled. "Uhh, that's a big fat *no*. She says she's not speaking to you."

"Why not?"

"Because she knows you'll tell her she still can't see her mom, and she doesn't want to hear it. But hey, would you expect anything less from the precocious little girl who busted out her screen, shimmied out the window, and hiked alone at night to a train station? She's pretty determined right about now."

"Understood. Well at least tell her I'm coming, and that I love her. And give her a big hug for me. I'll be there as quick as I can."

Two hours later, at a quarter past two in the morning, I stepped inside the tiny building that served as the Madera Amtrak station. Heather and Stu were sitting on a small wooden bench with Hope sprawled out between them, sound asleep.

"Hope," I said, nudging her just a little. "Hope, Dad's here."

She barely opened her eyes. "I'm going on the train," she mumbled half-consciously.

"How about we go in my car?"

She lifted her head and rubbed her eyes to clear the cobwebs. "No. I'm going to see my mom."

The drive from San Francisco to the train station had given me lots of time to think, and my number one thought was how close I'd come to losing Hope. It scared me to death. No, it scared me much worse than death. She was all I had left, yet somehow in my selfish stupor at the hospital I'd nearly convinced myself that she'd be better off without me.

That was about to change.

"I know," I told her. "It's time to go see your mom. I'll take you there myself."

She smiled—the big, beautiful smile she'd inherited from her mother. "Promise?" she asked.

"I promise."

Before I could say another word, Hope laid her head back on Heather's lap and was out cold. I thanked Heather and Stuart for all they'd done.

Well, for everything except the weekly allowance.

Hope stayed asleep the entire ride home. Dawn was breaking when we pulled into our driveway and parked in the garage. I carefully carried Hope from the car to her bed, then I found my way to the living room and crashed on the sofa.

My own bed looked plenty inviting, but I wasn't ready yet to sleep in it alone.

A few hours later, Hope woke me up by tapping my shoulder until I groaned. "Dad, you look like a gorilla."

I opened one eye without lifting my head. "I thought you liked gorillas."

341

"I do. *At the zoo*. But you don't want to look like that when we go visit Mommy."

"Oh right. That."

"We *are* going. You promised."

I sat up and stretched. "How do you even remember that? It was the middle of the night."

She shrugged. "I don't know. But you did say it. I heard."

"You're right. I did. And we will. But Hope, there's something I need to talk to you about before we go. Why don't you sit down for a second?"

"Is it about Mom?"

"Yes. Hope, I haven't been completely honest with you about your mom's accident . . . because I didn't want you to worry. But since we're going to see her, I want you to know what to expect. Honey, Mommy's car accident was very serious."

She tried to put on a brave face. "I know, Dad," she said softly, then began biting her lip.

"You do?"

"Uh huh. That's why you've been staying with her at the hospital, and why I haven't been able to talk to her."

"That's right."

"Uncle Stuart said that her mouth was hurt, and so she couldn't really speak."

"Well, that's one way to put it . . . sort of. But it's more than just her mouth. The accident hurt her brain, sweetheart, and it caused her to . . . *sleep,* for a long time. It's called a coma. She hasn't been awake since her accident."

Hope stared at me for several seconds. Then, with eyebrows raised, asked, "Like Sleeping Beauty?"

"Just like that."

"So . . . she hasn't talked to you either?"

"No, pumpkin. She hasn't talked to anyone. I was hoping she would pull out of it, and then I was going to take you to see her. But . . . now we're not sure that's even a possibility."

"You mean she might not wake up?"

The truth was hard, but I knew the time for lying was long past. "Yes."

"Yes, she *will?*"

"No . . . I mean, *yes,* she might not wake up. The doctor says she probably won't."

"Ever?"

I could feel my eyes getting moist, but I kept the tears at bay. "Ever."

She remained riveted on me again for a long time, refusing to look away. Her eyes were getting moist. Finally she asked, "Have you kissed her?"

"Huh?"

"Like Sleeping Beauty. Didn't that help her?"

"Hope, this is . . . It's not a fairy tale, sweetie. This is real. And as much as it hurts, we need to understand that Mommy is probably never going to wake up. She isn't going to be *Mommy* again."

Hope's tears started to fall.

"Do you understand what I'm saying?"

343

She replied with a stoic nod while wiping her damp face. Then she asked a question that I didn't want to answer in the worst way, because the honest response was a truth I didn't want to face myself. "But Dad, if Mommy is asleep and isn't going to wake up, what should I tell her when we go to the hospital?"

I could no longer look in her eyes, so I pulled her close and wrapped my arms around her. "I think maybe the right thing to say . . . is goodbye."

Chapter 25

"*T*he gorilla is gone," I announced as I exited the bathroom.

"There's nothing to eat," replied Hope.

I told her she could pick any restaurant on the way to the hospital. She instantly chose McDonald's. "We never went there the whole time I was at Stuart's. What's the point in having all that money, if you don't spend it on good food once in a while?" She seemed perplexed by her own question. Then she asked, "Isn't today Friday?"

"I believe so."

"Don't you usually work on Fridays?"

"Well . . ." I said slowly, trying to craft a suitable explanation for what I'd done. But the more I thought about it, the more I felt like she needed to know exactly what I'd done, and why I'd done it. "I decided I needed to be around here more for you. You're growing up so fast, and I don't want to miss it. So . . . I quit. I'll have to find another job, but I promise it won't be one that keeps me away so much."

"Really?"

When I nodded, she wrapped her arms around my neck. "I love you, Dad."

An hour later we arrived at the hospital, fully fed on hot cakes and egg McMuffins. Before we reached Anna's room, I warned Hope that her mother had some scars on her face, and that her hair had been cut short, so she might look a little different.

"I don't care how she looks," she replied. "She's still my mom."

As we walked down the final hallway to the corner room, several nurses passed by and did a double-take—like they sort of recognized me with a clean face and combed hair, but not quite. I smiled politely and kept walking.

I gave Hope a little squeeze of assurance before opening the door. "No matter what," I told her, "we're going to be okay."

Hope hurried straight to the bed as soon as I turned the door handle. I held back and just watched as she refamiliarized herself with her mother. Thankfully, the worst of the visual trauma from the accident had gone way down. Her left eye was no longer swollen closed, the black and blue was all but gone in her face, and even most of the bandages around her head had been removed. A pink scar across her cheek marked the site of a once-deep gash, but now that the stitches were gone even that didn't look so bad.

"Mommy?" she said softly, testing the waters. "It's Hope."

When no reply came, she called a little louder. Then louder still. When that didn't work she stood high on her tiptoes and gave Anna a kiss, then waited a few moments to see if Sleeping Beauty's spell was broken. She turned around and looked at me sadly when nothing happened.

"It was worth a try," I said.

For the next hour I had Hope sit next to her mother and just talk to her. She explained how she was feeling about the accident, how much she missed talking to her, what she thought about all of the scars—whatever came to mind. Hope shed a few tears along the way, but there were some happy moments too. Like when she talked a lot about all of the things she got to do with her cousins and how cool it was that Uncle Stu has so much money because they could buy whatever they want. She caught herself, then added, "But family is better than money." Eventually she explained how she'd managed to sneak out and get from the Burkes' house to the train station.

"Which, by the way," I interjected, "is something you're *never* going to do again. Right, young lady?"

Her sheepish nod made me chuckle.

We hung around the hospital for the rest of the day, just taking it easy. It was good for Hope to feel close to her mother. When I suggested we go to lunch—and later dinner—she made me pinky-promise that we were coming back before she would agree to go.

Stubborn little . . . just like Anna.

After dinner Dr. Rasmussen made a late visit to

check on Anna at the same time that Reg came to check on me. They both remembered Hope from the night of Anna's accident. She didn't recognize either of them, but she shook their hands without hesitation.

"You're looking better today," Reg told me while Dr. Rasmussen was examining Anna.

"And for good reason."

"Oh? Why is that?"

"Last night I was reminded of something Dr. Rasmussen told me right after the accident."

The doctor had been quietly listening to our conversation and turned around when I mentioned his name. "Me? Refresh my memory," he said, looking somewhat puzzled.

"You said I'm not without hope. Last night, for a little while, Hope was gone. Literally, disappeared—*lost*. But now that she's found, I'm seeing things a little more clearly."

He glanced at my daughter, who was at the table fiddling with the latch on Grandpa's old wooden box. "I think I understand."

My briefcase was lying flat on top of Anna's dresser. "Reg, before either of you go, there's something I need to give you." My hands started trembling, but I fetched the briefcase, opened it up, pulled out the manila envelope, and handed him Anna's living will.

He read the document with careful attention, with Dr. Rasmussen looking over his shoulder.

When he was through, he let out a small sigh and handed it to the doctor, who was still reading. "It can't be easy for you to give this to me."

"No. It's the hardest thing I've ever done."

"I think she'd be glad you did."

I tried to smile. "When I see her in heaven, there'd be hell to pay if I didn't."

Dr. Rasmussen handed the will back to Reg. "The fine print says one month."

"I know. I'm late. Are there legal penalties for withholding this?"

"Late?" replied Reg. "*Pfft.* The intent isn't that we measure this sort of thing to the very second, it's that we do our best to respect her wishes. Besides, there are thirty days this month, so in that sense you're right on time."

I gazed at the bed. "You hear that, Anna? For once, I'm right on time."

"Ethan, I assume the fact that you're giving this to me means that you're prepared to carry it through?"

Hope had rejoined the group. I placed one hand on her shoulder and pulled her close, painfully swallowing the lump in my throat. "Yes. It's time to let her go."

He nodded back. "Well, I think it's good that your daughter has a chance to spend some time with her. I suggest we wait four or five more days—it'll take that long for legal to get all of the paperwork in place anyway. And that will give you time, should you wish, to notify other family members and friends; maybe give them the opportunity to come here and say goodbye. How does that sound?"

Hope and I looked at each other for support, and then we both nodded.

"Dr. Rasmussen," Reg continued, "does it sound like a plan the medical team will agree to?"

"I'll talk it over with them," he said, "but given Anna's current status, I don't see why not. Ethan, you take the time you need to have folks say goodbye, and after that we'll turn off the dialysis. It should be very gentle. Okay?"

I *so* wanted to tell him it sounded absolutely awful, and that there was no way we could actually go through with it. *Stop dialysis and let the toxins shut down her system?* It would have been so much easier had we just left her off the ventilator right from the start, or not jump-started her heart when it failed in the ambulance and again later during surgery. But that wouldn't have been a decision I could have made either. I knew the dialysis route was the most humane— terminally ill patients do it all the time to themselves when fighting the disease becomes too much of a chore. And I knew Anna would feel no pain.

"Okay," I mumbled. "Five more days."

Chapter 26

*H*ope was adamant that we spend the night at the hospital, and I couldn't say no. That meant Hope got the room's second bed and I was relegated once more to the recliner. Whether it was the uncomfortable position or the firestorm of thoughts in my head, I couldn't sleep. With Hope completely zonked, I got up and paced around the dimly lit room. In the shadows of the corner, directly between the two windows, I spotted the dark form of Grandpa's guitar case.

I'd been avoiding the thing forever. But somehow that night the thought of picking up Karl—or at least looking at it—didn't seem so reprehensible.

With some lingering hesitation, I made my way to the corner of the room, grabbed the case by the handle, and walked it back to the recliner. Sitting down, I turned on a small reading light on the wall above my head and pulled the case onto my lap. The last time I'd opened it up was several months before the accident, late one night before a business trip that would have me away from home for two weeks. Anna had begged me to play for her before I left, so I favored her with one quick song before we both went to sleep.

Slowly, one by one, I flipped open the metal latches that held the case shut. Most of my anxiety was because I knew what would be waiting inside. Every time I'd looked at the case for the past month I'd known exactly what was waiting in there, sealed in a pink envelope and strung through the strings. For the first time in our marriage, I wasn't sure I wanted to read what she'd written. It didn't seem right that the last words I would ever hear from her were penned months before her untimely demise.

With unsteady hands I lifted the lid. My reluctant eyes scrolled up the neck of the guitar to where I knew the note would be waiting, woven carefully between the strings. When my gaze reached the tuners, I froze.

There was no note.

I didn't know whether to be relieved that I didn't have to face her final message or disappointed that for once she'd dropped the ball. I ran my palm along the smooth wood surface, then slid the case onto the floor while lifting Karl out, just to see how it felt in my hands. But as I tilted the guitar up, there was a faint, muffled thump from within its cavernous body.

When I flipped it over and twisted it just right, with the strings facing the floor, *two* pink envelopes dropped onto my lap.

I froze again.

I'd never received two notes before. "What did you do, Anna?" I whispered aloud. "One note . . . that was the deal."

I sat staring at the envelopes for who knows how long. Eventually, I put down the guitar and held them up to the light. Each one said "True Love Note" on the front in Anna's artsy hand, centered between musical eighth notes.

With precision, I broke the seal on the lighter of the two envelopes and used my fingernail to slide it open. The paper inside was dated four and a half months earlier. It was very short, and bittersweet.

Ethan,

Sometimes I feel like writing these notes is the only chance I get to tell you that I love you. That's so sad! I miss you. I wish you didn't have to go on your trip tomorrow. I miss having you to talk to. Hope misses you too. We both need you. Thanks for playing for me tonight, but I need to hear you play more often—because if you're home to play, it means you're home!

Come home soon.

Love, Anna

Glancing once more at the bed, I whispered, "I'm home."

An uneasy melancholy settled over me as I tore into the second envelope. I couldn't shake the feeling that something wasn't right. Why would there be two notes? When did she write it? Had she sealed the first one and then decided she had more to say about me always being gone? Was she going to rip into me for continually letting my family responsibilities slip by the wayside?

I gently slid the stack of papers from the envelope. My heart nearly leapt out of my chest when I read the date in the upper corner of the top page. I knew what date that was. It was the worst day of my life, and what could have been the last day of Anna's, exactly thirty days ago. *The day of the accident.*

Good evening Mr. Bright,

I can only assume it is evening that you are reading this—probably very late at night, since that's the only time I see you lately. Today was a bad day. I'm sure we both agree on that. I don't think I've ever been more upset with you, or more disappointed. As you may have observed, this note is not in response to you playing the guitar for me. I'm breaking new ground here, and I'll explain why. Today I was so mad at you that I honestly considered calling it quits. I wanted to give up. I was ready to walk; to take Hope and go. I thought maybe that would teach you a lesson about getting your priorities straight.

But guess what? I couldn't do it. And do you know why?

BECAUSE I LOVE YOU!

Which is why I needed to write this note now and get these feelings off my chest. For my own sanity, I couldn't wait until I see you tonight. We'll talk about this then, too, but for now this is an outlet for me to pour my heart out so the rest of my day isn't ruined by pent-up emotions.

But you know what? I kind of like writing to you "off schedule" for a change. This could be the start of something new, where I write any old time I want. Why should I wait until you play the guitar before I write down what I'm feeling? Maybe our tit-for-tat strategy wasn't well enough thought out. We can discuss that later too.

For now, though, it's settled: I love you. And no matter how little I see you, or how often I have to pick up the pieces for your absence, I'm going to keep on loving you. That's what I agreed to do when we got married. For better or worse, right? But that doesn't mean you're off the hook. Ethan, what will it take to convince you that this family needs YOU, not your inflated salary? I know it's me and Hope that you're working so hard for, but we were doing just fine back when you were writing jingles. We were happy. You were around. We did things together as a family. Can't we get that back? Think about it.

In the meantime, I want you to know that I'm

sorry for the way we spoke to each other today. I'm sorry for the feelings I had in my heart, and I promise those feelings are gone now. And just in case you're feeling a little guilty about today too, I want you to know that I forgive you.

Rest easy, my love. My heart is yours, forever and always.

Annaliese

I read, and reread her final note until my eyes were blurry. Three words remained fixed on my brain for the rest of the night, haunting me even long after I cried myself to sleep.

I forgive you.

Chapter 27

*H*ow does one man tell another man—*another father*—that you're ending the life of his daughter? If you live in California and he lives in Idaho, the answer is simple: *you do it by phone.*

Unfortunately, no amount of distance can make the task any easier.

"Octavius? This is Ethan."

"Good morning. How is Anna doing? We haven't talked in a couple days."

"She's . . . about the same."

"Oh. And Hope? How is she faring? Last time I talked to Stu he said she's really itching to visit the hospital."

"I brought her here yesterday. She sort of forced my hand."

"You know, I know you said from the get-go that there wouldn't be much value in me visiting until there was a change in her status, but I think it's time I came down to see her too. What do you say?"

I knew that was the perfect lead-in for the message I had to deliver, but I couldn't get the words out yet. "Umm . . . yes. I think it's time."

There was nothing but static on the line for several seconds. "You sound like something's on your mind, Ethan. Care to share?"

That was it. I couldn't avoid the matter any

longer. "Yes . . . you should come. Actually, I'd like as many members of the family to come as you think should."

He hesitated again. "This doesn't sound good."

"No. It's not. Years ago, when we were still living in Moscow, Anna and I created living wills which stipulate that, in such a situation as Anna's right now, we not suspend her life. The time frame that she felt was appropriate was one month. Which is . . ."

"Now," he added soberly.

"Yes. Based on the recommendation of the doctor, we've decided that the odds of recovery at this point are slim, and given the language of the will . . . we've agreed to move forward with Anna's wishes."

"I see. When?"

"They'll turn off dialysis in five days. She'll maybe make it a few days beyond that."

I could hear the quiver in his voice when he quietly said, "I'll be there to say goodbye."

The next call was to Grandpa Bright. The conversation went about like I expected. He let me do most of the talking, speaking only here and there to express his empathy. Once I explained about the living will and invited him and the family to come down to say goodbye, I told him everything that had transpired since he went back to Oregon, with particular emphasis on how I'd slipped into what I described as a "three-week despair" and how Hope's disappearance had pulled me back from that very dark place.

"Your father will be happy to know you haven't followed precisely in his footsteps when faced with adversity."

"Maybe. I was very close though." *Too close.* "I certainly have a better appreciation for what he went through."

"I'm sure. Actually, that reminds me, how is that young lady doing?"

"Hope? She's handling the whole thing much better than me. Sometimes I feel like she's the adult and I'm the child trying to learn from her example."

He cleared his throat. "I meant . . . the *other* young lady. What's her name? Abbey?"

"Ashley?"

"That's the one."

I wasn't surprised that he wanted to swing the conversation in that direction. Sometime in the middle of the night, after reading Anna's final note, my mind finally pieced together exactly what it was that Grandpa wanted me to learn from his concentration camp experience. In my head I rehearsed again what he'd told me during our previous discussion on the subject.

The sweetest things in life are usually right there for us to grab. That was the key, "sweetest."

In his journal, and also when he'd told the story in Anna's hospital room, he'd described one particular phrase as being the sweetest words he'd ever heard in his life. Anna had written that same exact phrase in her final note to me—three simple words that weren't simple at all. *I forgive you.*

The thought of forgiving Ashley Moore seemed so backwards to me as to be absurd, and yet I knew that's what Grandpa thought I should do. "I don't know," I admitted. "The last time I saw her, she was standing on her front porch, listening to me rip her to shreds."

"Yes, well . . . everyone makes mistakes."

I wasn't sure if he was talking about me or her.

"Did you finally figure out why I had you read about Mauthausen?"

"Yes."

"And?"

"And I don't know if I can do it. I don't know that I want to."

"It isn't easy, that's for sure. But having been on both sides of seemingly unforgivable deeds, I can assure you that the only way for everyone to heal is to forgive."

I'm sure he was hoping he'd shown me the light, or something wonderful like that. He hadn't. I still felt the same animosity toward Ashley as I had since I first met her. Rather than debate the issue, I slipped out of the conversation as quickly as I could. "Okay, well . . . I'll give that some thought. But right now I've got some more people to call. Will you please talk to the family and tell them what's going on?"

"Of course. And I'll be down there in a few days with whoever is able to join me."

"Good morning, Dad," said a bright-eyed Hope as soon as I clicked off. She was sitting up in the spare bed across the room. I'd checked before calling Grandpa Bright, and she was sound asleep. I hoped she hadn't heard too much of what I said.

"Good morning. All rested?"

"Yes. Was that Great Grandpa?"

"Uh huh."

She pulled back the covers and slid off the bed. "Who is Ashley?" she asked casually, as she walked to Anna's side and held her mother's hand.

Your brainless student teacher. "Oh . . . just someone who did a very bad thing."

"What thing?"

"It doesn't matter, pumpkin. You don't need to worry about it."

She let go of Anna's hand and came and stood right beside my recliner. "Did she say 'Sorry'?"

"Yes."

"Mommy says when someone says 'Sorry,' we should forgive them."

I pulled her close enough to hug, staring over her shoulder at the unanimated form of my wife. "I wish it were that simple. I really do." I really did, but I knew it wasn't.

"It is," she replied without pulling away. "Mom says."

Chapter 28

On the third day before *the* day, Hope and I left the hospital around noon to go home and freshen up. We also used the time to take care of a few other things that had fallen by the wayside during my prolonged absence, like shopping for groceries, sorting the mail, and paying bills. But Hope insisted that we go back to Anna's room at night because, "Mommy only has a few nights left, and she shouldn't have to sleep alone."

Who could argue with that?

Later that evening, while I was tucking Hope into her hospital bed, she asked a question that caught me off guard. "Do you say prayers at night?"

I wondered briefly if this was one of those unique moments where it would be better to tell a small fib to my child for the sake of setting a good example, but quickly decided that lying about praying to God was unwise, no matter what the rationale behind it. And the honest truth was that I gave up praying on the day we lost Hope's twin sister, Faith. "Not exactly," I ventured. "Do you?" It saddened me that I didn't know such a thing about my own daughter.

"Sometimes."

"Are you asking because you'd like me to pray with you? Because we can if you want."

"No. I was just thinking maybe if *you* prayed for Mommy, it would help. I've been praying for her every night since her accident, but I guess it's not working."

"Ah. Well, that's the funny thing about praying, I suppose. We pray for what we want most, but in the end sometimes God has a different idea."

"So it doesn't always work?"

"Afraid not, sweetie."

She looked disappointed, but asked, "Will you try anyway?"

"To pray?"

"Uh huh."

"For Mom?"

"Yes."

I ruffled her hair and gave her a kiss on the forehead. "You're so much like her; constantly trying to get me to do what I should be doing anyway."

"So you will?"

There was no getting out of it. "Yes, Hope. Tonight I'll say a prayer for Mom."

"Thank you, Dad." She rolled over with a smile and closed her eyes.

When I was sure Hope was asleep, I roused myself from the recliner and went to Anna's bed. Even though my wife couldn't hear me, it made me feel better to pretend she could. "Hey there. I suppose you know what's going on, right? Dr. Rasmussen has set a date to unhook your . . ." The thought made me cringe. "Look at me, I can't even say it without getting choked up. Did you hear Hope tonight? She wants me to pray. Unbelievable, that kid. But I promised her I would. Do you mind if I kneel down here beside you?"

I grabbed a pillow for my knees and tossed it on the ground. Once I was sure that the door was closed behind me, I knelt down and tried my best to say something intelligent.

"Um . . . God? Let's be honest, if you're as mighty and all-knowing as some people think, then you already know that I'm only doing this because I told my daughter I would. And since motive probably counts for a lot with these sorts of things, I really don't have any grand expectations. So let me say what's on my mind, and then I'll leave you alone."

Despite having the pillow underneath, my knees were already starting to throb. I shifted my weight around until it felt better. "Now then, about Anna." When I said her name, I opened my eyes and stared at my wife. She was lying at eye level right in front of me, so I couldn't miss her, even in the dark. I kept a picture of her in my head as I closed my eyes once more. "You and I both know that she got a raw deal in all of this. And the fact that it should have been me at the guitar store instead of her will haunt me until I die." I paused again. Something about hearing the word "die" spoken aloud, even coming from my own mouth, sent a chill of emotions through me. Those emotions spawned an onslaught of thoughts I'd never previously verbalized, though I knew they'd been simmering somewhere in my head ever since the accident. As long as I had God's ear, I decided to let him hear them. "Which reminds me," I continued, "I have a bone to pick with you. Far be it from me to point out flaws in your so-called plan, but the way I see it, you got this whole thing wrong. If you think it's so important that Hope only have one parent, you should have left *Anna,* not me. Don't you see that? I'm the guy who screwed things up to begin with, so let the consequences fall on me. Listen, when I married Anna, I found everything I wanted out of life. Have you seen her smile? It's like a piece of heaven, planted right there on her face. And then you added Hope to our family, and I found another piece of heaven. I don't *need* anything else. Seriously. Statistically, I know Anna's chances right now are not good. But you're God, right? If you're really there, then you obviously have a certain amount of sway in these situations. So let's make a deal . . . *Take me.*"

As soon as I said those words, I started bawling right there on the floor. I was kind of embarrassed by it, but I couldn't stop. I don't think it even had to do with Anna. It was more like a light had just turned on, and I was overwhelmed by the possibility that maybe, if God was really merciful and just, there was a solution to all of this mess that didn't involve Anna dying.

"Yes!" I exclaimed softly, making sure to keep my voice quiet enough to not wake Hope. "Take *me!* Take *my life,* and spare hers. Why should you care which one of us you get? I've found what I came here to find, and I'd be more than happy calling it quits right now, if it means Hope can grow up with her mother watching over her from somewhere a little closer than heaven. What do you say? Do we have a deal?"

I opened my eyes again, watching to see if, perchance, my bright idea would work. Keeping my focus on Anna's eyes, I sat perfectly still, hoping—*praying*—that they would miraculously open. From the corner of my vision I also watched her fingers, searching for any sign of movement— just a twitch would do; any indication that God was willing to strike a bargain. After five minutes of nothing, I bowed my head again.

"Fine," I muttered. "I'll stay, if that's want you want. I've still got Hope, and she needs *somebody.* So . . . I guess that about wraps it up. Thanks, and goodnight."

Did I just say goodnight to God?

"I mean, Amen."

Chapter 29

I couldn't sleep.

Three little words were giving me fits.

I forgive you.

Anna wrote that to me in her letter, but that was before she knew my actions would wind up killing her. Would she forgive me now? And even if she would, could I ever really forgive myself?

And then there was the matter of Ashley Moore. That had my stomach in knots too. Was Grandpa right? Did I really need to forgive her, and was that for her benefit or mine? Or both?

Was she deserving enough? Was she sorry enough? Or was she out there texting and driving right now, putting other innocent people at risk?

Would Anna want me to forgive?

The questions continued all night long. Every time I thought I had one answered, the answer gave birth to a flurry of additional questions.

By the time the morning light drew Hope out of a long night's sleep, I was more confused than when I'd laid down eight hours earlier.

"Dad?" Hope asked. "Why are you on the floor?"

"I couldn't sleep," I mumbled, staring up at the ceiling. "And I got tired of the recliner."

"How long have you been there?"

"A couple of hours."

"Isn't it cold down there?"

"Yes."

"Are you . . . okay?"

I pulled myself into a sitting position so I could look directly at her. She was so pretty, just like her mother. "I've been better," I admitted, "but I'll get over it. What do you say we run downstairs for some breakfast, then go for a walk? It looks like a nice day outside, and a quick stroll might help me get the blood flowing."

Hope and I took turns changing in the bathroom. When we were ready, we said goodbye to Anna, then caught the next elevator down.

Thirty minutes later, while we were walking around the perimeter of the hospital, my cell phone rang. It was a number I didn't recognize, but the area code was very familiar.

503. *Oregon.*

"Hello?" I asked.

"I hope I'm not calling too early."

My feet froze before taking another step. It was a voice I recognized immediately, but one I hadn't heard in several years. "Dad?"

"Hi Ethan. Is this a bad time?"

"Who is it?" whispered Hope.

"Your Grandpa," I whispered back.

"Grandpa Burke?"

"No, the other one."

"Great Grandpa Bright?"

"No, the *other* one."

My dad jumped in. "It sounds like a bad time. I'll call back . . ."

"No, it's fine. Umm . . . how are you?"

"I'm okay."

"Still working at that machine shop?"

"It's a job. In this economy, I'm not complaining."

Hope grabbed me by the hand and started tugging. "There's a bench," she whispered. "Let's sit down."

"So . . . what's up?"

There was a very long pause, then he said, "Tomorrow's the big day, right? How you holding up?"

I leaned back against the bench. "Did you talk to Grandpa?"

"Uh huh."

"Are you coming?"

"You and I both know I'd just be in the way. Besides, I have to work. But I'm sure Dad will fill me in. He's been keeping me posted right along. By the way, I wish you'd called me when all this happened. Sucks to hear bad news secondhand."

I clenched my fist. "Oh? Well it *sucks* even more to experience it *firsthand*. And I'm sorry I didn't call you, but when challenges arise, it's typical to turn first to the people you can rely on." This is the reason I hardly ever spoke to my dad. He has a habit of saying things that don't sit quite right with me, and I have a habit of responding with snarky remarks, and it escalates until we're both ticked off.

Hope gasped. "We shouldn't say *sucks!*"

"Sorry, sweetheart," I replied, covering the receiver with my hand. "I was just repeating what he said."

She lectured me with a stern frown. "That doesn't make it okay."

I didn't bother pointing out that she'd just committed the same offense.

Oddly, my father didn't seem affected by my comment. He actually sounded amused by it. "You know, you get that nasty streak from me."

The way he said it was surprisingly disarming, and not at all what I expected. Where was the counter-punch to my quick jab? His reaction diffused my emotions. Or maybe I had too many other things on my mind to engage in a petty fight. "You know what," I said, "I didn't get much sleep last night, so maybe now's not such a good time after all."

"I can make it quick."

"Is it important?"

"I think so."

I knew he'd just keep pressing, so I relented. "Fine," I sighed. "I'm listening."

"Are you sitting down?"

"Do I need to be?"

"No. But I do."

My ears perked up.

"You know," he continued more slowly, "what you're going through is like déjà vu for me, and I don't want you to make the same mistakes I made when your mother died."

Ah, that. I wondered just how much Grandpa had shared of our earlier conversation. "Dad, you don't have to say anything else. The last few weeks have really opened my eyes. I know how hard it was for you, and I don't blame you for how depressed you got."

"No you don't," he said, almost with a chuckle.

"That's what I said. I don't blame you."

"Nah, I meant the other part. You don't understand. You may have an inkling. You may even be going through it yourself. But until you've had years and years to suck on the regret, you don't understand it. Not like me."

Did he just shoot me down when I was trying to sympathize with him? "I beg your pardon?"

"Tell me, Ethan, how would you describe my reaction when your mom died?"

I thought about how I'd felt the last few weeks. "Sad? Depressed? Grandpa would probably have more clinical terms for it, but I think that sums it up."

"Then you and Grandpa would both be wrong."

It took me a moment to make sure I'd heard correctly. "How could you not be sad? That's an awful thing to say."

"Oh for crying out loud, of course I was sad. My

heart broke in a million pieces, like I'm sure yours is broken right now. But a person can get over being sad. Eventually the heart can heal from losing someone, even someone you love very much. I didn't dive into a tailspin on account of that." He hesitated, then asked, "Is Hope close enough to the phone that she can hear what I'm saying?"

I glanced quickly to my right. She'd found a ladybug on the bench and was trying to coerce it onto her arm. "No, why?"

"Because if she doesn't like the word *sucks,* she sure doesn't need to hear that I was *royally pissed off.* It wasn't sadness that sank me, Ethan. It was the anger. Anger at God, at the doctors, at anyone I could think to blame. The heart doesn't heal from that. It just festers, like the infection that took your mother's life."

My mind flashed to an image of Ashley Moore the last time I'd seen her on the front porch of her house, weeping in response to my vitriol. Grandpa thought I should forgive the woman because it might help *her.* Now my dad thought I should forgive because it might help *me.* Who was right? Or were they both right? Or were they both wrong?

"I think I understand," I muttered.

"Do you?" He didn't let me answer. "Do you remember the day you got married?"

The apparent shift in subject caught me off guard. "Of course."

"Do you? I hadn't spoken to you in almost two

years when I decided to hop in the car and drive to Idaho to see your wedding. When I finally got my minute alone to speak with you, do you remember what I said?"

An image of the white vomit-bag flashed across my mind. "Yes," I said. "You made me promise to learn to forgive Anna."

He snickered. "Close, but no. I didn't limit what I said to Anna. You promised me you'd learn to be forgiving . . . even when it's hard."

I didn't say anything.

For a minute, neither did he. "Ethan," he eventually continued, speaking more gently than I'd ever heard him speak. "If you're harboring anger, drop it. Just get over it. If someone is at fault in all of this—legally, I mean—let the consequences fall as they may. But let that be the end of it. Don't waste a single day being angry. Not even a single hour. It won't help you. It won't help whoever you're mad at. And it won't help Hope."

Hope? What did she have to do with any of this?

I looked at my daughter again when he said her name. She'd lost interest in the bug and was staring back at me, smiling. There was a spark of something in her eyes, a twinkle in the way she was looking at me. The only way to describe what I saw was *love,* which was a spark I couldn't remember ever having felt for my own father as a kid.

And suddenly I understood. There were more important things at stake than how I felt or thought about the woman who'd crashed into Anna. There was happiness. There was family.

There was Hope.

I took a deep breath. Maybe one day the feelings in my heart would magically subside. Or maybe my dad was right and they would fester until they erupted. But as I continued staring at Hope, I decided it wasn't worth waiting around to find out. I couldn't risk carrying around feelings that might ambush my happiness with her. And if there was a chance that it was really as simple as forgiving another, I was willing to give it a try.

"Thanks, Dad. I'm glad you called."

"Really?"

"Don't sound so surprised."

"No . . . I mean, you're welcome. It was good talking to you."

"You too." I hung up, not knowing how many years it would be until we spoke again, but certain that the next time we spoke I would welcome it.

"What's wrong?" Hope asked. "You look . . . nervous."

"I am. There's someone I need to visit—the woman who hit Mom."

"Can I come?"

I thought about it, then nodded. "Having you there might help me say what needs to be said."

. . .

An hour later we pulled up to the Moores' house. A full month had passed since my last visit. It looked different in the daylight. Less menacing. It was mid-morning, so there was no guarantee anyone would be home. I could've looked up their phone number and called first, but I'm sure they'd have split before I arrived.

Hope held my hand as we walked up the porch steps. "Are you ready to talk to her?" she asked.

Such a little nurturer. "No."

"Yes you are. Be brave."

I took a long breath, then rang the doorbell.

Nobody answered.

I rang again.

Still no answer.

Hope rang a third time, just to be sure. This time the door swung inward. In the entry was a very distraught young woman. It was obvious Ashley had been crying. She kept one hand on the doorframe and the other hidden behind her back. "Is she . . . gone yet?" she asked with a sniffle.

Hope gasped. "Miss Moore? What are you doing here?"

Ashley didn't smile. She hardly looked at Hope when she answered. "Surviving."

"So, you're the one who . . . ?"

"Crashed into your mom? Yes, that would be me. Sucks, huh?"

"We shouldn't say *sucks,*" Hope corrected.

Ashley just shrugged.

Hope looked appalled. Clearly, this was not the same bright-eyed, bushy-tailed young college student who'd spent a semester in her classroom. This was a woman who was suffering, just like I'd wanted her to.

"So . . . is she gone yet?" Ashley repeated.

For a moment I just stood there, taking it all in—the bloodshot eyes, the tangled hair, the wrinkled flannel pajamas, the ruined makeup, and the way she turned her body to keep me from seeing whatever she was holding in her hidden hand. That hand thing was actually a little unnerving. *Maybe she armed herself,* I thought, *just in case I go completely psycho this time.* I moved slightly in front of Hope, just in case. "You mean Anna?"

After an almost imperceptible nod she said, "I'm probably not supposed to know what's going on, but I have a friend at the hospital who's been giving me updates."

"No. She's not 'gone.' That process will start tomorrow."

"Is that why you came? To tell me that by this time tomorrow I'll officially be a murderer?"

"No."

"Then what? My parents are both at work, so they won't get in your way. Say whatever you want. I don't care anymore."

Hope squeezed my hand, nudging me on.

"It's not like that. Actually, I came here to apologize."

Skepticism marred her blotchy face. "You *what?*"

"He means he's sorry," Hope blurted out.

"Thank you, Hope, but I've got this. Ashley, the way I reacted—the way I treated you after the accident—it was wrong. There's no excuse for it, and I'm sorry."

Her eyes began watering. "You're serious?"

"Very."

Ashley's bottom lip was quivering, but eventually she managed a faint, "Thank you."

"There's more. I can hardly believe I'm saying this, but . . . I don't want to be angry at you anymore. I certainly don't condone what you were doing while you were driving that night, but I know . . . I know you didn't intentionally cause the accident. We all make mistakes from time to time. Sometimes big ones. We just have to learn from those mistakes, then move on."

"What he's trying to say is—"

"Hope. Really, I got this."

I cleared my throat. "What I'm trying to say is that this whole ordeal has been very hard on me, but only recently did I begin thinking that it is probably equally hard on you. Maybe even harder. I've never liked the phrase 'forgive and forget,' because I don't think we ever forget. But I like to believe that with forgiveness, maybe we can remember with peace. So . . . to get right down to

my point, I want you to know that I forgive you."
As soon as the words left my mouth, I felt like a
giant weight had been lifted. Like I was somehow
free. I pulled Hope closer to me, with one arm
around her shoulder. "*We* forgive you."

I could never have predicted what happened
next. Ashley crumpled like a rag doll, falling to
her knees on the floor in a big flannel heap. As she
fell, her previously hidden hand came forward to
catch herself. When her hand hit the hardwood,
the thing she'd been holding came free. In a split
second, the entryway was covered in little yellow
pills.

Hope gasped, and so did I. At first I thought
Ashley had stopped breathing. Maybe she did, for
a few seconds. But then she began sobbing—
giant, gut-wrenching sobs that hurt just hearing
them. "I'm . . . so . . . sorry!" she wailed. "So . . .
sorry!"

It took several minutes to get her calmed down
and moved from the entryway floor to a couch in
the living room. While I picked up the pills, Hope
kept an eye on Ashley, gently talking to her and
telling her that everything was going to be okay.
When I dropped the first few pills back in their
container, I discovered something else in there as
well—a tightly rolled piece of paper, like a
miniature scroll, with a handwritten message that
will remain forever seared on my brain.

After reading it once, I immediately asked

Ashley for her parents' phone numbers at work. The first one I reached was Mrs. Moore. I quickly recited what had happened and she told me she'd be home as fast as she could.

Then I read the note over and over until my eyes hurt. On the fifth time through, Hope caught me crying and asked if everything was okay. The only response I could muster was a feeble nod.

Dear Mom and Dad,

Please give this note to Mr. Bright. I'm sure you'll want him to know . . .

Mr. Bright,

You were right, but you already know that. I was stupid for texting in the car. It was impulsive. My boyfriend is a marine in Afghanistan, and he'd just sent me a note telling me he was safe. I knew he was in a dangerous city and I hadn't heard from him in more than a week. I was so excited that I couldn't wait to respond. But it was stupid and irresponsible. I'm sorry for that.

This past month has been unbearable. I keep having nightmares about the accident, about Anna, and especially about the things you said to me.

Every day I feel like I want to die. It should have been me, not your wife. It was my fault. What I did to your family is unforgiveable!

I can no longer live with the guilt.

Somehow I think there will be justice when I am gone. It's only fair. If Anna must die, then I should too.

Ashley Moore

PS Mom and Dad, I love you—and I'm sorry.

Chapter 30

"*I* did it. I visited Ashley today." Even if Anna couldn't hear me, I couldn't wait to tell her about everything. "I'm glad I didn't wait any longer. She was going to end her life. Just . . . end it. She had the pills in hand and everything, ready to swallow when I rang the doorbell. Can you believe that? Had I showed up a minute later . . . uggh . . . I don't even like to think about it."

My hand was trembling again. It had been doing that off and on since reading Ashley's suicide note.

"Mrs. Moore wasn't too happy to see me again," I continued, "but she was grateful that I showed up when I did. She and her husband admitted Ashley to the psych ward upstairs. The doctors want to evaluate her for a few days; I'm sure they'll get her the help she needs. Ashley asked to talk to me before they admitted her. She wanted to make sure she hadn't misunderstood me at the house when I told her I forgave her. Then you know what she did? She *hugged* me. The girl I'd berated last month stood on her toes and hugged me like her life depended on it. Then again, I guess it did."

I gently touched my wife's face, tracing the marred skin of the most prominent scar beneath my fingers. Feeling a fresh sense of remorse, I sat down and leaned back in the recliner. It had been a very tiring day. Hope was so exhausted that she fell asleep on the other bed almost as soon as her head hit the pillow. She was snoring lightly on the other side of the room as I talked to Anna.

No family members had come by the hospital yet, but they'd called to let me know they were in town. The Brights who were able to come—Grandpa, Aunt Jo, Aunt Beth, and my cousin Seth—checked into a hotel just a couple miles away. I told them they could stay at my house, but they didn't want to impose. Anna's dad and brother Lance were staying down in Fresno at Stuart's house. The plan was for everyone to meet at the hospital in the morning to say goodbye, after which the doctors would cease dialysis. It would still be a few days before she would be pronounced officially dead, but we at least wanted to be together to start the process.

Though I had resigned myself to what was going to happen, my heart still wished things had turned out different. I accepted the harsh reality, but I hated it. A large part of my grief was a lingering sense of regret. I wanted so badly to show Anna that I could be the man she thought I was. And there were still a million things I wanted to say to her and do for her, new promises I wanted to keep, and old promises yet to fulfill.

Old promises, I thought. *Like a special song, just for her.*

I sat up in my seat and scanned the room. Grandpa's guitar was staring at me again from its spot in the corner. How many years had passed since I was supposed to have written Anna a song? It was a promise I'd made on the first day of our marriage, and now, as the last day of our marriage loomed, there was still no song.

I sat up further, my gaze drifting from the guitar to Anna's face. *Even if she can't hear it, wouldn't she want me to finally write her a song?* "What do you say, sweetheart?" I said softly. "Is it too late to make good on my promise?"

Karl needed some tuning, but it wasn't long before my fingers were plucking and strumming gently next to Anna's bed. I warmed up with some good old-fashioned scales, then played a few of Anna's favorite songs from Shania Twain. Through it all, Hope kept right on snoring, oblivious to the private concert going on just fifteen feet away.

The wall sconce above Anna's head illuminated her face perfectly in the otherwise dark room. While I played, I imagined she could hear every note, and that she was humming along like she used to do. Though she did not move, her beautiful face *moved me,* and I gave her a concert like she'd never had before. For thirty minutes I went through all of the songs that had ever spoken to her heart—the ones she loved dancing to, the ones she sang in the shower, and the ones she said reminded her of me. I ended the set with *our* song—the first one I ever played for her on the streets of Austria—Pachelbel's "Canon in D."

I let the strings fade to quiet as I sat watching her. I thought of how happy she'd be to hear that song again. That's when I decided what *her song* should sound like.

I started over from the beginning of the canon, and took it very slow.

Sometimes writing songs is work. Other times the words and music kind of evolve together, and with some fine-tuning it develops into something good. But once in a while, when you feel something with your whole heart, the song just sort of *happens,* like it was there all along just waiting to be discovered.

Maybe there's a reason I never made it as a professional songwriter, and maybe that reason is because I wasn't very good at it—or at least not as good as I needed to be. Nobody ever bought one of my songs. Nobody ever heard one of my rock hits on the radio or downloaded one of my country songs on iTunes. But when you write a song for the love of your life, none of those things matter. There is no good or bad—there is only the guitar in your hands, the notes in your head, the words that you sing, and the love you feel.

Like I said, I started the canon slow at first, then a little faster. But I wasn't really playing Pachelbel's music anymore. This was Anna's song.

It was only for her—her lyrics, her melody, her story, all tied together with *my* pain. As I played the introduction, my fingers twisted the original just enough to make it current. What had been a classical piece only moments before was now a moody country ballad, built on the same chord pattern. Ignoring what my hands were doing, my mind pieced together words to adequately describe everything I felt. Those words took on shape and meaning as highlights of my life filled my head. Then the lyrics and tears started flowing in time with the tune's Nashville rhythm.

The first memory that came to mind was the very *first* worst day of my life: listening to the doctors explain that our oldest daughter had "expired." Then the image in my head jumped to a much more recent worst day. There I was in my mind's eye, crying uncontrollably beside Anna's bed a month earlier. She was hardly recognizable. I was so angry—at the girl who'd done this to her, at myself, and even at God for letting it happen. Where was the justice?

I cleared my throat and sang the first verse . . .

Have you ever sat and cried yourself to sleep?
Have you ever dreamed of things
you'd never want to see?
And have you ever questioned
what you don't understand?
Well I have . . .

Next my thoughts turned to what was about to happen . . . starting tomorrow morning. Where would Anna *be* after she was officially "gone"? With God in heaven, I hoped. But where is that exactly? Is it a long way, or closer than we think? In the same instant, I glanced up at Hope, who was still sleeping soundly on the other bed. She was the greatest gift Anna and I ever received. Seeing her reminded me of all the good things in my life. I also reflected on how she'd twisted my arm to get me to pray for Anna, thinking that it would magically reverse the irreversible. And just like that, more lyrics began pouring out . . .

> Did you ever hear that
> heaven's love is very far?
> Did you ever look for heaven
> deep within your heart?
> And do you ever thank the Lord,
> for all he's given you?
> Well I do.

The music shifted key for a brief refrain. I pictured myself kneeling next to Anna's bed with a pillow beneath my knees . . .

> And just last night,
> Before I went to bed,
> I knelt to pray to Him,
> And this is what I said . . .

Then the words of that prayer came spilling out of my mouth all over again in the shape of a chorus, but the only thing on my mind was Anna's beautiful face. Even with the scars, it was perfection to me.

> Take my life if you'd like,
> Because I found what I came to find.
> Or leave me here for a while,
> Cuz I found heaven . . . in her smile.

After the chorus, the melody morphed once more back to the classical version of the work that had been our wedding march. As my fingers kept time, plucking out Pachelbel's famous notes, I sifted through more memories.

I remembered the early years of our marriage. The struggles, and how we got through them together.

I remembered the constant ups and the downs.

I remembered miscarriages.

I remembered spending too much time away from my family.

The country ballad consumed the original melody once more. The second verse began as my mind rewound all the way back to when I'd first met Anna in Austria and how she'd asked how far I would go to be with her. All the way to Salzburg? To Moscow? To Timbuktu?

Did you really search the world
to find true love?
Did you ever ask the girl
if that would be enough?
And do you ever thank the Lord,
for all he's given you?
Well I do.
And just last night,
Before I went to bed,
I knelt to pray to Him,
And this is what I said . . .
Take my life if you'd like,
Because I found what I came to find.
Or leave me here for a while,
Cuz I found heaven . . . in her smile.

The words that I sang may be meaningless to the world at large. They will never be heard beyond my own room. They will never break records on charts or be sung by American idols. But to *me,* in that moment, they meant everything.

In the back of my mind I remembered what my grandfather had told me shortly after his own wife died. "The right words and the right music at the right time can heal the soul."

Like magic, I could already feel it healing mine.

As the final note sounded, I wiped away the residue of water from my eyes, and I thank God with all my heart that I did. With blurred vision I might not have seen the miracle . . .

It was small and weak—almost imperceptible, like the furthest star that appears before the sun is fully set—but I swear it was there.

A movement.

A wrinkle on her lips.

A miracle.

A smile.

POSTLUDE

*T*he walnut casket was propped up on a stand, not ten feet away. I wished I didn't have to sit so close. From my seat in the front row, I could make out my own reflection in the shiny lacquer finish, which only reinforced the fact that a very big part of my life was being laid to rest.

A pastor was at the pulpit giving pretty standard remarks. "Losing a loved one is never easy. We who are left behind invariably grieve the loss, whether those we have cherished are taken in their youth, in the prime of their lives, or in their twilight years . . ." Blah, blah, blah.

I tuned him out. I'd been to enough funerals of loved ones to know exactly what would be said, and to know that no matter what was said, the sting of the loss would still take time to fade.

Hope was sitting beside me, clutching my arm. Though I'd been to funerals before, this was her first, and she seemed to be taking it all in.

"You doing okay?" I whispered.

She nodded. "The flowers are very nice. I think Mommy would love them."

"I think you're right. I bet we can take some with us at the end."

After the service we followed the hearse to the cemetery, listened to another short sermon, and then watched as the casket was lowered into the ground. Afterward, family members came up and gave Hope and me hugs and words of encouragement. Some of them wanted to keep talking, asking how we were getting along and wondering if there was anything they could do for us. I appreciated the offers, but I really just wanted to go home.

At length we were able to head to the car.

"I need to make a quick call before we go," I told Hope as I turned the key in the ignition. "So I need you to keep quiet for a few minutes. Then you and I can talk. Okay?"

With a nod, she zipped her lips with her fingers.

I turned on the Bluetooth device in my ear and gave the voice command to dial my old boss.

"Hello, Jessica? It's Ethan Bright."

"Ethan? How is everything?" The sweet tone in her voice actually surprised me; I didn't know she had it in her.

"Fine, thanks. Listen, is it too late to apologize for how I spoke to you last time?"

"No need. It's me who should be apologizing. I had no idea what you were going through. By the way, I never really accepted your resignation. I've been waiting for a little time to pass to see if there's any way of getting you back."

"That's sort of why I'm calling."

"Oh, thank heavens! When can you start?"

"Wait—no. I wanted to talk to you about *a* job . . . just not that one."

Her sweet voice turned to confusion. "But this is where you shine. You're my number one guy, remember?"

"I do. I also remember that I wasn't very happy doing it. What I was actually wondering is whether there's a chance I can have my *old* job back. The one I started at. I think it fits my current family situation a little better."

"Didn't you start as a jingle writer?"

"Yes."

"But that job probably makes half what you're earning under me."

I shot a quick glance in the mirror at Hope. She saw me and smiled. "I know, but there are benefits of that job that you just can't put a price on." I'm sure Jessica had no idea what I was talking about.

With a dramatic sigh she said. "Well, if that's really what you want, then consider yourself a jingle writer. You can start whenever you like."

"Next week okay?"

There was a disappointed response that sounded like an *uh huh,* followed by, "I'll let your new boss know to expect you."

"Thanks."

"Take care, Ethan."

I tapped a button on my earpiece and the phone turned off. Then I put the car into gear, stepped gently on the gas, and pulled out of the cemetery parking lot, willing myself not to look back in the mirror at the handful of people still paying their final respects.

Hope and I chatted for a while, mostly about the funeral and how she was feeling. She was sad, of course, but all things considered she seemed okay.

When we were done talking I suggested that Hope take a nap. We had a long drive ahead of us, and she was looking tired. She fell asleep against the door in no time, leaving me alone with my thoughts.

Most of my thoughts were about Anna, and about all the things we'd been through together. I also pondered something Grandpa had said recently. After returning his wooden box so he could share its contents with the rest of the family, I told him I was gearing up to document the story of me and Anna in a journal, just as he'd done. There were details I didn't want to forget, and things I wanted Hope to know and remember as she got older. When I asked if he had any pointers, the advice he offered was perfect. "Writing your story is just like writing a song, only with more words and less rhythm. Start with the first verse, and take it one note at a time."

I can do that, I thought. *Heaven knows I've got lots of notes . . .*

We pulled into our driveway early the following morning, after driving most of the night. Our only break was a two-hour nap at a rest stop along I-5. Hope couldn't wait to get out of the car. She grabbed the flowers we'd been given from the funeral and rushed inside.

I left our bags in the trunk and followed her in. She was already in the master bedroom by the time I caught up with her.

"These are for you!" I heard Hope say.

"Oh, they're so pretty. Thank you!"

Anna was just waking up. The dialysis machine next to the bed was still finishing up its nightly cycle. My heart leapt at seeing her, as it had done a million times since she came out of the coma three months earlier. She still needed lots of physical therapy, and she didn't care much for the scars on her face, and we were finding small holes here and there in her memory, but none of those things mattered—we were together, and we were happy.

"Are these from Grandpa's funeral?" she asked.

"Yes," Hope replied. "I told Dad you would like them, and he said we could bring a few home. Smell them! They're still fresh."

She took a long whiff, then looked up at me. "How are you holding up?"

"I'm fine," I said. "It was sad seeing him go, but it was his time."

"I wish I could have been there. I missed you guys. The nurse came by every day, and Stu and the kids came by once, but it's much better being with you two."

"We missed you too, Mom." She paused; then her eyes lit up. "Oh, guess what Dad bought me in Oregon?"

"Umm . . . an Oregon coast T-shirt?"

"No, a guitar! He's going to teach me how to play!"

A broad smile swept across Anna's face—the one that reminded me of heaven. "Oh, how wonderful. Now I can have two people play songs for me." She tilted her head and winked at me. "Speaking of which, I missed your serenades the last few nights. How about a little concert in bed?"

"I'll never say no to that." I smiled.

Karl was leaning against the wall on the other side of the room. I opened up the case to find what I knew would be there: a pink envelope woven in the strings, with a couple of handwritten quarter notes on the front. I placed it on my pillow so I could enjoy it later.

Then I kissed Anna gently on the forehead and played her song.

♪

Have you ever sat and cried yourself to sleep?
Have you ever dreamed of things
you'd never want to see?
And have you ever questioned
what you don't understand?
Well I have.

Did you ever hear that
heaven's love is very far?
Did you ever look for heaven
deep within your heart?
And do you ever thank the Lord,
for all he's given you?
Well I do . . .

And just last night,
Before I went to bed,
I knelt to pray to Him,
And this is what I said . . .
Take my life if you'd like,
Because I found what I came to find.
Or leave me here for a while,
Cuz I found heaven . . . in her smile.

Did you really search the world
to find true love?
Did you ever ask the girl
if that would be enough?
And do you ever thank the Lord,
for all he's given you?
Well I do.

And just last night,
Before I went to bed,
I knelt to pray to Him,
And this is what I said . . .
Take my life if you'd like,
Because I found what I came to find.
Or leave me here for a while,
Cuz I found heaven . . . in her smile.

READING GROUP GUIDE

1. Ethan and Annaliese (Anna) met somewhat randomly in Vienna, Austria, where both of them were pursuing their passions. How much did the location influence their relationship? Do you think they would have hit it off as well if they'd run into each other somewhere else?

2. Going through a miscarriage, even just once, can be a real emotional trial. Anna miscarried repeatedly. How well did she and Ethan handle the losses?

3. Do you think the miscarriages made it easier or harder for the Brights to cope with the death of their eldest daughter, Faith?

4. Early in their marriage Ethan and Anna had big dreams for their future. Did their dreams change over time? How and why?

5. Ethan believes he is responsible, at least in part, for his wife's accident. Was he? Similarly, Grandpa Bright blamed himself for the death of Abel Richter and his twin daughters in the concentration camp. Was his guilt justified?

6. Forgiveness can be a long and challenging process. Is it more difficult to forgive others or to forgive yourself? Discuss which characters learned the most about

forgiveness, and what they learned. Who still has some learning to do?

7. Herbert Bright returned from war with two important items: a guitar and a door handle from Hitler's hideout in the Alps. Why were these things important to him? Did their value change over time? Is there any symbolism in Grandpa Bright finally ridding himself of the door handle?

8. After the accident, when it seemed unlikely that Anna would recover, Ethan was faced with a terrible choice: keep holding on— hoping that things would eventually turn around, or give the doctors the go-ahead to turn off life support? Was that burden greater because she had a living will, or did that only heighten his moral dilemma? Discuss what you would do in the same situation.

9. At times, Ethan seems to struggle finding balance between work and family. Does Anna make that struggle easier or harder on him? How? Would you say Ethan is motivated more by the lure of success, or by an honest desire to provide for his wife and daughter?

10. How important were the notes that Anna wrote to Ethan during their marriage? More important than the notes he played for her? Was there a *final* note?

Center Point Publishing
600 Brooks Road • PO Box 1
Thorndike ME 04986-0001 USA

(207) 568-3717

US & Canada:
1 800 929-9108
www.centerpointlargeprint.com